Scott Wellinger

Lansing Aerospace Company

Flight

a Warren Dennihan Novel

Flight

A Warren Dennihan Novel

by Scott Wellinger

World Wide Publishing Group

New York   Los Angeles   London   Toronto

www.WWPGroupInc.com

For information, address: World Wide Publishing Group.

wwpgroupinc@mail.com

Jacket design by Jason Goodchild

Printed in the United States of America

10 9 8 7 6 5 4 3 2 1

ISBN: 978-0-9861514-4-6   (Ebook)

ISBN: 978-0-9861514-5-3   (Print)

For Robbis ~
everybody's wingman

Epigraph

"Once you have tasted flight, you will forever walk the earth with your eyes turned skyward, for there you have been, and there you will always long to return."

~ Leonardo da Vinci

Preferred Air Flight 4273
Nonstop BOS→FLL
February 13, 2015

It was finally their turn to board the plane. Preferred guests, normally referred to as frequent flyers on competing airlines, were let on first. The people who fly for a living and have a special lounge in the Preferred Air terminals in which to relax with a cocktail before getting on a plane—in Boston and other major airports anyway—who rack up a ton of miles and sit in first class, get the added bonus of being the first to board and the first to exit the aircraft. The perks for those who spend more money than most people make in a year just in air travel.

The elderly were then asked to approach PA Gate 6 over the intercom in the massive Preferred Air waiting area by the airline representative. They would be more than happy to help those in wheelchairs or who would be slow to get down the jetway or through the boarding process. None would be on this particular flight to Fort Lauderdale, however.

Next, passengers with small children. This category was by far the greatest demographic on this flight. Christian Kane's children weren't small enough to qualify for early boarding, according to the lady making the announcements and acting as bouncer for the person accepting boarding passes. Small must be a relative term based upon some arbitrary criteria crafted by the airline, because Kane's two daughters were only six and nine years old. Zoe and Aria were well-behaved and needed no assistance, therefore were afforded no special perks.

Christian normally fell under the category of first to board— first to exit. As an outside sales rep for Diamond Advanced, a national distributor of electronic components based out of Dedham, Massachusetts, he spent most if not all of his five workdays per week traveling about the country trying to sell his company's wares.

A job he loathed with all of his being but more than paid the bills. The normal travel accommodations were forgone on this trip, however, trading in the flyer miles accrued from work for three seats —in his mind—one class-level above cargo. He hadn't until that moment fully appreciated the contradiction in treatment on an airline that purported to treat everyone equally and preferentially.

Preferred Air was a relatively new carrier to offer commercial airfare. Their niche of the air travel market was plush amenities for bargain basement prices. Every seat was marketed as business class or better. The planes were new with a modern look and feel. Each seat was as wide as first-class seating, three-quarter reclined, and was appointed with Napa leather. The snacks were larger in size and more nutritious. Attendants passed out full beverages. Passengers were treated with ample foot-room, enough for both a carry-on and human feet. It was all about the extras, for less money. They were taking air and public trading by storm; offering more destinations from more airports seemingly by the day, stockholders and passengers alike were reaping the benefits.

What made this flight less classy and more like commercial aviation's version of a public bus-ride, wasn't about the amenities. It was the sea of children semi-minded by their parents. PA flight 4273 was more akin to a bouncy room.

Christian reminded himself that he was on vacation and that he needed to try and relax. There was no reason to get worked up over boarding. No reason to stress-out over the crowds of people rushing throughout Boston's Logan Airport Terminal B to make their flight, or the swarm of travelers airing their grievances at the Preferred Air Customer Service desk in order to explain how they had been wronged and why they needed to be compensated. He wasn't getting on a plane for work. He was getting out of cold, mid-winter Boston to spend time with his family at Disney. Sunny Florida. The Kanes would trade their North Face winter gear for Hurley beachwear. One week with no school. No work. No sales calls. No conference calls. No God-awful meetings. Just Christian, his beautiful wife Sorina, his nine year old daughter, Aria—who looked like she could have a driver's permit—and his youngest, Zoe.

The threesome approached the jetway, each handing their boarding passes to the overly perky attendant. The process was an exciting change of pace for the girls, travel not in their normal day-to-day routine. Zoe had the week off from first grade at the Coffin School. Aria was a year ahead of other children her age scholastically and had the same week off from fifth grade at Village. Since both were located in the affluent township of Marblehead, Massachusetts, the winter breaks coincided. The level of bedlam at the airport made obvious that those two schools were not alone in sharing the time off.

"Why isn't Mommy coming?"

"Zoe, hun, for the twentieth time, your mother is already down there. Remember? She's there for work," Christian said as they each rolled their hard-case carry-ons down the jetway toward the plane.

Aria rolled her eyes along with her baggage at her younger sister. "She's doing another restaurant opening. You didn't notice that she was gone all last week, dummy?"

Sorina Kane, wife and mother of two, was also a corporate trainer for P.F. Chang's, a national upscale Chinese restaurant chain. In addition to overseeing the company's training staff, she managed to keep order in the Kane home like only a working mother could. She was not away from her daughters with nearly the frequency as Christian, but like her husband, felt that any time away was too much.

"Aria. Be nice to your sister. She just forgot."

"Sorry," she said, not hiding the fact that she didn't truly mean it.

They'd reached the end of the jetway and the door to the plane.

"Okay ladies. Decision-making time. Do you want to leave your bags here and grab them as soon as we get off in Florida, or do you want to try and fit them into the bins above our heads?"

Aria said, "I thought you didn't want to pay to check all of our bags, Dad?"

"You don't have to pay to put them under the plane here, but you do if they take it when you check in—before going through security. It's a game the airlines like to play. So what is it girls? Lug'em or leave'em?"

Christian left his bag with the cluster of others, as per usual. His laptop hung off his shoulder in a smaller, leather brief made by Tumi.

Aria mimicked her father, pushing the handle down on her pink, Ralph Lauren carry-on next to Christian's.

Zoe was having none of it. She had just picked out her purple *Frozen* roller depicting 'Anna' and 'Elsa' the week prior and was not letting it out of her sight. It had been a struggle to negotiate the terms of not allowing her to bring it to school every day since the bag was purchased at Macy's. It wasn't worth another fight or a tantrum, so it was brought onto the plane. He'd given her the choice, the six year old made it as though there had been one to make.

With only one bag to put into the overhead compartment, they were able to get into their seats in short order once they were able to get to them. They were sitting directly over the starboard wing, the right side when facing the cockpit.

Christian was a window man. He normally requested a window seat for his semi-daily flights. But he normally didn't fly with a six and a nine year old, so he was relegated to the aisle on the right side of the aircraft. Another sacrifice of fatherhood that he was all-too happy to make. Sort of.

An attractive flight attendant approached him when everyone who was supposed to be on the flight was inside the cabin, if not yet in their assigned seats.

"Hello, Sir. Are you willing to be my ABP for this flight?"

Christian knew what was being asked of him and what his duties would be in the unlikely event that the plane had an emergency landing.

"Sure. I don't know how much help my girls will be though," as he nodded his head to his right.

Zoe was already comfortable in her Napa leather seat, queueing up a video on her iPad mini by the window. Why she insisted upon the window when her eyes would most likely be glued to the tablet was anyone's guess. Such as life with a six year old female he reckoned.

Aria had fastened her seatbelt, popped in her earbuds, and was picking out the appropriate music to start their journey in the middle seat.

"As long as you can help get people out the door that will be fine. We have another across the aisle, two in front, two in the back so we'll be all set. If not, we can always exchange with a willing passenger," the attendant said. Her platinum name tag informed him that her name was Alice.

"They're all settled in, Alice. I don't want to move them."

"Okay. But they won't have too much longer on their electronic devices. We're probably going to taxi soon."

Christian nodded that he understood as Alice moved along, checking to make sure overhead bins were secure for takeoff and that passengers were taking their seats. He opened the front pouch of his Tumi bag by his feet, popped the top off his travel-approved size bottle of Advil, and poured two Ativan out of the white, plastic, trojan horse drug bottle into his hand. The two pills went down without the need of a beverage.

The Ativan was prescribed, but depending upon the TSA personnel at any given airport, on any given day, they sometimes confiscated it. Security was more likely leave the pills alone if the depression meds were smuggled in a travel-approved size container for a relatively harmless pain reliever. He'd been taking Ativan for the better part of a year, not because he was depressed, but because of his growing fear of flying.

Worldwide, an average of less than a hundred people die in a plane crash each year, the overwhelming majority of which are from private planes. With the number of annual flights on the seventy-eight major world commercial airlines—forget the countless private flights—the chances of being one of those hundred each year is approximately one in over twenty-five million. Many people chalk up their fear of flying, after being apprised of the statistics, as being a lack of control. Others, that if something should go wrong, falling thirty-thousand feet in the air to the ground is too much to survive. Oddly, those same people will get into a car without a second thought, while their death in a fatal accident on the road is roughly one in twenty-three thousand.

For Christian, his increasing fear was within the statistics. With the number of flights he took each week, each year, he felt he was playing with odds. One of these days, his number would be up. He would be the one in twenty-five million. The lottery mentality. People play Powerball or the ilk, week in and week out, because at some point their numbers will hit. It was just a matter of time. Only in his mind, instead of winning millions, Christian Kane would leave this world and his precious wife and daughters behind.

So he medicated. His primary care physician told him that Ativan would take the edge off. Help him to relax. His doctor was right.

Thoughts of impending doom subsided as the rituals of preflight occurred. An avid baseball fan—or more precisely, an avid Redsox fan—Christian likened the movements and announcements made by the flight crew to when professional batters get into the batter's box before each pitch. Each player goes through an exact ritual while in the batter's box, each and every time they get up to bat, before each and every pitch is thrown. Nomar Garciaparra adjusted his gloves in an exact way, then pushed his toes into the tips his cleats. Manny Ramirez adjusted his jock, stabbed the corners of the batter's box with the barrel of his bat, spit out some chew, and held the bat vertically toward the pitcher like a Samurai. Papi. Pedroia. Every batter, on every team, for each of their roughly four at-bats per game, times one hundred sixty-two regular season games. It was ceremonial and gave something for viewers to watch-yet-not-watch while waiting for the opposing pitcher and catcher to get on the same page. And so it was with the flight attendant on each flight demonstrating how to fasten a seat belt as if nobody had ever seen such a device.

Christian opened the air valve above his head, stale-smelling a/c spilled toward him as he looked around the cabin. Nothing out of the ordinary. Nothing to cause alarm or concern. Nothing to panic about.

As the plane was moving toward the runway, packed to the gills with vacationers anxious for the sun, electronic devices were being put away as instructed. People looked out the windows or at a book or at the SkyMall catalogue from the seat-pouch in front of them. Children carried on. Parents tried to subdue them. Conversations ran the gamut. The process took some time, planes from various carriers were queued up to go wherever they were destined. Maybe Florida. It was February, so probably Florida.

"Was she flirting with you, Dad?"

"Hmm?"

Aria asked the question again.

"The lady. Alice. Was she flirting with you?"

"I thought you were listening to your music."

"I had to put it away, remember? And you didn't answer the question," she said.

"No, Ari. She wasn't flirting. She was asking if I was capable of helping people out of the plane if we had to land before Fort Lauderdale. They call it an ABP. Able Bodied Person I think. They do it for every flight. Nothing to worry about."

"She's pretty."

"Mom's prettier," Christian said. His daughter smiled. Not only was it the right thing to say, it was right in that it was true.

Aria stared at the attendant. Alice, the red-haired, blue-eyed flight attendant was the closest and most visible of the crew, a few rows forward. She was buckling into her own seat.

It was finally time for takeoff.

As the plane accelerated down the runway, Christian white-knuckled his fingers deep into his thighs. His mind manifested the mild vibrations into the fuselage disintegrating and bursting into flames.

Of course nothing of the sort occurred. The thought was silly. Fear has a way of making the nonsensical seem not only plausible but imminent.

Preferred Air Flight 4273 left Boston, Logan Airport, just as planned and on time. The pilot told them so over the cabin speakers after the flaps made some noises and the landing gear was retracted into the aircraft. The plane then made a few hard turns and settled in for what was expected to be an uneventful three hour and ten minute flight.

After a time, another announcement indicated that it was now safe to use electronic devices and move about the cabin or recline your seat. They were traveling at an altitude of 31,000 feet, the weather was favorable, and the plane even had free Wi-Fi. The small icon lights above them forbidding certain behaviors went out, confirming the announcement.

Christian chuckled to himself. With the cost of airfare, nothing was free. How much could Wi-Fi cost anyway? His was bundled in with his cable bill.

Laptops and tablets and DVD players and MP3 players and portable video game units were produced in virtually every seat. Entertainment wouldn't wait for Florida.

The small screen on the back of each headrest allowed the passengers to watch a movie or keep track of where the plane was traveling. The East Coast and land west was tan on the left side of the screen. Each State delineated with black lines along their borders but the names were left unlabeled. The Atlantic Ocean a mass of blue on the right of the LED screen. An arched line depicted the flight plan in the middle. The line behind the icon was blue, the line in front was green. Each airport along the trip was red-thumbtacked and labeled. NYC/LGA. NYC/JFK. DC/Dulles.

Christian looked up from the book he was reading on his laptop, *World Gone By* - by Dennis Lehane, to see that the icon indicated that they had just flown past the RDU thumbtack. Raleigh-Durham. He nudged Aria and nodded toward the screen.

She pulled out her left earbud, unintelligible tween music blaring from it.

"What's that, Dad?"

"We're over North Carolina. Just a few more states to go. Do you know which ones?"

"Seriously? That's easy."

"Humor me. I don't get to spend all that much time with you and you're growing up so fast," he said as he closed his laptop.

15

"Okay Dad." Aria nudged her sister and whispered in her left ear before turning off the music app on her purple, bedazzled cell phone, turning on the video camera instead. She could share how much of a geek her dad was on social media to her friends later.

"Who were you listening to?"

"Nick Jonas."

"Who?"

"Never mind."

"Aria, it's not nice to be dismissive like that. I was just trying to take an interest in what you're interested in."

"You're right. Sorry. Nick Jonas is like super-ho—uh—uh—He's a good singer, Dad."

"Jonas? Like the Jonas Brothers?"

"Yeah."

"Aren't they Disney kids?"

"He grew up."

"Don't they all," Christian mumbled. "Zoe. Do you know the states we have left to travel over?"

He pointed to the screen.

She gave her father a look of surprise like she didn't know that there was going to be a pop-quiz. School was supposed to be in recess for the week.

"Don't worry, Zoe. I'll help you," Aria offered.

"Well …. I know that one," the six year old said as she pointed at Florida. Her mother had shown her where she would be working and where they would be vacationing on several occasions.

"Everyone knows that one, silly. It's shaped like a penis—uh—uh—Everyone can point out Florida," Aria said as she caught herself once again.

"Aria Kane. I don't know that I'm comfortable with the fact that *you* know what a penis is shaped like, let alone your younger sister. Hear me?"

"Sorry."

"Don't be sorry, just think before you speak. It's perfectly fine to not say out loud every single thing that you're thinking."

"Got it."

"Are you video taping me?"

"There's no tape, Dad. It's just video."

"Why are you recording me?"

"Because Mom always defends you when we call you a dork. I want to prove to her that we're right."

Christian looked at his youngest daughter. "You agree?"

Zoe giggled.

The plane icon flickered and moved down the screen a fraction of an inch. They were still flying above the Atlantic, east of the coastline, but were now approaching the ocean off the shores of South Carolina.

Zoe informed everyone in the area that she needed to pee by telling her father in a volume far greater than necessary.

"See Dad? I told you she shouldn't have the window," Aria said. "We better get her out before the cart blocks us." The beverage and snack carts were coming toward them from the front of the plane, Alice at the helm.

"She's small. Small people have small bladders. You're right, hurry up so she can get out please."

The three of them began to unbuckle their seat belts in preparation for the musical chairs they would need to perform to let Zoe out of her seat, when a loud noise came from the plane below them. A rumbling vibration that lasted about ten-seconds. At the conclusion of the rumble, the aircraft began to violently shake.

Christian had experienced his share of turbulence. He'd even researched it to find out exactly what caused it after a particularly rough flight.

The rumbling vibration was not turbulence.

The moment the rumbling stopped, the plane violently pitched upward, throwing anyone and anything inside the cabin toward the rear of the plane. People rolled aft for six-seconds before the plane leveled off.

Then, just as suddenly, the nose pitched downward. Drink carts and carryons and passengers were slung back toward the cockpit. The dive lasted as long as the ascent, then nosed back upward.

The aircraft and the people inside it were being tossed around as if they were inside an etch-a-sketch.

Overhead bins opened, luggage poured onto the passengers. Snacks and beverages were everywhere. Passengers were vomiting.

A loud ding sounded, indicating that everyone should be in a seat and belted in at the first pitch change. A blonde flight attendant made an attempt to make an announcement but was tossed into a swinging overhead compartment door and ricocheted to the aisle floor. Her head immediately began to bleed as she lay unconscious where she'd landed.

It wasn't Alice, but her yellow hair was reddening to match.

The plane nosed up and then violently down again. Three chimes dinged in the cabin, loud enough to be heard above the screams.

One of the other attendants made way toward their fallen colleague while Alice and the fourth attendant raced toward the cockpit as quickly as they could while trying to avoid being concussed themselves. A red light flashed above the cockpit door. Both women tried to brace themselves as they picked up phones in the forward service galley.

One was trying to say something to the passengers, but her voice was unintelligible. Probably something about safety or remaining calm. Bullshit about this all being normal.

Alice was speaking to someone else on a different phone.

Christian then looked for his daughters who had taken off their seat belts for the bathroom break and had been slung someplace within the cabin. He called for them but couldn't hear his own voice. Every other passenger was also screaming, praying, yelling, or whatever else they might be trying to convey in a state of fear at the top of their lungs. The attendant attending the fallen co-worker was trying to scream above the fray.

"Remain seated and stay calm! Buckle and secure your safety belts! Remain seated and stay calm! Buckle and secure your safety belts! Remain seated ...," the attendant repeated over and over and over again. Some listened. Most did not.

18

Christian did not. He was trying to find his children. He then looked at the seat number by his head as he tried to hold himself in place. He wasn't where his assigned seat was. He'd been thrown back three rows.

Getting his bearings, he looked toward his seat. Through the strong G-forces and people being tossed about, he crawled back to his children.

Where his youngest daughter had once been, through the small window and outside in the bright atmosphere, Christian saw something he had not seen on any flight he'd taken before during flight.

Panels on the front of the wing were open and mechanical parts were exposed. The entire wing seemed to be flapping like a bird taking flight. He wondered how much abuse the open panels could take at such a speed, or what the entire wing would endure, before each would break free from the body of the plane.

Christian heard an explosion just outside the window as the plane had turned back toward the heavens. Dark smoke began to meld with the blue sky and white clouds. Metal tore into the fuselage where his youngest daughter was sitting and continued a few rows behind. Neither daughter was in their row.

Masks fell from the over the seating as the aircraft nosed toward hell for the final time. The cabin had lost pressure.

Christian was launched toward the front of the plane, head bashed against hardened plastic, his body beaten before landing on top of Alice, the flight attendant. She was trying to get to her seat, phone no longer in her hand.

He vomited.

I'm dreaming. This has to be a nightmare.

He was all but paralyzed with fear. With pain. Finding his daughters is what kept him going.

He heard the repeated command from the aft flight attendant. It now had additional directives. "Remain seated and stay calm! Buckle and secure your safety belts! Utilize your air masks! Remain seated and stay calm! Buckle and secure your safety belts! Utilize your air masks!"

She could barely be heard above the commotion.

Very few people paid her any mind, also paralyzed with fear.

Maybe they couldn't hear her over their own screams.

Maybe they didn't care.

Maybe they were too busy vomiting.

Kane reached for a mask, desperately trying to find his daughters in the process.

Alice grabbed his arm. "If I'm unconscious when we land, take me out of the plane with you. Do you understand? You're the ABP. If I'm unconscious when we land, you need to take me out of the plane with you. Okay?"

"Sure, lady. You actually think this plane is going to LAND?"

"We're headed toward the water. One way or another, this plane is going to stop at some point. If I'm unconscious—"

"—I'll see what I can do," Christian said as he crawled aft. He had to find his girls.

A new direction was added and repeated.

"....While seated place your head between your knees and grab your ankles! Remain seated and stay calm! Buckle and secure your safety belts! Utilize your air masks! While seated place your head between your knees and grab your ankles!"

Head between my knees? Fat chance. I need to find my kids. Where are they?

He looked through the bodies. Some people were unconscious. Some were dead. Few others were still screaming. He crawled over bodies and through the tossed luggage and items therein stopping to get oxygen from a mask every few feet. He didn't see them. He called for them but they did not respond.

He vomited again.

Alice was pointing at him.

He made eye contact.

She pantomimed putting head between knees.

Only those who had been buckled into their seats initially were able to put their heads down, not that the position was going to save their lives anyway, he thought. If the plane was going to crash, a curved spine wasn't the difference between life and death. He decided in the fraction of a second he devoted to the concept that it was so the passengers wouldn't see death coming.

Now there was only one direction being screamed at them. "Brace! Brace! Brace! Brace!"

The remainder of the one hundred ninety-seven souls braced themselves for the inevitable.

Eastern Standard
Thursday
8:00 P.M. October 1, 2015

THURSDAY NIGHTS WERE USUALLY A GOOD NIGHT TO STAY in. Boston is a young city. A college city. Thirsty-Thursday is a city-wide ritual wear young adults look to unwind. Thursday being the first day of binge-drinking to close out the week. The fall semester was two months in and those learning how to think needed a break. Another excuse in an arsenal of them to get a head-start on the weekend.

October in Boston is also heavy tourist season, if there is such a thing. Boston always has tourists. Football. The Marathon. Summer at Fenway. In the fall, it's leaf-peepers. Or playoff baseball. Sometimes both.

There would be no bid for a pennant this year, but the city was abuzz with the final game of the final series against the arch-rival Yankees at Fenway.

Another reason he should go home to his future wife, he thought.

Too many amateur drinkers out there looking for fun, mixed with goddamn Yankee fans, culminated in trouble. He didn't need trouble. Trouble found him without having to turn over a rock.

But Warren Dennihan had gotten a call from his partner, Lisa Sheed, who said that she had to see him. Five alarm fire. So he didn't go home to Southie. To his girlfriend. To his dog. To his own, private Thirsty-Thursday.

Deni, as he preferred to be called, had just finished meeting with a client in Back Bay when he received the call on his cell. He'd had a tough day of trying to track down a former client who owed him money before attending a meeting with his current client.

Dennihan Investigation Services, a private investigation firm, was utilized to ascertain if a wealthy husband's suspicions of a cheating spouse were correct. He was correct. His wife was willingly plowed by anyone who stood when taking a piss.

Just another day at the office. Another few hundred dollars to keep the coffers half-empty. Another day of pseudo-profiting from other people's misery.

Lisa had been in Back Bay as well, finishing a meeting of her own with a client that Deni hadn't been apprised of. She was definitely fired-up when he took the call, but whether it was positive or negative, he couldn't quite tell.

They decided to meet at Eastern Standard, an upscale bar and eatery in Kenmore Square. The happening meeting spot was a cross between traditional and avant-garde. The woodwork looked old and was stained as dark as the sparse lighting. The staff dressed in white shirts, black ties with black vests. The marble bar ran the entire length of the left side of the establishment, high tables and chairs sat across from it, booths lined to the right of the open room with a cavernous ceiling. The menu and cocktails were non-traditional; the pricey offerings were created to set trends rather than follow them.

The meeting spot had been her idea and at her insistence that they meet immediately.

Had Deni thought about it, or Lisa for that matter, an alternate spot would have been better.

The Yankees were in town for the final time of the year. Eastern Standard was about a hundred yards north of Fenway park and a two minute walk around the corner on Brookline Avenue to Yawkey Way. Between the tourists staying at one of the adjacent hotels and the rowdy New Yorkers who were looking to put it the Sox one last time, the bar was packed four deep. Every high top table and chair occupied. Every booth filled to capacity.

Deni was the first to arrive and reinvigorated in the desire to have a glass of Irish at home.

He was only forty-two, but his need to be 'seen' had vanished years prior—if indeed he ever possessed it. Quiet was better. A place to have a drink and a bite without having to shout in order for your companion to hear you.

It took twenty minutes and a cash bribe to get two seats at the bar. Thirty minutes and still no Sheed, but that was down on the list of annoyances.

Several people were behind him; shouting, bumping his chair, trying to get noticed by the bartender to place their order. Deni couldn't hear himself think.

The bartender slid him a drink across the marble top that wasn't what he ordered, ten minutes after he ordered it. He'd ordered an Irish Whiskey, Redbreast to be specific, but he was made a Wilford Brimley, which had Irish Whiskey in it along with oats and fruit and some other bullshit. His libation was rectified with apologies after another ten minutes.

The food menu was called brasserie or charcuterie or some such nonsense. Frog legs. Bone marrow. A cheese selection. Deni was hungry and getting hungrier with every minute by annoying minute he waited.

The large screen TV, which was normally hidden behind dark wood cabinetry behind the bar—the place was too high-brow for such distractions—was forced to be on and turned to the game by the demanding crowd. The closed captioning across the screen blocked out the score, but Deni could tell it wasn't in the home team's favor.

Deni tossed back the remainder of his third glass of Whiskey and was about to give up on his partner, when he spotted her coming through the crowd from the front door.

"Wow, this place is packed. We really should have thought it through," Lisa shouted.

"Ya think?"

"You didn't object," she said as she shoved her way into her seat. Her coat was initially going to go on the back of her barstool, but she opted for her lap instead.

"Whatev-ah." There are Boston accents and there are Boston accents. South Boston falls under the latter. Deni's accent falls into an extreme South Boston category of its own, which means

24

it's nearly a new language. R's don't exist where they should, and are inserted into words where they have no earthly business.

"What took ya?"

"I couldn't find a place to park."

"They got valet, She."

"I refuse to pay for parking. I just can't do it."

"You live in Boston. If you own a car, you pay to park. It's what you do." *Cah. Pahk.* The stereotype doesn't do it justice.

Most people who live in Boston, don't own cars. Trains run everywhere. Cabs. Buses. If you need to get out of the city, or just get to the burbs, you can rent a compact by the hour or the day. If one decides to own a vehicle, that vehicle is likely to be very tiny and cost about the same amount per month to securely park it as it does for your apartment. Maybe more.

"The guy wants twenty bucks plus tip, when—if I apply myself—I can probably find a spot for free," Lisa said with a grin.

"The Yanks are in town. How far did you have to walk?" *Ther Yanks. Fah.*

"Over by the Pru. I should've just left it where I was on Boylston and hoofed it right after my meeting."

"Which was where?" *Whey-ya?*

Sheed ordered her drink instead of giving Deni an answer. A Wilford Brimley.

"You fuckin' kiddin'?"

"What?"

"I don't know how you can drink that shit," Deni said while shaking his head in disgust. "I Should'a just givin' ya the one they tried to give me."

"I get it all the time when I come here with Reg. When it's not crowded. It's normally not this crowded. I love this place. How was your day?"

"Oh aces. I had to find that prick that was duckin' me for the bill he owes us, before tellin' this other prick that his wife is a two-million-timin' whore. You?"

"Really good, but I'll get to that in a minute. Where's my drink?"

"You'll get it for Christmas. How's the wife?"

Regina was Lisa's other half. Deni called Reg 'the wife' though Lisa had repeatedly asked him not to. She let it go a long time ago. The wedding had finally taken place after the date had been rescheduled a few times because of this investigation or that one. Lisa's work-home balance was an ever-present strain on their relationship. Work was slightly ahead of Reg for first priority.

"Great. Being married is great. You should try it."

Deni didn't respond. Ani had been trying to get him to commit to a date since he popped the question earlier in the year. When he wasn't feeling the pressure at home, Lisa was there to fill the void.

But Sheed didn't let him get away without a response. "You and Ani set a date yet?"

"No and bite ya tongue. I just barely got her the ring."

"I know. I saw it when I bumped into her about a week ago, I don't know if I told you. I bumped into her about a week ago. That's some rock," Lisa said. Her eyes widened.

"It's the one she wanted. Two and half carats should buy me a couple of years before I gotta take the plunge."

Sheed laughed as her drink arrived. She raised the cocktail, saying, "You're a bastard," as a toast before sipping it.

On the TV behind the bar, Kristy Lee was briefly highlighting what would be covered on the NECN news after the game. According to the closed captioning, the Republican and Democratic races for the 2016 presidency and the latest developments in the Preferred Air 4273 crash last February were the top stories.

Deni returned his focus to Lisa. "So what's the deal? Where were ya? What's all the excitement about?"

"I was over at Taylor, Higgs & Pratt."

"Alex?" Alexandria Pratt, a partner at the largest law firm in Boston, arguably New England, had been the defense attorney of record for a case that Deni had been peripherally party to. A case in which he and Lisa ultimately solved and exonerated her wealthy client of the crimes for which he was accused. Alex had hired the small-time investigators on an ad-hoc basis on occasions since. Deni wasn't a fan. He had a defense attorney he liked to work with in New Hampshire, Ryan Wells. Ryan was a friend. Ryan Wells was someone he trusted. Alex Pratt was not.

Lisa, on the other hand—as a newly appointed full-partner in a business that Deni had started after quitting the Massachusetts State Police Crimes Against Persons division in Troop H years ago—looked forward to the calls from Alexandria Pratt. Pratt was tough but fair, and they never had to worry that the checks would bounce. Her firm paid top dollar without batting an eye. They paid for a result. DIS had always delivered thus far, thus the call for this next thing.

Deni let Sheed handle those cases whenever possible, preferring to work in southern New Hampshire or the increasingly infrequent other calls in Boston.

Find my biological parents. Can you do a background check? My child is missing. The police gave up on my stolen Audi, think you could give it crack? Stuff like that. It barely paid the bills. If he didn't have other ways to supplement his income, he and Ani would be struggling. As it stood, Ani was currently the majority breadwinner.

"Yeah. This is a big one. This will make our year. Maybe the next three," Lisa said while fidgeting in her chair. Her excitement was palpable.

"Then take it. You always do. I think you're doin' better than me with cases these days."

"Exactly. When it was just you, you went up to 'New Hampster' and took whatever Ryan sent your way. Between what came by you down here and the caseload up there, you made a pretty decent living."

"I got by, She. I also had to take fights, be a landlord, and do other shit to keep afloat. I told you hookin' up to my wagon wasn't gonna make you rich."

Deni, a master in Brazilian Jiu Jitsu, supplemented his meager income as a Mass Statie, back when he was a trooper, with amateur—and the occasional professional undercard—MMA fights. Those days were gone. He was too old and had suffered too many injuries to take on bouts now, though he still sparred at the gym owned by Kenny Florian in Brookline four to five days per week.

He'd just fully recovered from his latest injury—two dislocated shoulders at the hands of someone who got the drop on him during an investigation—which was another sign that he was slowing down a step.

He now owned his three-decker in Southie outright. He lived on the bottom floor—now with Ani—the top two floors were rented out and had been since he bought the place. The income from the leases more than paid the mortgage back when he had one.

Deni drove a Land Rover, which was purchased by trading in a Mercedes AMG worth over $100,000, which was given to him for services rendered on a previous case he'd worked a few years prior in South Carolina.

By outward appearances—with the exception of his daily attire and the tapestry of tattoos which covered his body from shoulders to thighs—it looked like Deni was beyond comfortable and well-off. By comparison to most, he was. But he had worked for it, year in and year out, and the mileage has and was taking its toll.

"Am I complaining?" Lisa leaned in to him, making her voice heard in the noisy establishment. "Have I once complained since coming to work for you?"

"You used to bitch constantly about bein' made a partner. Now you share half the bills instead of just gettin' paid. Sorry you went down that rabbit hole?"

"Not for one-second. I bring in money, and I'm bringing in more than you I might add. I'm paying my dues. I know what you did for me, and you didn't have to. I'm a big girl, I knew what I was doing when Hobbs and I caught that case with the floater. I followed you on that investigation even though I was told not to. I knew I would get fired if I got caught, and I did it anyway. I knew it would be a while before I could prove to you that I deserved to be made a full-partner, and I'm damn sure going to live up to my end now that I am one."

"You're doin' a good job, She. Wicked good. I'm happy you're happy. What's your fuckin' point?"

"I can't do this one alone."

"You want me to work with you on this Alex thing, whatever it is?"

She nodded.

"No. Forget it. I'll work anything else with you, but not for her." He waived at the bartender who miraculously saw him and nodded that another round would be served within the calendar year.

"Why do you hate her so much?"

"Hate's a strong word. I don't hate her, but she's a greasy, conniving, slippery ...." Deni shook his head ".... fuckin' lawyer."

"So is Ryan," Lisa said throwing up her hands. Her right hand hit a patron that was standing right behind her barstool. The offended man looked for an apology and received a 'get bent' look instead.

He shriveled back to his own conversation.

"I trust Ry. He's saved my ass, and I've saved his. We've been in the trenches. That bitch ...." He was back to shaking his head but trailed off, never finishing his thought.

"Well? 'That Bitch' what? Articulate your thought. Really. I'd love to hear how she's different."

Lisa Sheed, a lesbian former police detective for the same troop that Deni had worked in, was a strong advocate for equality. Whatever a man could do, a woman could do better and still take care of a family, if that's what she chose to do. Unfortunately, on the whole, they didn't get the same treatment or pay. She'd had to work and push to get where she was in the Staties, only to be tossed out by her male superiors. Successful women were often regarded as cheats or slippery when they rose to power over men. If that was where Deni was going, she was going to call him out on it.

"You've met Ry. And Ang. They're hippies. Greater good. This ain't a 'man versus woman' thing, She. This is a 'she's willin' to do whatever it takes to get her client off' kinda thing. Ry will do what he can to protect the rights of a defendant, or get a verdict if he thinks the guy's innocent. Alex ain't like that. No matter what sick fuck can pony up the dough for her retainer, she'll do whatever it takes to make sure the guy doesn't see the inside of a cell."

"Or girl."

"What?"

"You said 'guy'. Women go to prison too."

"But not as much. You know what I'm sayin'," Deni said with a roll of the eyes. "I saw her first hand." *Saw-r her*.

"Well, this time it's different. This time she's litigating a potential civil matter, victim's comp case. Defending actually. First she needs to know if there was any overt criminal act. If not, that negates the need for a civil case, meaning no need to award compensation damages. The case could be years down the road," Lisa explained. "Meanwhile, we keep billing Taylor, Higgs & Pratt."

Their new drinks arrived. At $25 a round, Deni could have purchased an entire bottle of whiskey for what this bar-tab would come to.

Deni took a sip. Lisa could see his wheels turning, a deep far-way look in his eyes. He was coming up short. He glanced at the TV for a beat, she did the same. It was between innings, the score was still unknown behind the closed captioning, and a repeated commercial for the upcoming NECN news came on.

"Im strugglin'. I don't get it. What the hell are we talkin' about here?"

Lisa pointed to the television.

Deni shrugged. Nothing.

"Flight 4273."

"The crash?"

Lisa nodded.

"I must be drunk. Are you out of your fucking mind? What the hell do we know about planes? Or crashes? Isn't that what the FAA does? No. Absolutely not. We would be completely out of our depth. Tell her thanks but no thanks. I'll go find a missing kitten first."

"I already told her we would do it, Deni. I signed some papers. We meet her client tomorrow morning at nine."

Friday
9:00 A.M. October 2, 2015

THE TAYLOR, HIGGS & PRATT EXECUTIVE CONFERENCE room, located on the twenty-eighth floor of the high rise building the prestigious law firm occupied, was known as the fishbowl.   The room was encased with sound-proof glass; the outer glass wall overlooked Back Bay and Boylston Street below; the three other glass walls separated those using the room from the attorneys, paralegals, support staff and the like who were amassing thousands upon thousands of billable hours on their behalf outside of it. Sharks met inside the bowl while a sea of smaller fish went about their business in the periphery.

Deni and Sheed carpooled, arriving twenty minutes before the nine o'clock meeting, which they assumed was plenty early, but the conference room was full and its occupants were awaiting their arrival. It took a few more minutes for them to enter the room where they could see the gaggle of anxious people, as the glass doors to enter were hidden within the glass walls.

Lisa wore an off-the-rack knee-length lace skirt and Jersey jacket from H&M, which was unusual to say the least. She normally donned pullovers and slacks, albeit from the same store. Her usual Sig Sauer was in its usual holster on her hip, however.

Deni wore a suit and tie, which he only did at funerals, forgoing his usual T-shirt and jeans. Ani had to dig out a pair of dress shoes hidden in a box in the back of his closet for him, or he would have been forced to where one of his usual pairs of Chuck Taylor All-Stars. Like his partner, his weapon was hidden under his suit jacket.

Both looked uncomfortable and nervous even to those in the conference room who had never met them.

Alexandria Pratt, who spent a considerable amount of her immense disposable income and more limited disposable time to ensure a proper appearance, stood with a few of her subordinates at the front of the room, welcoming the free-lance investigators into the fishbowl. She donned a 1940's style Jean Patou black wool and satin dress suit, showing just enough of her enhanced and ample cleavage to remain classy.

All but two of the dozen-plus chairs around the large table were filled with middle-aged men who looked very comfortable in their Armani. It was a boys club, the only women were Alex and Lisa.

"Thank you for coming, won't you both have a seat?" Alex said, like they'd just arrived at her home instead of her penthouse office space. "Allow me to introduce you to everyone." She pointed to the other end of the oval table, "This is Reid Lansing, President and CEO of Lansing Aerospace. He is the third generation at the helm of a truly great American company. To his left is Timothy Vahn, Chief Financial Officer, former CFO of Bank of America and McDonnell Douglas before the Boeing merger. Next is Art Connors, VP of Quality Assurance, I'm told he worked his way up to his exalted position from the factory floor, and has an encyclopedic knowledge of every nut, bolt and rivet on each of the aircraft Lansing manufactures. To his—"

"—Sorry to interrupt you, Alex," Deni said, still standing with Lisa. "But before you get too far into who's-who, we came in person to tell you that we can't take the case."

Pratt's frequent Botox injections didn't hide her shock and embarrassment.

"Mister Dennihan—"

"—Deni." She knew to call him 'Deni', 'Mister Dennihan' was for her guest's benefit.

"Deni. I was informing the Lansing senior leadership of your most unorthodox but effective investigation techniques. Services that have proven quite useful to our firm in the recent past."

"Yeah, thanks for that. Two hundred people are dead, somebody has to pay the piper," Deni said with a shrug. "Sucks to be you."

Reid Lansing stood up, fastening the button on his suit jacket. "Alex, we flew fifteen hundred miles for this meeting. Ten leaders of my company, who are in the middle of a crisis with probably a thousand other immediate demands on their time, took that time to be here to meet these so-called investigators that you insisted would be crucial to stifling, if not eliminate, these completely false accusations made against our company and our aircraft. 'Bruin in Body-Armor' you said. 'Unwavering dedication and tenacity'. You insisted that this two-person investigative team wouldn't rest until we could get a handle on this. I'm here because our legal team said that your firm was the best in Boston, in the best position to litigate a Boston case. I'm here because you said that this could be handled. I'm here at your word, Alex. We are all here at your word."

"Mister Lansing, please. There has been a slight miscommunication, one that can be resolved if I can just have a quick moment alone with my investigators."

Reid slowly returned to his seat with obvious reluctance about both the situation and leaving the room.

Alex all but shoved the two investigators out of the fishbowl and into the area in front of the sea of offices and cubicles beyond the glass. The three could still be seen by the Lansing executives, but not heard.

"Keep smiling or turn your back to them or so help me you'll rue the day you fucked with me," Alex said through her teeth. "Lisa? What the hell is going on?"

"You can talk to me," Deni said. There was no smiling or facial expression of any kind. "This is my call. She admits that this is too big for just her, I say it's too big for both of us. We ain't equipped to investigate a plane crash, but thanks for thinkin' that we can. I don't know the first thing about planes, for starters. I just know from the news that two hundred people are dead, two hundred people who were hoping for sunny fuckin' Florida never made it. You've seen the coverage. The papers. The simulations they show on TV. Those that weren't lucky enough to be knocked out or killed on the way down, drowned in the middle of the Atlantic and are still being fished out eight months later. I know what I see in the papers. On the news. FAA, TSA, FBI, NTSB, the Attorney General ..... They all got an iron in the fire. The federal fucking government. Not for nothin', but I been down that road and lost."

"Deni. I'm not asking you to impede any ongoing federal investigation. I'm asking you to go back in there and listen to what they have to say. Listen to what has happened up to date, and not reported on the news or in the 'pay-pahs'. I'm asking you to do what you do best. Investigate—as someone who is stubbornly impartial—what, if anything, happened to that plane. To see if they should just settle a class-action lawsuit, work up a victim's comp number that everyone can live with before it goes to the courts, or if they should take it to the hoop because they're innocent."

"I don't know how to spell it out for you, lady. I don't know nothin' about planes. You could show me anything you want and I wouldn't know if it went in a jet or a Tonka truck. I don't even work on cars. If I turn the key and it don't start, well that's about the extent of what I can do."

Alex shook her head. "You're a fresh set of eyes, Deni. You have instincts. Both of you," she said looking at Sheed. "You're right. One hundred and ninety-seven people are dead, only a fraction of which have ever been found, or ever will be. This tragedy has no answers. No finality. No dignity. Their families are angry and they deserve to know the truth about what happened. They are all devastated and pointing fingers at anyone and everyone. There has to be a reason. There has to be a reason all of those lives and the lives of their families have been irrevocably destroyed. The truth may be that sometimes things happen for no reason. Or, the truth might be that someone is to blame and that person or persons need to be held accountable. You both will aid in determining if they should settle with the grieving families quietly, or publicly point out that they didn't do anything wrong and welcome anybody to prove differently.

"The suit is based out of Boston. The plane took off from Boston, the lion's share of those passengers are from Massachusetts. If this goes to trial, it happens in a courtroom right here in Boston. It's my job to advocate for Lansing. Legally represent them. I need investigators to help me do just that.

"Not only is this the right thing to do, Deni—the thing that you are more than capable of doing—it's the thing that will get you well-paid in the process. High six figures plus expenses. For the truth, whatever that may be. Nearly half a million a piece. Will you go back in there and at least listen?"

She'd raised some good points.

The families did need answers. They deserved them. He and Sheed would at least try to find out what happened. What harm could come of that? He felt like the whore he'd outed the day before.

"I have one condition," Deni said after a time.

"I'm listening."

"We get paid by you. The law firm. Taylor, Higgs & Pratt. Not by them," he said as he nodded toward the glass box full of suits. "I don't wanna owe them nothin'. If they pay us, we work for them. Unbiased means unbiased. I don't care what you're charging them, we get paid by you. We work for you and let the chips fall where they may, if we find anything at all."

"That's fair. Now can we go back in there and try to pretend that this embarrassing episode never occurred?"

When they were all seated and all introductions were made, Alex began her presentation.

"Okay, here is what we know about flight 4372 to Fort Lauderdale last February."

Deni and Lisa were each given several thick binders with reports. FAA flight schedule for 4372. TSA. NWS. Witness deps. NTSB findings. PA Maintenance logs. Crew evaluations and psychological reports. NWS. ATC statements. Lansing ADs. It was all a foreign language at first glance. Deni stopped flipping through them as Alex Pratt continued with her presentation.

"The flight was scheduled for takeoff from Logan at 1:15 P.M. on Friday, February 13, which it did without incident. TSA reported no confiscated items or problems that day, which for Logan could mean one of two things—either they didn't screen thoroughly enough to have anything to report, or they had an unusually easy day where an abnormally high number of travelers did what they were supposed to. Boston seems to be where problems in the sky always originate, which is why they took it personally and conducted an exhaustive investigation. After three months, TSA produced the findings from that investigation and generated a seventeen hundred page report, which is in front of you, basically saying that they had nothing to report."

Deni raised his hand like he was back in school.

"You don't have to raise your hand, Deni, just fire off a question if you have one," Alex said.

"How can TSA have typed up a seventeen hundred page report if there was nothin' to report?"

"That's a fair question that only a government agency could actually answer, but they did. And as far as legal culpability beyond a reasonable doubt, they are in the clear. TSA covered their ass sufficiently from a legal standpoint. Bottom line; they didn't do anything, or by negligence, allow someone to do something that caused that plane to fall from the sky. No bombs. No hostage situation. No terrorist plot. But we're getting ahead of ourselves."

Alex took a deep breath and focused back on her presentation in the order in which she had prepared it.

"The carrier, Preferred Air, submitted a truckload of documentation about maintenance of the aircraft and every procedure they go through prior to takeoff and post-landing— including that the flight was scheduled to take three hours and nineteen minutes, and the weather was clear. We have another report from the National Weather Service, along with sworn statements from Captains and crew from other carriers; SPIRIT, JetBlue, American, and United, who were also flying passenger jets in the area to deliver their passengers to Fort Lauderdale, who corroborate the skies were clear with little or no chop. Two of those flights, a captain and first officer from each, have given four separate depositions about what they saw in the final moments of Flight 4273, before it dove into the Ocean near the Pelagic Sargassum Habitat.

"The plane, model—"

"—L530," Reid interrupted. "Our 530 line is a direct competitor to the Airbus A320 and the Boeing 737 commercial aircrafts. It is by far the best, newest, most state-of-the-art commercial widebody produced on the planet and was, by industry standards, brand new."

The VP of QA, Art Connor, spoke up. "Slightly more than a thousand hours is pretty much cherry. 530s are designed and built to fifty-thousand hours, twenty-thousand cycles. We test for three times that. We've been manufacturing this line for five years without so much as a hiccup. This particular plane was in the air long enough to detect any bugs, which of course there weren't any, but not nearly long enough where it would need any substantial maintenance."

"Again, PA made their service records public, along with every other 530 they currently have in service, which all indicate that they adhere to all suggested course of action by both the manufacturer and by the FAA," Alex said.

Deni raised his hand again.

"Again, you do not need to raise your hand. Question?"

"Yeah. What does that mean? Course of action?"

Art Connor took the question. "It means that over the course of time, every plane will need some part or another replaced. You can make the best aircraft in the world, which we do, and before that plane is put out to pasture, you are going to need to replace something. Normal wear and tear. Each carrier has to legally keep meticulous service records to provide to the FAA, or Lansing, upon request. On top of FAA mandates, we ensure proper maintenance and records are kept as part of the agreement when we sell a carrier our planes. We collect those records from each and every carrier, for each and every plane that we have active in the sky. The L530s, 60s, 70s, and the new 580 line—which is the largest commercial passenger aircraft in the sky, fifty seats larger than the Airbus 380. All of the data is then used to look for patterns. If we feel that one part or another is being worn too quickly or is best if replaced with an updated technology, we notify the carriers and demand that they replace it. Depending on the part, we may auto-ship them."

"Like a factory recall," Deni said.

"No. We don't have factory recalls," Reid Lansing said in a stern tone that wasn't lost on the occupants of the room. "They're called Service Bulletins. If the carriers refuse to comply with our SBs, we get the FAA involved, who then issue Airworthiness Directives, mandating compliance. If they don't, the FAA has the ability to shut them down if need be. We've been making planes for nearly seventy years. We have improvements that we recommend to the carriers that purchase planes from us. What Alex was saying was that PA, Preferred Airlines, the carrier who purchased the aircraft that went into the Atlantic, maintained their L530s and their records in accordance with both our SBs and the FAA's ADs."

Alex again took over her meeting.

"So the maintenance on the flight, as far as paperwork goes, didn't let them down. So we then looked at carrier staff. Captain Tim Raymond was seasoned and had never had a substantial issue with any commercial aircraft he'd flown—with PA or otherwise. Ex-military, L530 and C-17 by Boeing were his bread and butter. Over 20,000 hours between the two types. He moved to commercial flights initially for JetBlue and then PA. Solid as they come. His First Officer, Matthew Portman, was no slouch either. Over 9,000 hours after certification in the 530 and had first-seated as often as not. Re-cert was late last year, within a few months of the flight that went down."

It was Sheed's turn with a question.

"Do you have the black box? Don't they always know what caused the plane to crash by finding the black box?"

The execs from Lansing had a chuckle.

Deni came to her aid. "What's so funny?"

"The black box is a big myth," Reid Lansing said.

"There's no black box?"

"There are several of them. Fourteen, in fact. There isn't one box that, if found, will tell us anything and everything that happened with that aircraft. We've recovered two; the CVR and a QAR, along with approximately seventy percent of the plane. Mostly the fuselage and wings. We've just finished acquiring and reassembling 4273 at the plant, and will now begin to determine what caused the crash. We've not delved into diagnostics or recreating the flight in a simulator at all, we've been focusing on collection from the ocean in a nationally protected oceanic area and reassembling at the plant. The investigation truly begins next week. We're unsure what, if any, real data will be generated from the two so-called black boxes. What we do know is that at some point the starboard engine failed. A GE9X. Even the best jet engine, which General Electric makes, will fail with what that plane went through. The depositions Alex spoke of suggest that 4273 underwent severe pitch oscillations, which would put a tremendous strain on the engines. Suffice to say that, thus far, what we haven't been able to determine that a single thing was wrong with the 530 airframe we manufactured."

Of course you haven't, Deni thought but didn't say. He didn't need to, Lansing read his mind.

"Look, you're going to read or hear testimony about how the plane acted before it crashed. Supposedly. If what the competing airline pilots say is true, the crash wasn't because of either our airframe or their powerplant. As I said, GE makes the best commercial aviation engine ever invented. Puts all others to shame. However, we don't make the engines. We make the airframe and install whatever engine the carrier wants. Obviously the families of this tragedy need to blame someone. And while I feel for them on a personal level, we can't just admit to whatever wrongdoing we're accused of because we feel bad, take our wrap on the knuckles from the FAA or worse, and pay these people whatever settlement money their victim's comp litigator comes up with. It will destroy my family business. The business my grandfather built. It would be irresponsible business."

Timothy Vahn interjected. This was his territory. "One hundred ninety-seven souls—some financially worth more than others based upon age, health, and current yearly income—plus legal fees for both sides, a settlement would cost Lansing approximately $40.5 Billion in hard costs. It would also the slow if not cease all orders for future planes ..... Lansing, a great American success story the likes of Ford, Carnegie and Vanderbuilt, would fall. Ten thousand jobs at the 530 plant alone. Then there are the carriers who have purchased our planes, they would fold or be forced to buy a new fleet. Companies that manufacture our parts would fold. Our military contracts would go elsewhere, all of those defense planes would then need to be replaced ..... There is more at stake here than compensating families who've lost loved ones, we're talking about a national economic crisis that the President can't fix with a buyout."

The room fell silent as the words of the heartless finance guru took root.

After a time, Lansing spoke. "There is a litigator, a Trey Keating, who is waiting for the dust to settle on the various investigations and likely has a team of his own. He was hired on contingency by a ....." Reid looked at his iPad sitting on the conference table. " .....Sorina Kane, survivor of three of the passengers on the flight. Her husband and two daughters. All of these agencies, FAA, NTSB, FBI ..... They're all wringing their hands on behalf of the taxpayers. Their has to be a reason. The public wants answers. Well, when they rule out terrorism and airline negligence, the next deep pocket is the manufacturer. We make a safe product, Mister—Deni. We've been making the safest, most technologically advanced aircraft since we began making them seventy years ago. The military says so. Our safety record says so. Even now, the FAA still says so. What happened on that flight is not a manufacturing failure. There was nothing wrong with that plane. Period."

The room again fell silent, Alex used the moment to assess where she was in her presentation and to get the meeting back on track.

"Okay. So. As Mister Lansing just alluded, we do have recorded and eye-witness testimony about 4273, but nothing explains why. We requested all of that information from the National Transit Safety Board. We obtained sworn statements from all parties and the transcripts of the distress call to Air Traffic Control. ATC has a recording from their end. According to the statement by a David Moore, senior controller at Charleston AFB slash International Airport, he responded after the flight was handed over to him from

Wilmington International a few minutes earlier, while the plane was at cruise."

"Cruise?" Sheed looked around the room. Connors placated her.

"Cruise. Point eight mach, give or take, at 31,000 feet. Maintaining airspeed, altitude, angles, configuration, etc under autopilot. Wilmington didn't hand over a problem, they handed over a plane that was doing everything normally when it left their airspace."

"Gotcha."

Alex waited a few seconds.

"Before I begin this for the investigators, it is important for you both to understand that we can hear everything that Control is saying on this recording, not solely what was transmitted to 4273 by the ATC. When we get to the CVR, the Cockpit Voice Recorder, one of the so-called 'black boxes', the only thing we'll hear will be *transmitted* communications from the ATC, which you are also hearing on this recording. The CVR records sounds from three microphones; the cockpit and any ambient sound, and what each of the two pilots communicated. You will not hear any of that here, just what was happening at Air Traffic Control and what was communicated to and from 4273. Make sense?"

Everyone nodded. She pressed a button on her laptop. The audio from ATC was sent to the telecommunication system in the center of the conference room table.

"CHS Approach, this is Preferred Air 4-2-7-3. We have an emergency." The voice was calm.

"Go ahead, 4-2-7-3."

"Request priority clearance for emergency landing in Charleston, if we can get there."

"Okay, 4-2-7-3, copy your request priority. State the nature of your emergency."

"Wing and fuse damage. Passenger emergency," the pilot said. "Trying to recover. When we do, we'll need fifty ambulances on the ground, maybe more."

"PA 4-2-7-3, say again. Are you requesting fifty ambulances? Holy shit. Did he say fifty ambulances?"

"Affirmative. At least. I say again, we encountered severe wing and fuselage damage. Power plant is failing. We have severe injuries to passengers and crew."

"Do you need medical personnel as well?"

"Roger, Approach. We need everyone you can get."

"Mother of God. My data block reads Captain Tim Raymond, is that you?"

"Negative. This is first officer Matthew Portman."

"Can you estimate the nature of the injuries you're bringing in?"

"Negative."

"Is anyone unconscious?"

"Affirmative, Approach. Passengers and flight crew are unconscious and possibly dead, but I cannot give you a number."

There was a pause in the audio. ATC personnel are trained for these situations, though nothing can prepare them for the infrequent actual scenario. They knew everything was being recorded and going to be heavily reviewed. They also needed to remain calm and more importantly needed to keep the pilot calm, though that didn't seem to be a necessity here. Portman was steady. Most pilots are. Pilots are a cocky lot. They won't admit defeat. Lives were at stake. They controlled the plane and the lives of everyone inside their aircraft. Pilots don't think in terms of 'crash' and they certainly don't say the word. The pause in communication was for Moore to steady himself.

"4-2-7-3, what is the condition of the flight deck?"

"Losing the flight deck. Repeat, losing the deck. FDAU tracking multiple failures. We've just lost pressure and need an immediate place to land. Repeat. Need an immediate place to land."

"4-2-7-3, you are cleared for landing at CHS, all others are standing by and you have the green."

"Not going to make CHS. We're looking at a water landing."

"Holy ….. Copy. Can you specify the nature of the failures?"

"Airspeed over 400 knots. Altitude dropping fast. Rate of Descent 8000 plus feet per minute. Angle at 60. Configuration is dirty."

"Holy shit this guy's gonna crash! He's dropping at over 8,000 feet per minute! **Can you level it off? Can you make CHS?**"

Static.

"Repeat. 4-2-7-3, can you make CHS? Can you gain control?"

Static.

"4-2-7-3, do you read?"

"4-2-7-3, this is CHS Approach. Do you copy?"

Alex closed her laptop.

Deni looked at the room full of suits.

"Well, it sounds to me like you boys make a wicked good plane. Pissah." He stuck his thumb up like he was hitchhiking.

Reid Lansing didn't care for the sarcasm. "Mister—"

"—I mean, I'm no expert, guys, but it seems to me somethin' was fucked up with that plane."

Friday
7:30 P.M. October 2, 2015

DENI AND SHEED WERE ASKED TO MEET ALEX PRATT FOR dinner. She wanted to meet with them immediately after the meeting they'd all attended that morning with the Lansing executives; unfortunately, she had another meeting in that time-slot with said execs followed by babysitting her clients back onto their private plane.

Dinner would be at L'Espalier, a pricey modern French restaurant about a block away from the skyscraper Taylor, Higgs and Pratt majority occupied, closer to the Prudential Tower on Boylston Street. Alex had a standing table at the restaurant whether she actually dined there or not. When you pay over $200 a person, as often as Alex did, the restaurant made sure her table was always available.

Alex ordered wine pairings for the table, after each of them were handed menus without prices. She then explained to her guests that they were getting the prix fixe menu, three courses from which they could choose from five options for each course, and a wine would be paired to accompany it.

Deni told her he wasn't much of a wine person, preferring the whiskey he'd already ordered, but it made no difference. Wine came anyway, along with the plates they'd ordered. Food and beverages arrived and departed the table without a word. The staff at L'Espalier knew how to treat Alexandria Pratt and whatever guests she'd meet with on any given night. Service was felt yet not seen or heard.

"Lansing is concerned," Alex said after a demi-bite of her Cavendish Farms quail breast and a sip of 2012 Trimbach Riesling. "He thinks you're both amateurs and not on his side."

45

"We're not supposed to be on his side," Lisa offered.

"Not for nothin', but didn't you tell me in your little speech outside the conference room that all you wanted is the truth?" Deni asked. "Can't have the truth and be for or against either side right off rip."

"That's what I told him. He's absolutely convinced that his product is safe and that nothing went wrong with his L530. He thinks it's pilot error. Possibly powerplant. But he can't prove it. And with a record like Raymond's, the pilot, and a huge company like General Electric, those are very tough sells."

"What else could it be, right?" Deni said with an obvious snarky tone. "If it ain't us, it's gotta be them. No bomb. No terrorist. Gotta be somebody else. Why not GE? Or better yet, PA. Can't prove it with repair records, cuz there weren't any major repairs. Gotta be the pilot right?" Deni shoved a Diver scallop into his mouth and sat back heavy in his chair. He finished his thought while chewing his shellfish, a social faux-pas as far as Alex was concerned, but she let it go. "They're gonna shit all over these pilots cuz they're dead and can't fight back."

"It does seem like they're trying to protect their precious company," Lisa added.

"Of course," Alex said. "Ten thousand workers, just at that one Lansing plant. You heard the CFO. He might not be warm and fuzzy, but he's correct. If Lansing goes down, it won't be good for you or me or Joey or Janey taxpayer either. Did you know that each of those 530s goes for about $117 million? Do you know how many carriers consider the 530 the best plane in the sky? Times the number of domestic flights for each carrier each day, let alone international flights? Not Airbus who churns them out for about $97 million. Not Boeing for about $110 mil. Each of these manufacturers might be less expensive, but not better. Not according to safety records. Not according to anyone in and around the industry that knows anything about it. For what it's worth? I believe them."

"Is that it? That's what you're goin' with? That's why you're representin' 'em? Because you believe them? Why you? Why us?"

"Because the flight originated in Boston. Any criminal trial against them would be in Federal Court here in Boston, and the potential civil class-action/victim's comp suit is being instigated by Sorina Kane, a Massachusetts resident, who is represented by Trey Keating, a Massachusetts Tort Litigator and Vic Comp attorney. That's why my firm is representing them, and why I will use every resource at my disposal to defend them. Including you two."

"Nice speech," Deni said before downing the rest of his drink. Another arrived at virtually the same second he returned the highball glass to the tablecloth.

"They're going to do the unprecedented," Alex said. "Lansing is going to open up everything for you. Open book. Cart blanche. The VP of Quality Assurance, one of the execs that you met today, Art Connor? He's going to be your liaison at the factory. Any question you have, any document that you want to see ..... Anything. You'll get it. You just have to sign a confidentiality agreement. They can't have you going off to a competitor with proprietary information."

"So anything we find, has to be kept a secret? Doesn't that defeat the purpose?" Lisa asked.

"Anything proprietary. Technology ..... Anything patented ..... That stuff you can't give to anyone else. Negligence or criminal or things of that nature is fair game. I had a team of lawyers draft the contract this afternoon," Alex said as she handed each of them a copy of the thick legalese. "You'll need to sign that before you officially start your investigation."

Deni shook his head. "I'll sign it but it's all a waste of time. I can't believe I let you two talk me into this. They've had eight months to cover their tracks. And even if I knew where to start—which I don't have the foggiest fuckin' clue—I wouldn't be able to tell you what's-what because I don't know nothin' about planes. And the cherry on top? The best part? If it involves anything they got a patent on, I can't tell anybody or they can sue me for everything I got or will ever have. This case is a real shit sandwich." He pushed his plate away, toward the center of the cloth table, but was taken away before it reached its destination. The service negated the desired statement he was looking to make.

"That's why you'll have the VP of QA by your side the entire time," Alex said. "You'll have unfettered access to the recovered plane, the entire assembly line, the administrative offices ..... The entire place. You fly out on Monday."

Deni leaned in. "Excuse you? What did you just say?"

"Monday. You fly out to Joplin on Monday. They'll have a car waiting, a hotel suit for each of you, for as long as you stay."

"Joplin?"

"Joplin, Missouri. That's where the remnants of the plane are. The factory where they built the 530. Lansing. Where did you think it was? Here in Boston?"

Deni sat back in his chair, hand waiving at his neck like he was cutting his throat. "I'm done. That's it."

Lisa moved toward him. "Deni ..... We're committed."

"Nuh-uh."

"What do you have against Joplin?" Alex asked.

"We got a business here. Cases here. Both of us can't go. And for how long? To the mid-west? Nope. Not this kid."

It dawned on Lisa.

"Flying. It's the flying. You're afraid."

"It's a private jet," Alex said. "They'll have one waiting for you here on Monday Morning. A couple of hours. Tops. You'll be there by mid-day."

"I ain't afraid to fly. I've flown before. Costa Rica. Ireland. California. South Carolina. But you want me to get on a plane made by the very company that put one into the drink? The company that I'm supposed to be investigating? They could decide I'm a liability and just nose that fucker into a corn field. Nope. Line drawn."

"What is the safest airline to fly the day after a plane crash?"

Nobody responded to Alex's question, so she answered it herself.

"The airline that crashed. Lansing is under a microscope."

"Not me. And it was eight months ago, not yesterday," Deni said.

"Well, I'm in," Sheed offered. "I'll go it alone if I have to."

Alex shook her head. "I'm hiring the both of you. Package deal. Take it or leave it. I thought we agreed this morning? Outside the conference room? Two hundred people are dead and you said you were dedicated to learn why. Yes or no? Once and for all."

Deni shook his head.

Lisa said, "Deni I signed a contract."

"I didn't."

"Can I have a minute?" Lisa asked, standing and pulling Deni to his feet.

Alex waved toward the rest of the small dining room with her left hand. *Be my guest.*

Outside the restaurant, on Boylston Street, Lisa punched Deni in the chest. "What the fuck? I thought you were in? Justice for the families and mid-six figures in our pockets. *EACH.* This will keep us busy for the rest of this year and probably next. This about the greater good, Deni. What's your deal?"

"My deal is that we're over our heads. We're gonna get chauffeured around the factory on a guided fuckin' tour and we're supposed to figure this out? Planes crash. People die. I want to know why, everyone wants to know why. But we ain't gonna be the people who solve it. Federal agencies are combing through every shred of evidence to hold feet to the fire and have come up with jack shit so far. But we're gonna save the fuckin' day? She, we're two ex-detectives who are tryin' to make a buck on the private side. This is a big case. A big deal. *That's* my deal."

"I've never know you to be a coward, Deni. You don't back away from anything."

"I'm not backing away. I'm bowing out. There's a difference."

"Alexandria Pratt is going to defend Lansing in any case or courtroom that she needs to, with or without us. What harm could we do? We'll kick the tires on this thing and see if we can ask the right questions. Maybe we'll get lucky. Maybe we don't find anything and we still get a fat check. Maybe we get justice for the families. Maybe we'll make a difference. Isn't that why we do this? That's why I do it. It's not the hours. It's certainly not because Reg loves it. This case moves us up to the big-time. I know I can handle it. I know you can handle it, even if you don't."

Deni took in a deep breath. The autumn air was cold. Pedestrians moved around them on the sidewalk in front of the restaurant, continuing on their path down Boylston toward the Marathon finish line. Cabs and traffic moved in the same direction on the one-way street. He looked at his blue Chuck Taylors, continuing to think.

He'd worked on big cases in the past, both for the Massachusetts State Police and privately. Organized crime. Big Pharma. Attorney General. High-profile murders. This seemed too big a monster. But the others did at the time also, and he managed to get through them. Not easily, but he managed.

He looked back up at the shivering Lisa Sheed. She waited for an answer. She was waiting for the correct answer. She wouldn't give up. When that woman wanted something, she went after it as relentlessly as he did.

And she wanted this.

He shook his head and looked out at the traffic. At the leaves falling from a tree being allowed to grow from the sidewalk on the opposite side of Boylston.

"I'm not getting on one of their planes."

"So we'll book a different flight on Monday," she said excitedly.

"And how do I know if that's an L530 or not?"

"See? You're learning something already."

"Very funny. Fuck it. Let's do it. But I'm drivin' out there."

Saturday
3:15 A.M. October 3, 2015

COFFEE WAS ALWAYS MADE AND AT LEAST ONE CUP consumed before a conversation took place in the Dennihan household. It was an unwritten rule that even the Boston terrier, Hobey, understood. Don't bother the man until he's had a chance to wakeup, which on that morning was very early. It had taken two cups for Deni to get motivated for the journey that was to come.

It was still dark, the sun would continue to rest for a few more hours. The lights on the bottom floor of the three-decker illuminated the apartment and leaked out onto empty Bowen Street.

Deni was moving slowly, but Ani was abustle in trying to make final preparations for the trip.

"Bae, are you sure you want to take Hobey?" Ani asked while painstakingly adding another outfit into her suitcase.

"I don't wanna pay to keep him in that dog-hotel you looked up. He'll get sick and lonely. Besides, I don't know how long this thing is gonna take. My preference is that you *both* stay home, but we had that argument last night and we both know how that went."

"It'll be fun. We never get out of the city. I rarely take any time from work, and if I don't take it by the end of the year, I'll lose it."

As an advocate for battered and abused women, Ani had constant demands on her professional time. She felt that time away from work put women at risk of suffering through life with their abusers rather than attain exit strategies and garner a support system. She was well-paid for her efforts, both financially and emotionally.

"It ain't gonna be fun, hun. I'm gonna be workin'—"

"—I know. That was your default argument last night," Ani said. She now had their bags packed and was dragging them toward the front door.

She'd been mentally getting ready for the trip since the subject was first brought up when Deni came home. It had been a little over six hours since she was told that Deni would be going to Missouri. In that time; Ani had argued in favor of coming along, found a place to keep their dog—which they weren't going to end up using—notified her work that she would be taking some time, took a nap, and had now fully packed for the both of them.

And Deni was the one who was looking tired and ragged.

"It's oh-dark-thirty and this conversation is pointless. You're coming and anything I say against you makin' the trip is just going to get you pissed again."

"For the twentieth time, I wasn't—nor am I now—pissed. I just think it will be nice to spend some time together outside of Boston. Outside of Massachusetts. Hobey and I will be able to keep ourselves occupied while you and Lisa do your thing."

Deni shook his head.

"It's Joplin, Missouri. What kind of entertainment is going to keep you both occupied in the middle of nowhere?"

"Have you ever been?"

"To Joplin? No. And I'll bet everybody that lives there is wicked stoked about the day they get to leave."

"Mmmm-hmmm. Just go get dressed. You said you wanted to get an early start, and we still have to pick up Lisa, so chop-chop."

Deni slowly made his way down the hall toward the bedroom he shared with Ani. "Yeah. This is gonna be a real hoot."

"You ladies are outta control," Deni said. They were approximately six hundred miles into the fifteen hundred mile drive and he was losing his patience. Ani and Lisa were getting on nicely, conversing a mile a minute in his right ear. Ani would lean between the bucket seats in the front to say something to Lisa or Hobey in the back of the Land Rover, and Lisa would lean forward between them to say some other unimportant nonsense.

Deni was always a fast driver. Speed limits were merely a suggestion. As the front and back seat cackling became more annoying, his foot grew more heavy on the accelerator. They had only been on the road for a little more than five hours and they were already nearing Ohio, two hours and change ahead of schedule.

He'd made several suggestions for the two women to take the back seat and Hobey could ride 'shotgun', but the suggestion was disregarded each and every time.

"When did you get to be such a grump?" Ani asked.

"He's always been a grump, Ani, you're just late in realizing it," Lisa said into Deni's right ear.

"And stop switching my music. The two of you are drivin' me nuts."

Deni found technology to be the death of the human race. To say he hated it was an understatement. His Rover's bluetooth capability could share up to four devices for music, sound, navigation and the like. Until he met Ani, none had ever been linked to the Meridian 29 speaker 3-D sound system. It had been a revolution for him to use Pandora.

He filled the changer with Compact disks—which for him was a concession made years prior since he preferred vinyl—and shuffled through them or listened to Pandora.

Ani and Lisa were playing music battles with their phones through the SUV stereo system, each taking turns sending a song from their music collection. They shared a taste and a love for music, but none of it was familiar to Deni.

"How can you have a sound system like this and not appreciate music?" Sheed asked.

"Oh he loves music. Look at his T-shirt collection."

Deni always wore graphic tees, usually associated with rock bands. Or sports. Boston sports. Today's shirt depicted art and the song title 'The Heavy Persuader' from a now defunct California band, Buckfast Superbee. "He just hates *new* music. If it's not Nirvana or Metallica or classic rock, don't bother. I never get to listen to my music unless he's not around," Ani explained.

"You don't listen to music, hun. You listen to crap. That thing you were listening to the other night, 'Bitch where my money at?' or whatevah. That ain't music."

"It's 'Bitch Better Have My Money', Deni. And Rihanna is insanely popular," Ani said.

"I like her too, Deni."

"It's fuckin' terrible."

"He's so old for forty-two," Sheed said with a laugh. She tapped a button on the screen of her smartphone. Miley Cyrus' *Wrecking Ball* was replaced by *Funeral* by Band of Horses.

"How's this? Better?"

"At least it's music, but I still can't understand a single word. Have I heard this before? Who is it?"

"Probably not, and you probably wouldn't know the band if I told you," Sheed explained. "But the 'to know you is hard' lyric should ring pretty true."

Ani began to laugh.

"Do you two do this all day long?"

"We mostly have our own cases. If we're both in the office, or if one of us needs help with the computer," Lisa said nodding toward Deni, "otherwise we catch up or get advice over the phone. So the answer to your question is, no. I take it he doesn't share very much of his day with you?"

"He hates talking about his cases. He'd rather let me vent about my day," Ani said.

Lisa nodded. "You must need to vent, what you do is rough. Admirable but rough. I had to live through an abusive relationship once upon a time and that was the most horrible time of my life. For you to have to live through each of the stories that all these women that you help have to go through, over and over and over again, each and every day?"

"That was back when She liked dick," Deni explained. "Speakin' of which, why didn't Reg come along?" Deni said.

Ani reached across the vehicle and slapped him on the chest.

"Hey! I was just kiddin'."

"You can be such an ass sometimes, Deni," Ani said. She then turned to Lisa who was still leaned forward between the bucket seats.

"I'm sorry for him. That was uncalled for. How is she? Reggie right?"

"Yeah. Or Reg. For Regina. She's good. She would have loved to come. She's been anxious to meet you. We couldn't really afford the big wedding so we just JOP'd it, so she hasn't really met Deni either. Not more than to say a few words. Anyway, she couldn't get the time away. Honestly, the biggest thing between us is how many hours I spend doing this, and the fact that she thinks it's dangerous."

"It is dangerous, Lisa. In the time I've been with Deni, he's been concussed, had both shoulders dislocated, broken ribs, been shot at …. I'm going to be a widow before I'm even married."

"If you could not share that information with Reg, that would be great," Sheed said.

"Of course not. I'm just saying that I understand her worry. I'd love to meet her. I feel like we're just getting to know each other."

"I know, right? Not to change the subject," Lisa said, "but how are your plans coming along for the wedding?"

"*SHE*?" Deni gave her the look through the rearview mirror that was unmistakeable.

"What? I'm just curious."

"There are no plans. Just the Pre-Cana class we signed up for at church. We were lucky that Father Donnelly was willing to handle our class personally."

Pre-Cana marriage classes are mandatory for couples who want to be married in a Catholic church. The classes generally last six months prior to the ceremony and derived from the bible passage in John 2: 1-12, the feast at Cana in Galilee, where Jesus turned water into Wine. Irish Catholics have their traditions, new Pope or not.

"He's making you get married at Holy Cross? Don't let him fool you, he never goes to mass on Sundays," Lisa said.

"Oh, he's not making me. I'm making him. And he goes now, Father Donnelly insisted."

"Huh. This might sound ridiculous, but you're Asian. You don't hear of too many Asian Catholics. Right?"

"Maybe not in Boston, but believe it or not there are millions of Asian Catholics. Not to get into a history lesson, but crusaders brought Christianity to the Mongols during the Tang Dynasty and was widespread in the thirteenth century by Genghis Khan's grandson, Möngke. My grandparents were Catholic, my parents, me ...."

"Wow. Never would have guessed," Lisa said.

Ani chuckled. "We're not all Buddhists."

Sheed joined in the laughter.

The Rover was nearing the end of I-90 West near Cleveland, where Deni would then head South on I-271. Lake Erie was to their right, just north of the interstate, and about to be behind them. The Mass Pike slash New York Throughway slash Pennsylvania Highway and now interstate 90 West in Ohio was a toll road, necessitating payment every time a vehicle entered or left the interstate. In an effort to curb the number of vehicles on the exit ramps, and of course to make money, rest stops were designed for easy pull-off and not only had gas stations but had an assortment of eateries as well. One such sign indicated that the upcoming rest stop had a Dunkin' Donuts.

"Can we pull off?" Lisa asked. "I could use a Dunkies Turbo."

"Sounds good. I need a cup before tackling a new highway," Deni said, "and I think Hobey could use a stop."

"I need to pee also," Ani offered.

"It's unanimous. We're stoppin'."

The pit stop was as time consuming as it was frustrating for Deni. After topping off the tank—which the price of gas was exponentially higher than anywhere else in the known universe—and giving Hobey a much needed stretch of the legs, he wandered inside to see what was holding up the ladies. It was now after eight in the morning and it appeared that the Dunkin' Donuts on I-90W in Willoughby Hills, Ohio was the place to be. Both of his travel companions were still in line, Ani doing a little dance, the international sign for having to use the toilet.

"You haven't gone to the bathroom yet?" Deni asked after approaching them in line.

"No. This place is a mob-scene," Lisa said.

"Whattaya want? I'll order for everyone, you guys can go do your business."

"Coolatta," Ani said before racing away.

"Iced Dark Roast, Turbo'd." Sheed hustled to join Ani who had already made it halfway to the restroom.

"Hey. You can't cut the line, Mister."

Deni turned to see a tall and wide, mountain of a man, staring down at him. Deni was just shy of six feet tall and was shoulder-height to the offended party.

"Look, don't even try to start with me, guy. It's already been a wicked long day and I got a ways to go."

"Can't you see where the end of the line is? Back there," the large patron said, pointing about a dozen parties behind him.

"I didn't cut, there were two girls here holdin' the spot. They had to go take a leak. So relax there Sasquatch."

The man took exception and moved closer to Deni, index finger moving toward his chest like he was about poke him with it. But Deni was having none of it. Deni's right hand grabbed the man's forefinger and he used his left hand to push in on the man's elbow. The finger popped and if the man hadn't gone to his knees, his elbow would have also. The man's right pointer finger was broken, his right elbow only slightly hyperextended, just shy of tearing ligaments.

Deni looked to the rest of the people in the crowd, as he stepped on the man's thigh, holding him the kneeling position. *Was he going to get the bum's rush from someone else in line?* He squirmed his jacket open enough for the handle of his pistol to be seen, in case anyone was reading his mind about rushing him.

But nobody moved, they just stood in absolute shock as to what they'd just witnessed. A six foot-ish, one hundred seventy pound man dropped a six-five mammoth—who probably weighed close to, if not over, four bills—to his knees in about a second.

Deni let go of the finger and elbow when the line moved. He took his foot off the massive thigh as he warily turned toward the counter.

It was finally his turn to order drinks.

Only the lady behind the counter didn't understand a word Deni was saying.

The back of his neck was burning as he ordered a 'Lodge Regul-ah'—Regul-ah' for the third time, when the ladies returned.

"What's going on?" Ani said. She could see that the wheels were about to come off of the bus.

"Tons of fun behind me wanted to take a shot at the title, and now this thing doesn't understand english."

It took a millisecond for Ani to fully comprehend the events that took place in the short time it took for her to relieve her bladder.

"Deni ...." Ani said, closing her eyes, "GOD .....I've got this. She turned to the lady behind the counter. "He wants a large regular coffee with cream and sugar, I want a Coolatta .... "

Lisa spoke up and explained what she wanted, an iced dark roast with an extra shot of espresso.

"And whatever he's having," Ani said, nodding to the man who was still in line behind them despite being humiliated and in pain. "I swear sometimes, Deni ...." she said as the man ordered.

"What? I don't go lookin' for trouble, hun, it just seems to find me."

"He's sorry," she said to the man behind them before turning back to her future husband. "Well, you don't go out of your way to avoid it, do you?"

Sheed chimed in. "Looks like someone could use a little Buddhism."

When they were back in the SUV, they decided not to discuss the Dunkin' Donuts ordeal again. Ever. Ani had said her piece. Deni insisted it wasn't his fault. And Sheed just continued to laugh to herself.

He promised to slow down but didn't as they merged left onto I-271 South. The vehicle was silent except for the music. The two ladies were no longer playing music war, Lisa had complete autonomy over the selections.

Ani sat in the passenger seat in silence. Hobey was no longer interested in the traffic outside, laying down in the backseat next to Sheed.

Deni silently kept his eyes peeled on traffic and for police. At ninety-five miles per hour or better, he would be in for a significant fine if pulled over.

Sheed selected a new song from the music on her phone, which came over the Meridian sound system. The acoustic guitar and falsetto voice of Bon Iver's 'Holocene' was hauntingly beautiful.

Deni'd not heard the song before but decided he liked it. It couldn't be new, nobody actually made decent music anymore. He wanted to ask Sheed what it was but decided to remain silent. Listening in silence, he stared straight ahead at the highway to come.

"..... *Saying nothing, that's enough for me*

and at once I knew I was not magnificent
hulled far away from the highway aisle
jagged, vacance, thick with ice

I could see for miles, miles, miles ....."

Saturday
4:45 P.M.   October 3, 2015

THE REMAINDER OF THE TRIP ON SATURDAY WAS CHILLY— to put it mildly. Ani only spoke to Deni when she was spoken to, and her responses were curt. She and Lisa continued to enjoy their time together; however, Ani opted to move to the back seat—as Deni had suggested at the beginning of the trip—when she grew tired of turning to her kindred spirit in the backseat.

They stopped for the night in Indianapolis, Indiana, making the fourteen hour trip to Indy from Boston in under twelve. Nine hundred miles is a lot to put in for one day. Nine hundred miles with an angry spouse-to-be is that much more excruciating. But the bulk of the trip was behind them, Deni thought. They would put in a six hour day of travel on Sunday—at most—another five hundred fifty miles to go. They would get to Joplin with plenty of time to check into a hotel and get situated before having to go to the Lansing plant first thing on Monday morning.

He was hoping that checking into their room might settle Ani, and the process of making up could begin. But she had decided to take Hobey for a long walk with Lisa instead. Deni brought all of their luggage to the room he'd share with Ani, and Sheed's to hers, before deciding to hit the nearby bar. Alone.

The Holiday Inn Express had not been the best choice, it turned out. Sheed had argued that since Taylor, Higgs & Pratt were paying their expenses, and that his girlfriend was using this trip as a pseudo-vacation, nicer digs were in order. Deni said that it was just a half mile away from I-70, where they would head toward Joplin the next day, and the dive motel was located on Massachusetts Ave. It was a good sign, he'd said.

He'd been wrong.

If Ani had any inclination to forgive the mild violence earlier in the day, that notion had passed. She simply said that she wanted to take the dog for a walk, asked if Lisa would like to come along and stretch her legs. And just like that, the two women left the motel.

So Deni went into the restaurant that practically shared the same parking lot, P.F. Changs. They carried his favorite Irish Whiskey, Redbreast, which was a pleasant surprise. Not many places carried it, not even in Boston, the Irish mecca. An Asian chain restaurant carrying an uncommon Irish Whiskey was unheard of. He thought it another good sign. Redbreast Irish Whiskey on Massachusetts Avenue in Indianapolis, Indiana.

Okay, maybe not. He'd been getting his signs mixed up as of late.

Three whiskeys, an order of pork dumplings, and an Oolong Chilean Sea Bass later, he still hadn't heard from either Ani or She despite the repeated calls from his cell. He even looked at his texts —and made a few—which he never did.

His mind ran riot.

They must have taken one hell of a walk. It's been two hours. Did something happen to them? They have Hobey. Nobody is going to mess with them if they have the dog, right? Did She bring her piece? She can handle herself, firearm or not. Ani is no pushover either. They'll be fine. I'm sure they're fine. Ani is just trying to tell me she's pissed.

He tried to shake off the feeling that something was wrong, but couldn't.

Deni paid the bill, went back to the room long enough to make sure they hadn't come back and to get an extra clip for his Taurus PT-1911.

He left the motel in search of them.

He searched for over an hour and found no trace of them. He again went back to the motel room. They hadn't come back. Full-on worry began to set in.

Deni had called their phones. Off. Directly to voicemail. He'd left messages for them to call him as soon as they heard the message, trying not to sound panicked. But he was.

At a little after nine o'clock, Ani and Hobey entered the motel room. Deni didn't know if he was more angry or relieved. He concluded after a few deep breaths that another fight, more like a blowout the way he was feeling, wouldn't help the situation. He decided to go with relieved.

"Thank God. I've been worried. Where the hell have you two been? I mean ..... I was worried."

"Now you care how I feel?"

"I don't want to fight, okay. I've been callin'. You guys were out for like four hours, so yeah, I got nervous."

"It's a gorgeous night. It's, like, in the sixties. It sure beats Boston this time of year. And there are some great art studios around here. We took Hobey for a walk, and we came upon one. They were cool with dogs, so we had a glass or two of wine and checked it out. Then another, then another .... "

"I was callin'."

"They don't like cell phones at art galleries because people take pictures, so we shut them off. I'm sorry you were worried, but I can take care of myself." Ani squatted down to take off the dog's leash. "And Hobey was there to protect me, huh?" She covered his face with kisses. "And Lisa. We were fine. Plus we figured you'd be getting cocked anyway."

"You made your point. We can check outta here and go get a nicer hotel if ya want," Deni said.

Ani smiled and shook her head. "You can be the smartest idiot sometimes. Do you think that's what this is about? I don't care where we stay. As long as it's clean and pet friendly."

"Then what? This morning? With the coffee?"

"I'm over it. It happened and I'm moving on."

"Then what? You're trying to get back at me, make me worry. You had to know I'd get worried after four hours. You've got a psych degree, is this a game?"

"No, Deni. No game. No ulterior motive. I just had fun with my friend, your partner, for a few hours after being cooped up in a car with maniac driver who likes to hurt people. Beginning, middle, end."

"You know that Attila the Hun guy at Dunkies would'a hurt me, right? It was that prick or me," Deni said.

"Maybe. But you don't exactly do things to avoid confrontation, do you? Charge right in, guns blazing."

"I didn't use my gun."

"You know what I mean, Deni."

"Look, cards on the table? You and me here? I'm really not lookin' forward to this trip. This case. I think She has us in way over our heads and to tell you the truth I think Pratt and this Lansing outfit like it that way. Their bankin' on the fact that we're not going to find anything that puts them within a frequent flyer mile of any wrongdoing. Two hundred people died and nobody wants to own the fact that they fucked up. So they act like they're concerned and spend some coin on top-dollar outsiders to augment three or four other federal agency investigations. I don't like bein' played. I don't like it when somebody who thinks they're bigger and badder than the next guy does whatever they want and fuck'em if they can't take a joke."

"So you beat up the big guy," Ani said.

"I didn't beat him up. He came at me thinkin' he was the one, and I just knocked him down a peg or two."

"So walk away, Bae."

"Not that simple. She got us into this. We're on the hook. Documented."

"I'm sure there's a way out. You haven't even started investigating yet. No harm, no foul. Call Ryan. He's a lawyer, he'll know how to get you out of it," Ani said. "It's probably just simple contract law or something."

"One hundred and ninety-seven people, hun. Some never to be recovered. Into the drink, bye and bye. Fish food. Empty fuckin' coffins, hun. And nobody knows why. She is in this thing for the dough, at least a big part of it. I have to admit, they are throwin' big money around."

"Oh yeah, I know. Look at all this," Ani said, looking around the motel room and chuckling. "Look at all the money and elegance. Very classy."

"Very funny. Those people, those families ....."

"I know why you're doing it. I knew why from the moment you told me. You act all rough and tumble, but I know how big your heart is." She closed the space between them and kissed him on the lips. A long kiss.

"Don't tell anybody," Deni said after the kiss.

Ani unfastened the button on his jeans, unzipped them.

"I can be bribed," she said.

They kissed again. Harder. More intense.

He tossed Ani on the bed, lowering himself on top of her. Pressed himself into her. Hobey found a new place to rest.

She nibbled on his ear, groaning. Whispering.

"You're secret is safe with me."

Sunday
October 4, 2015

IT WAS AS IF THE EVENTS OF THE PREVIOUS DAY HAD been forgotten. Nobody in the threesome mentioned the altercation at the rest stop. Nothing was said about the four hour walk the night before. Instead, they met in the lobby for the continental breakfast that was really just cold pastries and terrible generic k-cup coffee.

Deni, Ani, Lisa and Hobey piled into the Land Rover and began the second day of travel after stopping at a Waffle House for an actual breakfast. Ani's phone told her that they were eight hours from Joplin, but knew it wouldn't take them that long.

It would be six hours of windshield time. Maybe. In six hours or less, they would check into another hotel, rooms in which they would call home for the entirety of the investigation.

The Drury Inn & Suites was the anthesis of the lodging accommodations the three had experienced Saturday night. The Drury was not a motel. The hotel had both rooms and suites for those needing an extended stay. The suites were more like apartments.

True, it didn't look like much from the outside, but Ani and Lisa's independent internet searches for the best hotel in the area of Joplin from their smartphones produced just one choice.

The hotel had a business center, indoor pool, jacuzzi, a gym —though if guests didn't like the one provided, they could attain a free day pass for a number of local gyms—a restaurant in the lobby and three others shared the parking lot, free laundry service, a dog walking service as pets were allowed .... More comforts than home.

They took two adjoining suites, separated by a locking door —one suite for Deni and Ani, one for Lisa—both with small but fully functioning kitchens, dining, and living areas. It wasn't the Waldorf by any stretch of the imagination, but it was as good as could ever possibly be expected in a small midwestern city like Joplin, they reckoned. All of these amenities would set them back—and ultimately Taylor, Higgs & Pratt—a whopping $80 a day for each suite.

The City of Joplin became such with the discovery of lead and zinc in the late 1800s after the Civil War. The mining camp flourished and attracted an influx of travelers, many who stayed to build their fortune, as railroads were built to accommodate said westward travelers and mining concerns. Rail lines, trolleys and historical Route 66 made Joplin the hub of the 'Tri-state District'—southwest Missouri, Oklahoma, and Kansas—the lead and zinc mining capital of the world.

As the city became mined beyond resource after the turn of the century, and with mine shafts caving to create enormous sink-holes, entrepreneurs took advantage of the falling real estate prices and the existence of a national rail system. Mining became Manufacturing. Low-paying mining jobs converted to factory assembly line jobs.

The turn of this century has left Joplin looking to redefine itself yet again. Tornadoes destroy the area seemingly every few years. Factory jobs are being outsourced to other areas, other countries. What was once a thriving community, rich with historical buildings, is now desperate to hold on to what they've built. The city of 75,000 people depend heavily upon the three major employers that remain for survival; Lansing, employing roughly ten thousand workers at their Joplin facility; Con-way Truckload employs almost three thousand; and Tamko, which provides work for about one thousand laborers.

The rest of the major factories made like Bonnie and Clyde, holding fort in Joplin for a short time, then ran off with a fortune at the expense of the citizens, which were left high and dry.

An average Joplin household income today is under $50,000 per year. Men average $38,000—the mean brought up by the strong union presence—while women earn under $30,000. Even with the

UAW, nearly a quarter of all households live below the national poverty line. Their Walmart, however, is thriving.

The parking lot of the Drury Inn was shared with three restaurants for those that didn't want the family-style fare of the restaurant in the Drury. The hotel took up one side of the rectangular parking area, The Olive Garden on another, juxtaposed to The Outback Steakhouse, which sat adjacent to yet another P.F. Chang's. Surrounding them, on 36th and 37th Streets, were the other hotels that fed the chain restaurants. The Sunrise Inn. Best Western. Baymont. Candlewood. The Hampton Inn. None could compete with the relative luxury of the Drury.

Ani and Lisa wanted to dine at P.F. Chang's, which suited Deni though he had eaten there the previous evening. They had Redbreast he assumed. If one had it, they all must.

The three sat at the bar. Deni chose the middle seat so he could discuss how to approach the start of the investigation the next day at Lansing over a plate of Mongolian Beef he shared with his partner, while infrequently checking in with his future wife to see if she was enjoying her Ma Po Tofu.

At the conclusion of the meal, Sheed and Deni decided to take the guided tour at Lansing, listen, and formulate a plan of how to proceed with the investigation. Deni would be the bad cop when necessary, Sheed would be the delicate female. The voice of reason. It was how they always played it, much to Lisa's chagrin.

Ani decided that she and Hobey would take in the sights of Joplin, since their bartender assured her that there were many, while her man and friend went back to the Drury and called their client.

Deni and Lisa talked to Alex Pratt on speakerphone from Lisa's suite. They'd arrived in Joplin, and they had a plan.

67

His smartphone vibrated next to him on the dining room table. The ringtone, a snippet of the song *Learning to Fly* by Pink Floyd, further indicated that someone needed to speak with him. The look from his wife was the international signal for not caring who it was. It was dinner time, another attempt to gather and spend quality time as a family was ruined.

It was the same thing every evening at the Connor residence, even on Sundays. The teenage kids would watch TV while eating supper, if they bothered to come to the table at all. Art would either be working on his laptop, on his tablet, or speaking with someone from Lansing. None of the family members cared about what was leaving their plates and entering their bodies, nor about how much care and concern was put into preparing a nutritious meal.

Jessica Morley-Connors was a stay-at-home mother of two who felt under-appreciated and silently resented her husband and the comfortable yet loveless life they'd created.

The illuminated screen on Art's smartphone read that it was none other than Reid Lansing who was calling. Art picked up his phone, pressing the green phone icon as he watched his wife place her utensils on her plate and leave the table in a huff. The kids didn't seem to care either way.

"Good evening, Reid."

"Hello, Art. As you know, we have the investigators coming to the plant tomorrow. Are we prepared?"

"We're as prepared as can be expected. The plane is as reassembled as it can be unless the trawlers dig up more parts. I'll show them around and have the engineers give their presentation, as we discussed."

"I don't have to remind you what's at stake with this investigation. Do I, Art?"

"No. Of course not."

"We're already in a spot, we can ill-afford for these hack investigators to find anything. You're the VP of QA. It's your head. It's my family, my company, but at the end of the day it's not going to be me who suffers if this goes sideways on us."

Art looked around his dining room. The expensive china on the designer table. The large flatscreen on the wall, one of seven in the expansive house that his seven-figure salary from Lansing affords him. He looked to his left, seeing the toned posterior of his comely wife scraping plates at the kitchen sink. If he was fired, her carefree days of hair salons, nails, and pilates would come to a screeching halt.

"You've made your position abundantly clear, Reid."

"What's the mood on the floor?"

"Everyone is nervous, of course. One of our planes crashed into the Atlantic eight months ago. Our product is a point of pride with these workers. They want to know what happened as much as anybody. They don't like the thought of these outsiders coming in, but if it has to happen, they want them to help prove what everybody at Lansing already knows—that our planes are the best in the air."

"Then why the nervousness? We DO have the best planes in the air."

"They're nervous about their jobs, Reid. The writing is on the wall. It doesn't take a genius to see what has happened in the last months since the crash. We have finished planes that are piling up in the paint shed, none of them getting carrier paint schemes on them. Every jet coming off assembly is green-tailed."

"The frozen orders will come back in full-swing once we finally put this crash behind us. PA, Virgin, Quantus and Lufthansa will all come around once we are officially cleared and these legal matters are put to bed once and for all."

"Of course. Everybody gets it. But what happens if we don't get cleared? What happens if the IRT or the investigators find something that puts our feet to the fire? What happens if the orders don't come back? You asked what the buzz on the floor is, well ..... That's it."

"Appease them. Do your goddamned job, Art. Keep the peace. I could have forced layoffs. I could have shut down the whole fucking plant. I could have shut down all of our plants. But we keep pumping out planes even with the suspended orders. I want to hit our production goals. Period. As far as these investigators go, my money is on the fact that they couldn't find their own asses with a map and a flashlight. Make sure of it, or you know what will happen."

"Again, I fully appreciate your position. But there's also the union. The union doesn't like having outsiders coming in to investigate their workers. They hate the IRT, but this? This is going to get ugly."

"How do they even know?"

"You're kidding, right? Reid, the plant is like high school. Half of the workers knew about the visitors before the decision was even made. They manufacture as much gossip than they do planes."

"We have visitors all of the time. Potential buyers, department of defense, carrier reps ..... We have more guided tours than the White House. This won't look any different."

"With all-due respect, this is very different. None of those tours are conducted as a perceived witch-hunt. Look, I've explained why it's important to Bob. He's the local rep for UAW, he's supposed to help keep everyone calm, but he's done nothing but stir the pot. I worry that they may cause a job action, or worse."

The United Aviation Workers on the floor have absolute control over the production line. The sales team, marketing team, and PR team can line up sales until the turn of the next century; but if the plant cannot produce the product the admin teams are working tirelessly to sell, those orders will dry up in a hurry. The plant workers pay their annual dues to the union, who look out for their best interests. Safety concerns. Pay. Benefits. Working conditions. The union even has a say in sales meetings as it relates to production goals. One word from their local UAW rep, Bob Flannery, and workers could slow down, sick out, break tooling, and create hundreds of other intractable problems—none of which could ever definitively point to worker negligence, though obvious.

"Fucking union. The bane of my existence," Reid Lansing said. "Talk to Bob. Make him understand that all of his constituents are going to find themselves out of a job if they decide to put Lansing belly-up with their bullshit."

"I have. I will again."

"You'd better. Make sure these two idiots that Pratt shoved down our throats stay in the dark. Take them by the hand and send them back to Boston as clueless as they started. I want this behind us, and I want it done yesterday."

"Yes sir."

"I want updates twice per day. Minimum. On top of the Incident Review Team briefings."

"Okay, Reid."

"I'll see you tomorrow."

Art placed his cell phone back on the dining table. He looked around the table, his children were still engrossed in the Kardashians. His wife hadn't returned to the dining room, she was still in the kitchen picking up from the unappreciated meal. He pushed his untouched plate away from him. He'd lost his appetite.

In every sense, his plate was full.

Monday
9:00 A.M. October 5, 2015

LANSING AEROSPACE COMPANY WAS A CITY WITHIN THE city of Joplin. Of the 36 square miles of Joplin, Lansing comprised nearly twenty of it. LAC had fifty buildings on the secure property; their own gas station, a supermarket, and even their own police force which was little more than a team of security guards. Anything one could possibly need could be found on the premises as a means of keeping workers producing without having to leave the facility, including three Starbucks locations.

On the north side of the Lansing property was the border between the aerospace company and the airport, which LAC had a controlling interest. It made flight tests as well as incoming and outgoing freight much more convenient.

Deni and Lisa arrived at the front gate, on the south side of the property, a few minutes before 9 A.M., as was instructed. They were told by the security guard to park in the lot just on the inside of the gate, and someone would be with them 'forthwith'.

As Deni exited his SUV, he looked toward the sky. It was warmer than Boston this time of year, in the low sixties already, but it appeared as though the clouds were going to spill on them.

When the guard had said, 'forthwith', he wasn't kidding. They were no sooner out of their vehicle when they spotted their guide.

The Vice President of Quality Assurance had arrived in a clean electric vehicle, which proudly displayed a General Electric logo on it. He parked directly behind Deni's gas-guzzling Land Rover, and was climbing out of the compact four-door within the few moments it took for them to take in their surroundings.

Deni stuck out his hand, "Art right?"

"Art Connor, correct. I'm the VP of QA for Lansing. I visit all the plants these days, but I spend the vast majority of my time here. Especially with this latest event," he explained as he released his hand from Deni's to shake Lisa's. As she offered her hand, her one and only short blazer from H&M slid up to reveal her Sig Sauer P224 SAS in its waistband holster. He turned to Deni and noticed for the first time his Taurus PT-1911 in its shoulder harness under his jacket.

"We cannot allow those guns here," Art said. "Investigators or not, you can't bring those in with you."

"My weapon goes where I go," Deni said.

"We simply don't allow them. Period. Even our security personnel carry tasers instead of firearms."

"That might be a deal-breaker, Mister Connor."

Lisa stepped in. "We can leave them in the car. Will that be okay?"

"Of course. As long as they aren't carried with you. Not that you'd need them anyway. We've never had any occasion for that sort of violence here at Lansing. I started my career here right out of college, right on the factory floor in that building over there."

He pointed in a far-off direction. The flat expanse was a sea of separated buildings, each more than two football fields wide, but those with good eyes could see the building he was pointing toward had a number 30 tattooed onto it.

"So you know your way around the joint," Deni said.

"I do. I'll be your contact throughout your investigation. Whatever you need, I'll make sure you have it. We want to be as transparent with you as possible, without divulging any trade secrets of course."

"So no secrets other than your secrets," Deni said with a roll of the eyes.

Turner looked at Lisa, then back at Deni.

"I'm not the adversary, here, Warren."

"Nobody calls me 'Warren'. It's Deni."

"I want what you want, Deni. We have a special team set up to investigate the aircraft and the events that led to the tragedy. The IRT will report to you every day to let you know the progress of their investigation. Incident Review Team. I assure you, we both want the same thing here."

"I doubt that. I want to find out what happened to flight 4273. You want to be off the hook. I wanna know what caused two hundred people to disappear into the Atlantic Ocean, most of them never to be found."

"As do we. Believe me. Both of you. That is exactly what I want as well. I have spent my entire career ensuring that Lansing makes the very best planes in the world. Everyone within this entire facility takes pride in what they produce. We make a safe product. We make the safest product in our industry. The only way to prove it is to figure out what happened," Turner said.

"Which you conveniently haven't been able to do," Deni pointed out. He was going to be the bad cop, as decided the night before over dinner. He was being antagonistic, literally, right out of the gate.

"I think what my partner is trying to say, Mister Connor, is that you designed the aircraft that went down, built it, sold it to carriers who put it in service, and are now housing the remains of it. It's a very convenient scenario and if you can't figure out what went wrong, who can?"

"Oh, we *will* figure it out. We've just been too focused on finding and putting the puzzle together to really start investigating it yet. But let me put things into perspective for the both of you. We build roughly three hundred planes per year at this facility, every year. We had one incident. One. It's very unfortunate. Yes, we are concerned with why. But our safety record is unparalleled in our industry. Do you know how many incidents Airbus had last year? Boeing? That plane was virtually brand new and I will stake my reputation, my company's reputation, that what caused that plane to crash had nothing to do with our design or how we build it. Now, if you're ready to proceed, we can get out of the sun and start building a foundation of understanding. An 'Aircraft Manufacturing 101', if you will."

He handed each of them a large name-tag which read 'VISITOR' under their names in a larger font. On the back was a barcode. Connor explained that all personnel carry them and the barcode is scanned not only for access to the buildings, but can also be used to purchase goods and services. No need for cash or debit card when you get a sandwich or coffee, just scan your ID and it will come directly out of the employee's payroll direct deposit.

Lisa clipped hers to the bottom of her V-neck, which weighted the collar further down her chest. She never wore that type of top, preferring crew necks, and she'd picked the wrong day to start a new trend. She immediately regretted leaving her jacket in the SUV along with her pistol.

Deni clipped his to the pocket of his sport jacket. Today's tee —from the band Cocoon which read '*My Friends All Died In A Plane Crash*'—peered from under the unbuttoned jacket. It was yet another subtle rebellion not lost on the VP. Nobody commented on it.

"Today, I'll take you through the entire process of designing and building the Lansing 530."

Art Connor drove the small electric vehicle almost five miles, passing mammoth building after building. Some were slightly larger than others, however with the exception of the large numbers assigned to them, they were indistinguishable to the two investigators.

Each building could have had its own exit ramp off a freeway, they were so enormous. All were wide, some were a mile in length.

Building 65 was the design building. Connor parked the tiny four-door in the designated spot, then connected it to the GE WattStation to recharge it.

He showed them inside, guiding them into the largest conference room for the design team on the third floor. A baker's dozen were waiting within it, all with laptops open in front of them. As the trio entered the room, none of the dozen or so in the seats made any attempt to take their eyes off their respective computer screens to greet them. Whatever was on their laptops was more important than they were, Deni and Sheed separately yet simultaneously thought.

Connor then made the announcement to the room who the vistors were, like it wasn't already known. He then introduced the design team, one by one, and still not one of them looked up for more than a millisecond.

"Looks like they all have something better to do with their time," Sheed said after the last designer in the room was introduced. They both took their seats.

"I'm sorry. Please don't take it personally. These folks are the design engineers that collaborate with our build team," Art said as if they weren't in the room. "Our engineers are geniuses, what they lack in social etiquette is more than made up by their collective achievements. They designed the 530 to be the most comfortable, safest, most state-of-the-art aircraft on the planet. It is the most sought after plane by both domestic and international carriers."

"Even now?" Deni raised an eyebrow.

"Even now, and that's a fact." Connor said. "This incident notwithstanding, we max out our production orders at about 320 per year, which I alluded to earlier. We currently have more than 1200 ordered, which is admittedly slightly down, though still four times more planes than we can possibly make this year."

"Your customers are ordering planes four years out?"

"Yes and no. Some place orders to show their stockholders that they are expanding, yet have no intention of purchasing new planes. Some will cancel their orders, or purchase an out-of-service aircraft from another carrier. It's complicated and we are getting ahead of ourselves. We'll go through manufacturing and sales for the 530 at some point in the near future, but for now just know that the premise is the same for all of our aircraft. At this sight, we produce the L530 and parts of the L580, which is the largest commercial aircraft on the planet, seating almost 1300 passengers. More than the largest Airbus, which holds 1255."

"Great. More people to kill at one time," Deni mumbled to Sheed.

"Pardon?"

"Nothing," Deni said to Art. "Go on."

"Our other facilities produce the 550, 60, and 70. We also have a plant in New Mexico specifically for our defense contracts, but we are obviously going to focus on every minute detail of the L530. Good?"

Deni and Sheed nodded.

"Great. First, it is important for you to understand the complexity and the redundant safety precautions designed into the L530. We have a presentation prepared."

As if on cue, the lights dimmed and a curved screen dropped from the ceiling. The Lansing logo shown off the screen into the dark room in 3-D, with the sound of an aircraft taking off to accompany it.

Sheed realized that she wasn't wearing any 3-D glasses, and yet the visuals presented were three-dimensional. She elbowed Deni. "Neat."

The skeleton of an aircraft spun in front of them, floating over the conference room table, giving them a 360 degree view of the structure. A deep voice mimicking Morgan Freeman began to narrate the animation.

These guys ARE geniuses, Deni thought. The voice was soothing. Assuring. It was a voice of someone projecting confidence and stability about the projected imagery.

"Man has always had the dream to fly, dating back to Mythology. To Icarus. We looked up at the sky and dreamed of soaring through the clouds."

The image changed to an animated dramatization of a winged man soaring toward the sun.

"That dream has been fulfilled and yet we still dream. We want to fly farther, higher, faster, safer.

"At Lansing, we make those dreams a reality. We build aircraft that are designed to be lighter, using alloy framework that is stronger yet lighter than any other aircraft."

Three dimensional depictions of various planes manufactured by Lansing were projected toward the center of the room. The engineers still had their faces buried in their laptops.

"Lighter means faster. Whether choosing the Rolls Royce 1000-Ten engine, or the Pratt & Whitney PurePower PW1200G, or the new General Electric GE9X—which is two-thirds lighter and the most energy efficient jet engine ever created—you will get passengers there in less time, using less fuel.

"Less Fuel not only means operational savings through efficiency, it also means a drastically reduced carbon footprint. At Lansing, more than seventy percent of the entire aircraft is made from renewable and-or recyclable materials ...."

"This is some propaganda machine," Deni whispered to Sheed sitting on his left. She nudged him and gave the signal for silence. She was eating this up.

The projected image changed again as the narrator spoke. Now, the exterior of one plane was peeled away, revealing only the skeleton, just the frame of the fuselage was visible. The wings had also been removed, as were the tail and the nose. Just the cutaway of the barrel was shown.

The faux-Freeman voice went on.

"Our latest and most innovative commercial jet, the L530, is the most state-of-the-art conveyance since the invention of flight. Made from proprietary alloy material, the frame is the strongest yet lightest. Working with carriers to determine flight capacity and amenities, we then fabricate the interior to the custom specifications of each airline."

The airframe skeleton was then shown to have an outer skin, then turned to look inside the barrel. Animation then added insulation onto the interior, followed by a web of wires and sensors, then the interior panels.

"Each Lansing 530 has 2.65 million parts which need to be installed and tested. Compared to a modern luxury car, which has only 5,000 parts and no redundant safety features, each aircraft is a technological marvel."

Seats and galleys were then added to the floating image as it spun for each person sitting around the conference table to see. The engineers were still looking at their laptops, rendering the image-turning unnecessary.

Next the nose, wings and tail were added.

"The barrel, nose, wings and tail, are manufactured separately, then assembled prior to test flight.

"The nose contains the cockpit and the standard yet innovative instrumentation technology, as well as the additional specifications requested by each carrier.

"The wings are made with a proprietary carbon resin, which is layered over the wing frame, then loaded into an oven to cure, which becomes harder than steel, yet a fraction of the weight. The wing is the most important part of the aircraft, as the shape and functionality determines the thermodynamics necessary for flight. The wing of the L530 is the next generation in wing technology, with innovative winglet technologies, slat, flap, spoiler, and alleron technologies which create 25% more wing area, 30% greater fuel efficiency, and 22% better aerodynamic efficiency. Lansing has even developed a patented engine housing unit below the wing, which easily adapts to Rolls-Royce, Pratt & Whitney, or the new GE9X from General Electric. The wings are then tested for torque and tensile strength before test flight."

While the voice was speaking about the wing, the image was focused on only the wing and the parts being mentioned. The wing was then virtually shaken, like a bird who would flap to take flight, before the image zoomed out to the entirety of the aircraft. The plane took another spin over the table before zooming in on the tail.

The narrator went on to speak about the Lansing innovations in the vertical stabilizer, elevators, rudder and horizontal stabilizers. Deni was trying to pay attention but was getting lost in the technical minutia. Technology was not his forte, another reason he felt ill-suited for the investigation at hand.

Lisa was consuming every detail, however. She furiously jotted down facts and questions that she would pose after the elaborate presentation. There were several pages written on her notepad, front and back.

Aircraft Manufacturing 101 was only being appreciated by one.

Monday
11:30 A.M. October 5, 2015

AFTER THE NEARLY TWO-HOUR PRESENTATION IN BUILDING 65, Art Connor guided the two investigators over to building 60, the Wing Production Line, stopping for Starbucks on the way. Their IDs were scanned and hot beverages were produced in record time.

Deni needed it. His head was swimming.

Sheed didn't need the caffeine, she was already amped from the presentation. She was getting an education in commercial aviation, a foundation not only necessary for the task at hand, but also just generally interesting.

It was like the Discovery Channel, only live.

People fly from point A to B every day, of every month, of every year. Some to get away. Some for work. No matter the reason, commercial flights connect humans with the world. Without flight, the world would be limited to see only what was closest around them. Limited in culture. Limited to experience only what could be visited by car or train or sea, in the short amount of time allotted to them for vacation time. Travelers scurry about airports griping about layovers or connecting flights or security, not taking into account what goes into the convenience of traveling around the world. Sheed found it fascinating and had a new appreciation for air travel.

And it was only the beginning.

As the threesome entered the building after finishing their cups o' elaborate Joe, Art mandated that they wear hardhats and neon yellow vests the color of a highlighter marker. He also told them that since they weren't wearing safety glasses or steel-toed shoes, they would need to stay within the uber-designated walkway paths. OSHA regulations, he said, were designed for their safety as well.

He further explained that while at Lansing, they would be required to wear their PPE, Personal Protective Equipment, in every building where manufacturing took place.

Building 60 was one of them, and the word enormous doesn't describe it. That one building consumed three-quarters of a square mile in real estate. The pathways moved both along the perimeter of the assembly line, but also within it.

Art spoke to them as they walked, pointing out what they were seeing.

"As it said in the presentation, the wing is the most important part of the aircraft. Ninety percent of aviation technology lies within the wing. It is the most technical part of the aircraft, because without aerodynamics, the fuse and the passengers therein don't get off the ground. Aerodynamics is a form of fluid mechanics, which really means airflow. Boats and submarines have laminar flow, measuring force and drag, planes have airflow which is mathematically solved using the Navier-Stokes Equations."

Sheed looked puzzled. Deni's eyes were glazing over.

"No need to get worried. There won't be a math test, that's a fact. Just know that it's a complicated formula that's needed to ensure the wing has the correct amount of lift, by manipulating the amount of air pressure below the wing versus on top of it. As the jet engine propels the plane forward, the wings cut through the air and deflects the flow of air downwards, which provides lift. In order to shift the air downwards, we have to manipulate how the air interacts with the wing at various points on it, meaning we have to change the shape of the wing at various points throughout the flight. One shape forces the plane into the air, another to descend, another to slow it down when it lands, and still another to minimize the drag while in flight."

He guided them toward the skeleton of a wing, being wheeled toward another section of the building. The wing seemed to them to be as long as a football field.

"Holy crap," Lisa said. "They look big when you're on a plane, but down here they look absolutely ginormous."

"Given the size and weight of the 530, each wing is about 200 feet long. This is just the innards, if you will. The mechanical parts. All of these tracks and cables and hinges have primary and secondary motors which move various parts on the wing. See here? The leading edge of the wings have these doors on them called slats. They increase or decrease lift during takeoff and landing by increasing or decreasing the surface area of the wing, which manipulates how the air interacts with the wing." Art pointed to the rear part of the wing. "There are several slats on each wing."

He paused to make sure they understood what he'd explained. He didn't get a reading either way, but continued regardless.

"In conjunction with the slats on the leading edge, the doors on the aft portion of the wing, flaps, also help with lift but increase drag when landing." He pointed to the back side of the wing.

"And here in the middle of the wing is a spoiler, designed solely for drag. The door at the aft tip of the wing is the aileron, which the pilot uses to change roll." Art put his hand flat ahead of him and changed the angle left and right in a so-so motion.

"At the far tip of the wing is the winglet. The shark-fin looking thing. The winglet is a modern marvel. It adds wing area without needing a longer wing and adds stability and aerodynamics by decreasing drag which allows the carrier to use less fuel. In order to hold as many passengers as we do on the 530, we would need another twenty feet on each wing to give us enough lift to takeoff, making our wings 10% longer than the 200 feet per wing and much more expensive. That fin saves us, and the carriers, vast sums of money."

"When are we gonna see what's left of the crashed plane?" Deni was getting impatient. "Let's get past the walk around Disney, okay? I don't care how the magic is made, I do care about what killed all those people. That's what I'm here for. You got better things to do than hold our hands, and I got someone else who I like holdin' my hand."

"Actually, I don't have better things to do with my time, Deni. And that's a fact. I'm the Vice President of Quality Assurance at Lansing Aerospace and earlier this year we had the unthinkable happen to one of our planes. We don't make little innocuous gadgets, sir. We make a product that we put a great deal of time, money, and resources into ensuring that is safe—because it has to be. If we manufacture a bad product, people die. It's just that simple. So we take great pride in the fact that we don't make a shoddy product and we haven't since the first plane we built. We continue to make the best in the business. That's not boastful, that's fact. So this is my business. If by providing you with enough knowledge to aid in our investigation to prove what everybody here at Lansing already knows, then I believe that this is time well-spent."

The awkward pause was palpable. Laborers were pretending not to notice the threesome moving about the plant. Sheed gave Deni a look which he interpreted to mean that she wanted him to apologize. No apology would be forthcoming.

After a time, the VP continued his tour.

The next area of the Wing Production Building, was called 'Feathering' by those that worked in the building. It was the area that applied the outer surface of the wing. Forty or so workers moved around the long wing, each operating machines with robotic arms which were applying layers of black strips along the wing surface.

"Looks like duct tape," Deni said.

"Very perceptive."

"Wait. That is duct tape? No wonder the plane—" Sheed elbowed Deni in the ribs before he could finish his insult.

"It's not duct tape. Not exactly. These machines lay down many layers of tape over the wing components. The tape is made of a proprietary carbon fiber resin, which is nothing like duct tape other than it comes from a roll. When all of the layering is done, or what the workers call 'feathering', the wing is then rolled into that oven," Art said. He pointed to the next position in the assembly line. The oven was nothing short of vast.

"We can have as many as ten wings curing at once, enough to outfit five planes, obviously. Once out of the oven, the wings become harder and stronger than steel, more flexible than aluminum, at a fraction of the weight. Once upon a time we used to rivet everything. This surface is smoother, allowing less drag, and is stronger. Rivets pop out with stress and fracturing. Once cured, our wings can withstand more than ten times the tensile stress of any of its predecessors."

On the other side of the oven was a giant glass booth. Workers inside wore what appeared to be hazmat suits and masks. Ten cured wings were being applied with what looked like lime-green paint.

"This is the final stage of the wings before they are wheeled over to Building 30 for final assembly. As you can see, a final coating is sprayed onto the surface."

"Like a primer," Deni said.

"Yes and no. It's an epoxy. The carbon resin surface, as I said, is very smooth and it's crucial that it stay that way. The surface is very expensive and any knick or ding can change the way air moves around the wing. The epoxy protects the surface for when it is being mounted onto the fuse—the fuselage—and, yes, readies them for when the custom paint and graphics are applied for the carrier over in the paint shed."

The VP stopped speaking for a beat, letting all the information from the Wing Building marinate."

"Questions?"

Neither of the two investigators had one.

Art looked at his watch.

"Okay. I have a quick meeting to attend, which shouldn't take more than an hour. Now is a good time to break for lunch anyway, so I'll drive you over to Building 10, the Admin Building, where you can eat in the executive lounge. I'll zip over to my meeting, then we can meet up so I can show you where we build the nose. The cockpit. Sound good?"

He was headed toward the exit door before either of the investigators could utter a sound.

Monday
1:30 P.M. October 5, 2015

"HOW'S SHOW-AND-TELL GOING?"

"As you might expect. Slow and painful," Art said to Reid. He was in the President and CEO's office on the top floor of Building 10. "It's like trying to teach calculus to a kindergartener. That Deni character isn't going to take much more of it, I can tell you that much. He's about this close to going off the rails. The girl? She's the more pliable one. If I can keep her in-line, maybe she'll keep the wild card under control."

"Where are they now?" Reid Lansing was behind his desk, leaned back in his chair. His hands steepled under his chin.

Art pulled up an application on his smartphone and showed it to Reid, who didn't scrutinize the image.

"Main floor. Eating. Their badges will allow me to keep tabs on them."

"Then what?"

"Then I take them over to Nose. Then Tail. Then QA. That should eat up the rest of the day today. Tomorrow, I'll bring them to the IRT Hangar and show them what's left of 4273. I have to tell you, Reid, this might be a waste of time and a big thorn in the side of the IRT. We just got the wreck assembled and the Incident Review Team is slated to start diagnostic tests any day. With these two underfoot ...."

"You're preaching to the choir, Arty."

Art hated to be called Arty and Reid knew it. Everyone who'd ever called him by that name was made aware that he hated it.

"Alex Pratt said she wanted these guys, and we need her firm if this actually goes to trial. We need them to *avoid* a trial, for that matter. Our lawyers agree that Taylor, Higgs & Pratt is the best firm to represent our interests in Boston and could have heavy influence over all involved if this thing even proceeds. These two knuckleheads could save us billions in victim compensation. So, If we have to, if *YOU* have to hold their hands like little kids to keep Alex happy. If that's what it takes to put this to bed, then sure as shit that is what you'll do."

"I am doing it, Reid, and that's a fact. I'm just saying that having them around prolongs an outcome rather than speeds it up. I had to explain what a slat is for Christ's sake."

"Maybe expediency isn't the answer here. Dragging this out might make this Keating litigator give up on the civil matter. Or give time for the public to forget. With everything that happens these days, everyone has a short memory."

"I don't know about that. Sorina Kane, that surviving wife and mother of two, is hell-bent for justice. She's on TV or writing letters to editors every chance she gets. If she has her way, she'll be changing the name to Kane Aerospace before she burns the place to the ground—or worse—sells us off to Boeing."

"Without a criminal trial, it will be all but impossible for her or any of the other victims to get a dime of our money. The real question is, will it be cheaper to buy them off or wait them out? Without any proof from any of the investigations underway that we made a bad plane, which they won't be able to do, I don't see how we could lose," Reid Lansing said.

"Court of public opinion, Sir. Orders are frozen. We are green-tailing three hundred-odd planes per year until the public feels safe in our planes again. Carriers won't buy them if passengers won't fly on them."

"That's for marketing to deal with. In the meantime, we have our own public opinion polls to worry about. Did you speak with Bob?"

"I left a message. He hasn't called me back," Art said. "And I've been kind of busy."

"Call him again. And Again. And again and again. Make sure the UAW keeps the minions calm. A lawsuit will probably kill us, but a series of union job actions definitely will."

"I'm on it."

"You'd better be. And keep those investigators happy. Buy them lap-dances over at Sensations if you have to. I think the girl—Lisa is it?—might even be into tits and g-strings in her face, if you get my meaning."

Art rolled his eyes, failing at concealing it.

"I'm not sure that's going to do it."

"Then what?"

"They're investigators. Right now they're on a tour. Deni keeps bitching about seeing the wreck. About justice for the dead. They want to investi—"

Reid Lansing was nodding his head in agreement, he was already there.

"—Investigate. I know I know. So let them. They are our two newest members of the IRT," Reid said.

"Their heads will be swimming."

"Like trying to take a sip of water out of a fire hose," Lansing added.

"Genius. And that's a fact."

Monday
1:30 P.M. October 5, 2015

THE EXECUTIVE LOUNGE, AS IT WAS REFERRED, WAS REALLY nothing more than a cafeteria with nicer seating. Deni and Lisa ordered their food and found a small table in the corner while waiting for their lunch to be prepared. A small LED screen above the order counter displayed the orders that were completed and ready for pickup, like the DMV, in lieu of someone bellowing out completed order numbers.

When their number was illuminated on the screen, Sheed approached the counter to retrieve both orders while Deni remained at the table. Her grilled Portobello sandwich wasn't made correctly. The twenty-something male behind the counter said that he would fix it immediately.

"I don't know how that kid still works here," a women said. Lisa turned to the voice. The lady behind her was well-dressed in a khaki Victoria Beckham business suit, hair pulled up off her neck, with eyeglass frames matching her brown eyes. "He takes the orders wrong so the chefs in the back don't have a chance at getting your order right. It's a daily occurrence. He must know somebody or has some kind of dirt on somebody in craft services, because no matter how many times we complain, here he is." The women stuck out her hand. "I'm Macy. Macy Dunn. I don't think I've seen you in here before ..... Lisa."

Sheed looked puzzled then remembered her name-tag, which hung from her V-neck and exposed more cleavage than she wanted.

"Oh. Yeah. I didn't want to ruin my top with the teeth of the clip, so I stuck it here. I had it clipped to the glowy vest for a while but ...... Never mind. Nice to meet you Macy." The handshake was firm.

"You must be one of the investigators from Boston. That your partner?" Macy nodded toward the corner. Her Missourian accent was now prevalent.

"Yeah. Yes. How did you ..... ?"

"Everyone knows. Quite frankly, rumors fly around here, darlin'. No secrets, no matter how you try. Everybody knows everything minutes after it happened. Sometimes before. People with the day off are fully briefed."

"I see."

"Y'all aren't going to be revered around these parts, best let your partner know it. That shirt of his is just pouring gas on a fire."

Lisa turned toward Deni, who was still sitting at the table, watching the interaction from afar. He must have been warm in his sport jacket, since it was now on the back of his chair. His *My Friends All Died In A Plane Crash* T-shirt not even remotely hidden.

"He doesn't mean anything by it. It's just his sense of humor. He's a good guy once you get to know him."

"And how about you? How does one get to know you?"

Lisa began to blush. She was at an obvious loss for words.

"Didn't mean to rattle you, dear," Macy said. "Your lunch is ready."

Sheed turned toward the counter, the remade sandwich was on the tray next to Deni's bbq pulled pork. She collected the tray and turned back toward Macy.

"Care to join us? Maybe you could give us some other pointers. The lay-of-the-land so to speak."

"Love to. Maybe I can clear up some of the rumors going 'round here."

Macy collected her tray and followed Lisa to their corner table.

"Deni this is Macy. Macy, Deni. Macy is a, uh, what is it that you do here?"

"I'm VP of CAS—Commercial Aviation Services," Macy said.

Deni raised an eyebrow. "Is everybody a Vice President of something here?"

"Kinda sorta. They throw around titles pretty regular. Throw something over your shoulder and it'll hit a Veep. In this building anyway."

89

Macy sat down at one of the two unoccupied chairs. Deni and Sheed took their lunch items off the tray while their new lunch companion got settled. She shook her head when she looked at her order and pushed her lunch to the empty place at the table. Deni looked at Sheed, who gave the international signal for 'I'll explain later.'

"Fancy shirt you have there, sport," Macy said. "People 'round here aren't going to find that kind of thing very funny."

"I'm gettin' the sense that not many people here have a sense of humor. Fuck'em if they can't take a joke."

Sheed kicked Deni's shin under the table.

"Let me give you a free piece of advice, Deni. The corporate culture 'round here, 'round aviation in general, is real serious. About not screwin' up. We have systems that check systems to make sure that systems are checked. You get my drift? We don't make mistakes or people get fired. We catch a variance long before it gets to the next step. With a record of infallibility comes arrogance. A sense of knowing that you're right a hundred percent of the time. You're here to point a finger. You're here to point out where we all screwed up and rub our noses in it. You won't make anyone's Christmas card list to be sure, and be damn careful out on the floor. These workers are union. Local UAW 1514. Accidents happen, if you get my drift."

Deni had dealt with southern accents before. He'd been to Charleston, South Carolina on an investigation a few years before. That investigation had taken its toll. Macy's accent wasn't southern, it was mid-western, but it reminded him of that time in Charleston. He'd made the mistake of stereotyping the accent with ignorance. Hick accents with hillbilly upbringing. He'd been wrong then. Just as many people were wrong to mistake his accent. He used it to his advantage, making people underestimate him.

Carina Fischer, who he'd met in Charleston, was as sharp as a tack, and she'd pointed out that he didn't sound too swift with his yankee Boston accent. An underestimation that had worked to his advantage more times than he could count.

Macy had a thick accent as well, but she too was smart. Deni was sure of it. Lansing may throw around VP titles like they're bread crumbs, but it was clear from the onset that this VP had earned hers.

"I don't do well with threats," Deni said.

"I'm not threatening you. I'm telling you where the bear shits, 'scuse the language."

"What is a VP of Commercial whatevah-whatevah, anyways?"

"Commercial Aviation Services. CAS. We have several departments under CAS. Customer Support. Material Services. Fleet Services. Integrated Services. At a hundred and seventeen million bucks a pop, you best have some perks that come with that bird. We help with everything from start-up airlines, like PA, to maintenance and parts allocation, to flight training if need be."

"PA. Preferred Airlines. You helped to get them started?" Lisa wasn't eating her lunch. Deni was using the moment to shovel in a bite, yet Macy now had both of their full attention.

"Yes Ma'am. Their entire business model was to provide luxury flights on a penny budget. A hundred dollar plane ticket gets you a more comfortable flight than you'd get on say ..... Emirates, and at Southwest pricing."

"And?"

"And ..... Lansing planes are more expensive than Airbus or Boeing. Off the line. Before spec add-ons. But neither of the other companies can prove savings in fuel and maintenance over the course of the life of the plane. Our planes last longer than their design life. Fifty-thousand hours or twenty thousand cycles is nothin'."

Macy read the look on her lunch-mates. They didn't have any frame of reference as to how long that was.

"We measure everything by hours. But you're basically looking at twenty years plus. They're built to last twice that—forty years as far as you're concerned."

"Airlines fly planes that long?"

"They can. Or they sell them to another airline who flies them. We have planes that are nearing forty years old still in service. Figure an average of five hours per flight, two or three times a day, seven days a week, for twenty years? A hundred thousand hours isn't surprising for a Lansing Jet."

Deni was shaking his head. He was finished eating.

Macy read the body language.

"You can get disgusted if you want, but running an airline is about as risky as opening a diner. Most fail. Only instead of losing a few hundred thousand, airlines stand to lose a few hundred *billion* dollars. US Air became part of American Airlines. Continental was bought by United. It's make money, merge, or fold. Preferred needed a niche and a partner that could help them navigate to solvency. Lansing is that willing partner. Two hundred planes with one hundred locations, that's a $23 BILLION deal for planes alone. Damned straight we'll help."

Lisa did some quick math. "Wait. Art said you can only produce three hundred planes per year. Doesn't that mean that PA is getting most of your planes? What about all the other companies? The other airlines?"

"At this facility. Larger hubs like Chicago, Atlanta, LA, have more passengers and therefore the airlines need larger planes. 550s, 60s or even 80s for international carriers. We build the other types at the other plants. Lansing has the same perks for every carrier that wants those services. If they don't, they don't. But in this case, we outfitted PA with what they needed, on time, and on budget. It was a big deal for both of us," Macy explained.

"And then there was the crash," Deni said.

"You said a mouthful there. So tell me 'bout 'yerselves. Long way from home and clear as I'm sittin' here don't know what you've gotten into."

Lisa took the question.

"We work for the law firm that is going to represent Lansing in Boston, should it come to that."

"I heard. Either of you know anything about aerodynamics? Fluid dynamics? Thermodynamics? Electrical engineering? System analytics?"

The table was silent for a beat.

"No?   How 'bout metallurgy?   Material manufacturing? What about advanced math or physics?"

"Still nothin'? Weekend flyer? Does sport here have a pilot's license? Hang glide?"

And still nobody spoke.

"Uh huh.   That's what I thought.   Y'all are gonna need a friend, and I don't see anybody linin' up for the position."

Out of the corner of her eye, Macy spotted Art Connor entering the lounge from the other side of it. She slid her business card to Lisa as she rose from her seat.

"You need anythin', sugar, you give me ring."

She'd left the table with the same abruptness as she'd come to it.

Deni leaned in toward Lisa.

"I told you we were in over our heads, She. I ain't the kinda guy so say I told you so, but if I were—"

"—I know, I know. I think she was hitting on me."

"Maybe.   Probably.   We might need to keep that in our pockets. She could be handy."

"I'm very recently married, you ass."

"You don't have to ..... Do whatever it is that you do with her, you just have to make her believe that you would."

"I'm not that kind of person, Deni."

"Then let's hope we don't need that friend she was talkin' about."

"There you are. How was lunch?"

Art Connor was standing over them.

"It was okay," Lisa offered.

Connor noticed that both of the lunches were left mostly uneaten.

"There are other places to eat at the facility, you'll get to know them for however long you're here. My favorite is the food truck by Building 30. Anyway, I have some good news."

"Oh yeah? For who?" Deni stood.

"You, of course. Both of you."

"Once we get through the tour of the facility today, you'll meet with the IRT. Incident Review Team. Anytime there is a concern or an issue with the 530, the Joplin Division IRT investigates and follows up. We have a dedicated team for each aircraft that we make. You both will be on the team here. Our diagnostics and flight simulators for 4273 begin tomorrow. You'll meet three times per day and report directly to me."

Deni liked the idea of actually beginning his investigation, but didn't want to wait another day.

"What about Lansing? Reid?"

"I'll keep him apprised of the results as needed. To be honest, I thought you'd be happier. You said you wanted to get your hands dirty, this will be your opportunity. Instead of the 4273 team reporting to you like I said this morning, explaining the disposition of the investigation to you, you'll be part of it. And that's a fact."

"That was how it was supposed to be all along, Art. That was our understanding," Lisa said. "And *that's* a fact."

"Then consider this your confirmation. Shall we continue on to the nose?"

Monday
2:30 P.M. October 5, 2015

THE NOSE OF A LANSING 530 LOOKED MASSIVE FROM THE exterior, as the threesome moved toward one inside building 40. Deni and Sheed further concluded its monstrosity as they climbed the portable scaffolding to get inside one. But inside the cockpit, everything was as congested as a sub-compact car. The three of them could hardly occupy the space without being in each other's way.

What wasn't windshield was a barrage of knobs, levers, buttons, and gauges. Deni was afraid to touch anything for fear that any one button would cause the plane to takeoff like in a cartoon. It was a silly thought, of course, the cockpit wasn't attached to anything. The nose had yet to be attached to the fuselage, the wings, or the tail.

The control center for the remainder of the plane hung from I-beam rails and moved on the assembly line from one end of Building 40 to the other as it was being built.

"Tight space for the pilots, Art."

"Not once they're seated. You want your captain and first to be in the seats, not roaming around the cockpit. At any rate, carriers need to maximize plane space with paying customers. A larger cockpit means less room in the cabin for seats. For PA, they already made a concession for larger seats and increased foot-room, so our smaller cockpit design is both desired and necessary. Here, take a seat."

Art pointed to both of the pilot's chairs.

"No thanks," Deni said. He stood where he was.

"Sit here then." Art reached behind Deni and pulled down the folding third seat, installed for instructors or dead-heads if no seats were available in the cabin.

"I'm good, Arty."

"Please don't call me that."

Lisa had already wiggled into the captain's chair.

"Deni, be nice. Hey, this isn't so bad. I don't know about four or five hours, but it's roomier than it looks. What happens if they have to go to the bathroom?"

Art chuckled. "That's why there are two of them. The one pilot takes over while the other uses this lavatory," he said, pointing to the small closet door to his left. "We'll get into a little bit more of how everything works once we go into the simulator. I just wanted to give you a sense of what goes into building the 530. All the circuits and gauges are checked by connecting the harnesses up to a test-computer. Those harnesses test each system and the override to ensure they work before those harnesses are attached to the plane. It's called a CET. Cycle Electrical Test. If there is a problem when we assemble the nose to the fuse in Building 30, we know it's not in the nose and can isolate the issue."

"How many times is there an issue?"

"Almost never, Deni. I see where you're going with this, but even if there was an issue, it's caught long before the carrier takes delivery. We test each plane extensively in the hangar, before we then take it out on test flights. The 530 has almost a hundred hours of flight time before a paying passenger sits in a seat. Flight 4273 had a thousand hours of commercial flights after our test flights, flying day in and out with passengers for Preferred Air, before it crashed."

Sheed was tired of craning her neck as Deni and Art conversed behind her. As she left the captain's chair, her knee pushed the throttle on the middle pedestal. She looked up as it happened, trying to determine if anyone had noticed or if there were consequences for her clumsiness. Art noticed.

"I'm sorry. I didn't break anything, did I?"

"Of course not. Just next time, you can release the seat to make it easier to get in and out."

"How often does that happen, Art?"

"I'm sure it happens, accidents happen. But if either the captain or first officer decide to leave their seats, it would be at cruise. Meaning autopilot would be operating the aircraft."

"What does that shifter do?"

"It's the throttle, Deni."

"Would moving the throttle while the plane is flying itself take it out of autopilot? Like cruise control in a car? Hit the gas or break and cruise shuts off?"

"It's not that simple. We'll get into all of that in the simulator, but every system in the aircraft has a backup system.   We build redundancies into virtually everything on the jet," Art said.

"That doesn't really answer the question, does it?"

"It could, but as soon as something like that would happen, they would get a clack."

"A clack?" Sheed asked.

"A warning sound. If auto didn't reengage, either of the two pilots could then take over.   At any rate, not only are we getting ahead of ourselves, but if what the four depositions from supposed eye witnesses are true, the drastic pitch oscillations wouldn't have anything to do with the throttle."

"What would cause it?"

"If it's accurate?"

"Yes," both Deni and Sheed said simultaneously.

"Could be several things. Slats. Flaps. Elevators on the tail horizontal stabilizer ....."

"Slats and flaps are on the wing," Deni said.   "You just showed us those about an hour ago."

"What controls those?" Sheed was still closest to all of the controls, she was pointing at several on the pedestal.

"They are activated with hydraulics and cables. Separate systems.   There isn't one control for all of the things, as I mentioned."

He was stalling, avoiding an explanation.   Deni knew it, Sheed was beginning to sense it.

"Which knob, Arty," Deni said.

"I asked you not to call me—"

"—Which knob?"

"The small lever on top of the throttle controls the slats."

"The throttle that she just accidentally bumped with her knee?"

"Yes. But there's a protective guard over the top of the slat controls. You're being quite reductive, don't you think?"

97

"Sometimes the simple answer is the right one, don't *YOU* think?" Deni took a quarter-step closer, which was all that could be afforded. The two men were uncomfortably close, a clear lack of personal space.

"Listen, I know you think you've quite literally stumbled onto something, but the guard over the top of the slats lever would have to be lifted open on the hinge and moved out of the way before an adjustment could be made. That's what pilots have to do normally in-flight so accidents don't happen, that's a fact. However, even if those very unlikely occurrences accidentally happened, autopilot would reengage. The pilots would hear clacking. Within a few seconds, maximum, the plane would correct itself. Redundancies, remember?"

"But what if the pilots shut off the autopilot?"

Art Connor shook his head. "Experienced pilots know how to fly a plane. That's why they're certified pilots. But, for the sake of getting along, If the scenario you just proposed actually occurred; a knee or a clipboard or something bumped the pedestal, which opened the door over the slats lever on top of the throttle, held the door open and then depressed it, which engaged the slats on the leading edge of the wing, which caused a great deal of drag at cruise speed, which nosed the plane upward, causing clacking and autopilot to reengage and retake the plane, followed by either pilot shutting down autopilot only to then crash the plane? It's beyond the realm of possibility.

"But, IF that scenario occurred? The overriding pilot would just have to manually fly the plane like they're trained and certified to do. You remember the personnel files you were given? The two pilots were seasoned, to say the least. I don't mean to be condescending or dismissive, but that's not what happened to 4273. Can we move on?"

Art Connor turned away from the investigators, heading toward the scaffolding to leave the cockpit and nose, but Deni stopped him by grabbing his arm.

"Not so fast. Not for nothin', but you said the slats on the front of the wing control pitch, which makes the plane turn toward space or down toward the ground, right? Doesn't that explain what happened to 4273?"

Sheed chimed in. "Yeah. I read the depositions from the other planes in the area. That's what they said happened. How can you be so dismissive?"

"Because we've dealt with this problem when the L530 was first designed."

"So this has happened before? You fuckin' people been spewin' off about safety—"

"—When it was first designed, Deni. Not since. Have you ever built something? I don't mean furniture from IKEA, I mean design and build something? You run into problems. That's why we design and test and use simulators and then redesign where necessary and test some more. Shirtsleeves and clipboards and things were occasionally bumping the slats levers. So we built the safety lock, the little door over the top of it which is a three dollar part. The lock solved the problem—or more appropriately the possibility of a problem. We never shipped one plane that didn't have the lock, and not one 530 has reported an issue. Fact."

"That you know of."

"As I've told you, we review all maintenance, all issues, from all of the carriers, from all of your planes in service. If there was a problem, we would know about it and issue a 'heads-up'. A Service Bulletin, which tells the carriers that we've identified a potential problem, and how we recommend to fix it. If the problem is severe enough, the FAA gets involved with an Airworthiness Directive, which requires them to fix it. We told you all of this at our first meeting. You called it a 'factory recall' if I remember correctly. Every aircraft ever built has ADs. Lansing has fewer than any other plane manufacturer. Period. Don't take my word for it, look it up."

"But this slats thing. It seems pretty legit. Like what happened to your plane," Lisa said.

"Miss Sheed. Our teams have been collecting and rebuilding 4273 since it crashed eight months ago. Experts in various aspects of design, engineering, avionics, maintenance and so forth. We've run simulations up to this point and will conduct actual tests on the actual aircraft now that we've recovered enough of it to do so.

99

Speculating that a pilot—with a flawless record mind you—and a first officer—also with an unblemished record, accidentally or otherwise deployed the slats during cruise which ultimately crashed the plane with one hundred ninety-plus occupants inside is literally ignorant speculation. Redundancies, remember? Autopilot would have taken over the plane. I think I've indulged this hypothesis for about as long as I can."

The VP of QA left the cockpit and made his way down the scaffolding. Deni and Sheed didn't follow him.

"We've got a problem with the investigators."

"You have a problem with the investigators. What is it, Arty?"

He grimaced as if someone had just scratched a chalkboard. He'd found a private spot to make a call from the foreman's office.

Each manufacturing building at the Lansing facility had jamming mesh built into the high ceilings to block cellular signals. It was essential in certain buildings, like building 40. Cell signals could adversely affect instrumentation testing once installed in the cockpit. The mesh was considered a necessity in other buildings as well for a number of reasons.

The first was because they were near the airport, and erroneous signals could possibly interfere with takeoff, landing, and control tower communications.

The second, because cell phones create a distraction and a potential safety hazard for the workers.

Or the signals could interfere with Lansing's sensitive test equipment in those buildings as well.

And yet another in the long list of reasons to jam cell signals was because their work was proprietary. Not for public eyes.

Art could see the two investigators moving down the scaffolding as they left the nose through the office's one-way window as he spoke with his CEO. He didn't have a great deal of time for an update.

"They think it was an involuntary slats deploy."

Reid Lansing slammed his left hand on his desk. His right hand was ready to crush the phone against his ear in lieu of not being able to squeeze his VP's throat. "Not this again. How did they come up with that?"

"One of them jammed her knee into the pedestal when we were in the cockpit. It came up," Art said.

"We should have fixed that design problem from the onset, Arty. How in the hell did it come up'?"

"We did fix the problem, Reid. Instead of having to retool and reconfigure the deck and pedestal, we fabbed a lock for a couple of bucks. We haven't had a problem since, and we still haven't. You know as well as I do that with the seasoned pilots PA had in the cockpit, that it wasn't an involuntary slats deploy that ended 4273."

"Slats certainly would explain the eye witness accounts. How can this be happening?" Reid sat heavily in his chair behind his desk in his office.

"It's not happening. There's another explanation. Remember Alaskan Air 261? That was the tail, and that's a fact."

Alaskan Airlines flight 261 crashed in January of 2000. The plane was not made by Lansing, rather by McDonnell Douglas. The MD-83 suffered a catastrophic loss in pitch, as did this flight. It was ultimately concluded, after a two-year investigation, that the horizontal stabilizer had failed in-flight.

"Was that supposed to be a joke? I'm not laughing, Arty. There is no more McDonnell Douglas. They're Boeing now. Is that what you want? You want to work for Boeing? This isn't going to bolster your resume."

"No. It wasn't a joke, and no I don't. I was just trying to say that there's another explanation. I'll make sure there's another explanation. I'll take care of it."

"If they go running back to Boston and tell a slats story to Alex Pratt, she's going to push a settlement. The victim's attorney, this Keating character, will inevitably see the bulletins we sent out back when we rolled out the 530 line, in discovery. He'll hang his fucking hat on a design flaw, and point out that we knew about it and covered it up. Literally. Add in these investigator's statements and we'll have no choice but to payout the billions in victim's comp money. If that happens, Arty, we're fucking ruined."

"That's not going to happen. Calm down. I can handle it."

"Whatever you have to do. Handle it."

"I'm on—" The conversation was disconnected. "—It," Art Connor said, to himself, as he looked at the phone in the foreman's office.

Monday
4:30 P.M. October 5, 2015

IT WAS LIKE DEJA-VU ALL OVER AGAIN. The flight simulator, in Building 20, was a complete nose and cockpit attached to robotic arms to simulate the aircraft's movements in-flight. On the inside of the cockpit, instead of windows, ultra high-definition screens displayed realistic graphics depicting what the pilots would see while flying.

Deni and Sheed were thankful they didn't have to occupy space in the small cockpit while watching the two pilots in the simulator. Fifteen cameras at various angles in the cockpit fed the LED screens in the observation tower less than twenty yards away. Inside the comparably expansive observation tower, those conducting the simulations not only have the ability to see what the pilots are doing, but get readings from the displays the cockpit. Computers analyze the data and generate real-time feedback for both the simulator operators, engineers, test teams, instructors and the ilk.

There was such a need for these tests and results, that time in the simulator needed to be scheduled, necessitating Lansing to employ a full-time booker for the facility. Carrier pilots sometimes needed to be trained and re-certified. If their employers didn't send them to one of the myriad outsourced training facilities, the Lansing facilities were used. Engineers and designers needed time to ensure that new designs were functional. Incident Review Teams, like the one for 4273, needed to use the facility to investigate any problem reported to Lansing regarding the 530. Every Lansing plant had a simulator for each model the aerospace company produced.

In the tower, the operators have complete command over what is inputed into the simulation software. Weather. Aircraft malfunctions. Flight deck misreads. You name it, the operators can control what happens during the simulation by entering new conditions into their computers. How the pilots and the aircraft reacted to those planned and spontaneous inputs determined certification, or influenced designs.

A simulated crash is a definite fail for all concerned.

Deni and Sheed loomed over the shoulders of the two Lansing techs that were running the simulator. Two experienced Lansing pilot instructors sat inside the cockpit for their own re-cert, easily running through take-off communications to a simulated tower. The Captain and First Officer spoke into the simulated CVR and to the non-existent ATC. One of the techs in the tower would go through the normal communications as if an Air Traffic Controller existed, but nothing said would 'break the fourth wall' in actor's terms. The pretend flight was real as far as all participants were concerned.

When the plane was up to thirty-one thousand feet, Deni wanted to see what would happen if the slats were accidentally deployed.

"Can you make one of them bump the slats lever thingy?" The simulation operator, Jeff Green, turned over his left shoulder to the guest.

"Deni," Art Connor said before Green could respond. Art was sitting on the couch on the rear wall of the observation tower.

"I want to see what happens."

"What do you want to see?" Green asked.

Sheed explained. "We want to see what happens when one of them bumps the pedestal, triggering an involuntary slats deploy. Did I get the lingo right?"

"I thought I explained that that isn't what happened," Art said.

"Humor us," Deni insisted.

"It's not even worth the—"

"—Sit back down and let the guys humor me," Deni said pointing to the operators. "Your boss wants us to investigate, so we're investigating. Stay there and shut up."

Art Connor did as he was told.

"You got the lingo right," Green said, "but I can't just ask one of them to recreate what you just said."

"Sure you can.   Just call in there and tell'em to bump the pedestal like She said. You been talkin' to them for twenty minutes." Deni leaned back in toward Green.

"Of course I CAN talk to them, but we're supposed to play the part."

"Just this once."

"Okay.   But even if I did, to what end?   Do you know how difficult it would be to 'accidentally' bump the throttle lever on the pedestal, lifting the slat cover, deploying the slats? I could tell him to do it a hundred times in a row and it wouldn't happen."

"I tried to tell him," Art said from the couch.

"And I tried to tell you," Deni said turning toward the VP. "Say one more thing. Please. Say one more thing and see what happens."

"Deni, stay calm.   Mister Connor, please don't antagonize him. Jeff is it? Jeff, there must be a way to recreate it," Lisa said trying to keep the testosterone in the room on an even keel.

"Make him do it two hundred times in a row if ya have to. Just make it happen."

The other operator, Drew Randle, interjected.

"We could just deploy the slats from here. Without the bump. We could just extend the slats to see how the pilots react. We won't break the fourth wall and you'll get the result, even if you don't see the cause."

Green looked at the investigators to see if his colleague's suggestion would be acceptable.

It was.

"Ring their bell, Drew."

He punched a few keys on his computer keypad and watched the video monitors and computer screens.

Inside the cockpit, both pilots were enjoying an uneventful simulated flight. They were at cruise with a clean configuration.

Suddenly, they experienced clacking with a simultaneous response from the plane. The nose drastically moved upward, the non-existent plane along with it.

The Captain assertively responded by adjusting the yolk and throttle inputs, the aircraft resumed its original orientation. The event was but a hiccup in an otherwise normal flight.

"That was odd," the Captain said to his First.

"They were just throwing a test at us."

"Record the incident for the CVR."

"Done."

It happened again.

The plane nosed toward space, toward the heavens, after the clacking alerted the pilots to a problem.

"We must have not handled that right. Here we go again."

A loud buzz filled the cockpit, much more ominous than the previous alerts.

"Auto kicked off."

"It will reengage."

The Captain again adjusted the inputs, trying to correctly situate the aircraft, succeeding in leveling it off.

Autopilot engaged, retaking control of the plane.

"Here we go. Okay. Note it and be ready for it again."

Drew Randle turned around in his chair. "Satisfied?"

"Maybe," Deni said. "Does autopilot always kick back in?"

"It's designed to at cruise alt," Green said. "But even if it didn't, you just saw that pilots know how to fly the plane. Redundant systems. There is a backup plan for everything. Auto is there just in case. It's like luxury cars now. If the person driving the car doesn't know enough to brake, the car knows to stop the car instead of crashing into whatever is coming ahead. Every single thing on the plane has a redundant system."

"I've explained that," Art again said while typing something into his phone on the couch.

Sheed nodded. "But the slats aren't the only part of the plane that controls pitch."

"You're a quick-study," Green said.

Randle turned to his colleague. "Do you want me to flip the tail?"

106

"Horizontal stabilizers, a-la Alaska Airlines," Green said as he spun back around, away from the investigators.

Art interjected from the couch, "McDonnell Douglas MD-83. Not a Lansing aircraft, and that's a fact," referring to the Alaska Airlines flight 261 in 2000.

Green nodded to Drew Randle as if Connor hadn't said anything. "Hit the tail."

The pilots were ready for the incident this time. Virtually the same thing happened. The nose pitched upward after the plane warned them that something was wrong. They corrected the aircraft and steadied it. Another hiccup, but nothing more.

"We can do this all day long, but these pilots are ready for it now," Green said.

"They were ready for it when it happened. They're pilot instructors being re-certified. They never would have been in the plane in the first place if they couldn't overcome something so routine," Connor said, again without looking up from his phone.

"Well we didn't *imagine* that 4273 went down. *We* didn't say that the plane went up and down like that," Deni said. "Gotta be somethin' like that happened."

"Unlikely," Art said. "Portman and Raymond were very experienced pilots. You saw how these pilots reacted. You're right, something happened. But if either of them did accidentally bump the middle pedestal, you just saw how quickly experienced pilots would overcome it." He stood up, put his phone away, and headed toward the exit door. "I think that's enough for today. I'll meet you in the same place we met today, at the same time tomorrow morning."

And then Quality Assurance VP was gone.

It was well after the evening IRT briefing had begun and probably had ended. The three had missed it. Clearly Art Connor believed it was for no reason.

Deni said to Sheed, "I think we made a friend."

"Macy was right."

Monday
8:15 P.M. October 5, 2015

IT TOOK SOME TIME AND EFFORT FOR DENI AND SHEED TO sort out how to get back to Deni's Land Rover from Building 20. They'd spent the day being driven around Lansing Aerospace in Art's electric vehicle; but their chauffeur had left them in a huff, and nobody volunteered to give them a ride. They were forced to walk back to the main gate, navigating past the many buildings which were not necessarily in numerical order. A couple of wrong turns here and there added to the several mile walk and to the time it took to get back to the hotel.

It'd been a long day for both investigators. Lisa wanted to get back to her suite and take a long, hot bath after room-service prepared and delivered a meal. Deni needed a drink and to rest his brain which was still swimming from all of the information that had been thrown at him all day.

Lisa got her wish.

Deni didn't. Ani was waiting for him at their suite at The Drury, anxious to talk about the day. He couldn't blame her, yet he didn't have the same level of enthusiasm about it.

Ani and Hobey had gone for an afternoon run, after which the dog was exhausted. Ani was not. She then went to a nearby gym which was recommended for their pilates classes by the concierge. Exercise amped her up, gave her more energy. She was chomping at the bit waiting for her man to walk through the door, practically attacking him when he did, still in her jog-bra and yoga pants.

"So how did it go? Have any leads? You're back later than I expected."

"We didn't solve anything, if that's what you're askin'."

"Nobody expected you to wrap it all up in one day, Bae. You'll figure it out," she said while hugging him. The door to the suite had not yet closed.

"I'm not so sure. I thought we were on to somethin', but everyone at Lansing thinks it's ridiculous. Who knows? I don't really want to talk about it. Can I come in? How was your day? Wicked boring?"

"No, not at all. It was kind of fun to just relax. I unpacked our stuff, had a late breakfast, then explored a little bit. They don't have a Dunkies in this town, but they have a cute little coffee shop. Hobey and I went for a long run, which is why he's passed out on the couch."

The dog was practically comatose on the small couch in the efficient living area of the suite. Deni was thankful not to have someone else vying for his attention.

"Then I went to a pilates class. It was okay. I was dressed differently than they do here I guess, so I was getting some eyes. Come to think of it, I was getting some looks in the coffee shop too, but who cares? New in a small town, right? Anyway, want to go get some dinner? I'm starving."

"Yeah, I could use a drink. And a minute to breathe."

"Sorry. Didn't mean to get all aggro on you, I'm just glad to see you," Ani said as she walked toward the kitchen. She then opened a cabinet, removing a bottle of Whiskey. It wasn't Redbreast. It wasn't even made in Ireland. It was from Tennessee.

"I found a packie. They call them ABC stores here. No Redbreast, but it's the best I could do. Collier and McKeel. The guy there said that it's the best."

"Tennessee?"

"It was that or Jameson. They didn't even have Bushmills. Should I have gotten Jameson?"

"No. No. Thanks. Collier and McKeel. At least it's made by Irishmen. Very thoughtful. I love you."

"And you should," she said, giving him a kiss as he entered the kitchen. Have a drink, I'll go shower."

"Where do you want to go? We should hurry up before they stop serving food, so you might want to make it quick," Deni said.

She pulled on the front of his jeans.

"We could have a quickie."

"You're in a mood," he said.

"We're in exotic Joplin, how could I not be in the mood?"

"I told you this wasn't going to be a fun trip. For any of us."

She kissed him on the mouth again. Then his neck. "Are you going to pour yourself a drink, fuck me, or keep yapping?" She grabbed his groin and unzipped him. "Hello big fella. I think Joplin has you in the mood also."

"It ain't this town that's got me in the mood."

After making love, they both showered and realized the late hour. Deni called down to the front desk to ask what times the nearby restaurants closed. He was told by the young man that most restaurants in Joplin closed early on Mondays—within the hour in fact—but offered to have their order picked up for them from a nearby diner, and he would deliver it to their suite personally. Deni took him up on the offer.

When asked what they would like, without the benefit of a menu, Deni tried to make the order as simple as possible. A burger and, since they didn't have a turkey burger for Ani, a chef salad.

Less than an hour after the phone call, a knock came to the door.

Deni was told by the same young man that he would add the cost of the meal to their room bill. Deni handed him a twenty as a tip with thanks.

Ani came toward the small table from the bathroom in her robe. "What did we get?"

"I got a burger."

"What did I get?"

"They didn't have turkey burgers, so I got you a salad."

"Oh, Bae. I'm starving. A salad?"

Deni was unpacking the takeout bag, then suddenly stopped when he read the note that was inside. On a folded piece of paper was a hand-written note.

GO BACK TO BOSTON

"I was hoping for something a little more ..... What's wrong?"

110

"Don't eat anything," Deni said as he flew to the door of the suite and out into the hall. The person from the front desk was still in the hallway waiting for the elevator as Deni rounded the corner and tackled him as if they were both in the NFL.

Deni had him pinned to the carpet in the hallway.

The twenty something let go of the twenty dollar bill that was still in his hand.

"Explain the note."

"Wha-wha-wha what note?"

"'GO BACK TO BOSTON' - the note."

"Sir. I have no idea what you're talking about. Did you give me too much for the tip?"

Deni could see the twenty-something was ernest. He had no idea why he'd just been tackled in the hallway and was taken aback to say the least. More like shitting himself.

"Where'd you get the food?"

"Little place around the corner. The diner. What's wrong? Did they screw up your order? They're closed now. Yours was the last order. I had to call in a favor to get them to cook it. Can I get up now please?"

Deni let him up, but pushed him against the wall by the elevator.

"They left me a surprise. How did they know the order was for me? Explain."

"I have no idea. I just placed the order like normal."

"Did you tell them who it was for?"

"I don't think so. I just said that I needed ….. Oh wait. Yeah. I think I said something like, 'It's for the other suite. Or the other investigator. I don't know. I just said that I needed it and that I was sorry that I was calling it in so late."

"The other suite? You got food for She? Fuck!"

Deni turned to look toward Lisa's room. "Gimme the key," he said to the kid.

"I, I, I don't have one with me. I'd have to go back down—"

The concierge was interrupted by the ding of the awaiting elevator. The door was finally opened and waiting to take any occupants, waiting or already inside, to lower floors. The car was empty.

Deni shoved the young man into the empty elevator and ran toward Lisa's room.

Her door was locked. It was always locked for occupant security.

Locks, however, were not even a speed-bump for Warren Dennihan. Deni had forged a skill from the time he'd spent as a kid in South Boston. Before he was a teenager, he was stealing car stereos and the occasional car. He'd given up that particular road he was on, leading to a life of petty crime like most others in his neighborhood, and decided to go the police academy instead. Deni was no longer a thief. No longer a cop. But he could still pick a lock in less than time than it took you to find your keys.

He reached into his wallet, retrieving his two titanium pins, and was inside the room in a matter of seconds.

Everything was dark. The room quiet. He wished he'd had his gun, but then realized that whomever had poisoned the food had done so from a distance.

Chicken shit bastard.

A few steps into the dark room, Deni could see a bit of light coming from the direction of the bathroom. Lisa's suite was the mirrored reflection of his and Ani's. Her kitchen and living area was to the left as he entered the room, the bathroom to the right next to the bedroom.

Deni moved toward the bathroom.

"She? You okay? She?"

No response.

The light, the only light in the suite, came from the bathroom. The door was slightly open. Deni slowly pushed the door open. On the toilet was a precarious stack of binders, the various documents handed over to the investigators.

Next to the toilet, Lisa was lying, naked, in the filled bathtub. Her eyes closed. Motionless.

"She?"

Her eyes slightly opened, then screamed as she frantically pulled the earbuds out of her ears, standing up. Faint music could be heard as the earphones hit the tile floor. The clinging bubbles from the bath were not doing a good job of covering the necessary areas.

"*WHAT THE FUCK ARE YOU DOING IN HERE*?" Sheed yelled as she tried to cover herself.

"Shit. Sorry," Deni said as he averted his eyes.

"Jesus Christ. Throw me a towel."

He did from the nearby rack. He turned his back toward her so she could cover herself, but turned toward the mirror over the vanity. It seemed no matter where he looked, his eyes found a naked Lisa Sheed.

"Just get out."

He stepped out of the bathroom.

A few moments passed before Sheed emerged from the bathroom in a hotel terrycloth robe.

"Did you get a good eye-full?"

"Sorry, She. I just thought ….. "

"….. You just thought what?"

"We ordered food from the same place you did. The kid at the front desk. We got a note in the bag. Said, 'GO BACK TO BOSTON'. Did you get one?"

"No. A note? I don't get it."

"Not very ambiguous, She. Get the fuck outta dodge seems pretty clear to me. No gray area. No room for interpretation."

"So somebody from the restaurant wants us to leave town? Why? They must know somebody at the plant? We should look into it."

"We got enough on our plates. How do you feel? Sick?"

"No. I feel fine. Why?"

"Oh I was just askin'," he said sardonically. "They fucked with our food."

"Or they wanted you to think so."

"Whatevah. Either way, I'm not takin' any chances. I'm wicked hungry but I ain't that hungry. And I'm sending Ani and Hobey home. We're not makin' friends and I can't have anything happen to them."

113

"Are you sure it's not all bark, Deni?"

"I'm not sure of anything. I'm not sure what I'm doin' here in the first place."

"We're trying to find out—"

"—I know, I know. But are we going to? I mean really. Let's call this what it is. A payday. Lansing doesn't want us here. The workers don't want us here. The town clearly doesn't want us here and is willin' to poison us if need be. Ani said she was getting looks today. She thinks it's 'cuz she was wearin' a jog bra in public. I didn't have the heart to tell her different. I just know that this is no place for her. Or the mutt."

"So now what? Are you quitting? Running scared? I've never known you to be scared of anything."

"No. I can't quit, even if I wanted to. We're locked in. Contractually. Written by a fuckin' lawyer."

"So you putting her on a plane?"

"Are you outta your mind, She? A plane? No. Look into getting a rental. Tonight. I'll pack her up right now and send her home in the Rover. You and me? We stay frisky. Locked and loaded at all times goin' forward. Clear?'

"Clear."

Tuesday
9:15 A.M. October 6, 2015

IN THE WORDS AND ADVICE OF DYLAN THOMAS, ANI DID NOT "go gentle into that good night".

It had not been a good Monday for Deni, and it was shaping up to be an even worse Tuesday. He verbally wrestled with Ani for hours, trying to make her see that Joplin was not the place to be at present. It wasn't a vacation spot. Though he'd never served in the military or been involved in an official war, Deni felt as though the current situation was the equivalent of being a soldier on the opposing side of an enemy line. And said enemy had just given fair warning.   Go away before you get hurt was the not-so-subtle implication, and Ani was undeterred in her pursuit of rest and relaxation with her fiancé.

She insisted that he was overreacting. Her rebuttals were just as emphatic, resolute in not going anywhere. She was staying with her man, come what may.

Deni tried to enlist the help of his partner, but Lisa wasn't getting involved.

Light had begun to break before Ani and Hobey were packed into the Land Rover along with their things. He watched her drive away, realizing that he had to be at Lansing in a few hours and hadn't had a wink of sleep. And there was too little time to get any now.

He'd need a keg of coffee to get through the day, and he decided to get started on one.

They were fifteen minutes late in getting to Lansing because Enterprise was late in dropping off the car.   No explanation was asked for, none was given.

Art Connor simply met them just inside the Lansing south gate as he did on Monday. He'd been waiting for the investigators as they pulled their rented Ford Fusion from Enterprise into the parking spot. How long he'd been waiting was unknown, but it was long enough to have gotten hot in the already seventy-plus degree weather, and remove his suit jacket. He looked steamed in more ways than one, but didn't vocalize it.

Today he had a female assistant with him, who also looked warm in her charcoal pencil skirt and ivory sleeveless top. They had two General Electric vehicles, each behind the wheel.

The two investigators were handed an itinerary by the assistant, after she left the driver's seat of her vehicle. The itinerary consisted of meeting times in the Building 10 conference room. They would be required to attend, at the very minimum, if not report any of their findings to the IRT members.

They'd already missed the first briefing.

Not much else was said, a simple exchange about seeing them in Building 80, and again in Building 10 for the remaining two briefings. Connor and his assistant left the two investigators in one of the electric vehicles, leaving one for them. They stood at the gate with agenda in hand as the VP and his assistant drove away.

Deni wanted to mention the poison attempt, but Lisa advised him before arriving at the plant that accusing him and/or Lansing of wrongdoing without proof was against their interests.

Alexandria Pratt had said so as well, through the car speakers, using a bluetooth connection to Lisa's phone. Pratt also said that he might be overreacting.

He didn't like it, but he agreed. With the plan, not about the possible overreaction.

The curt interaction hadn't produced a comment about Deni's daily T-shirt choice or the fact that both were wearing their firearms under unnecessary sport jackets. Maybe Connor hadn't noticed.

The first order of business was the 4273 wreckage that had been reassembled in Building 80. Today was the first day that diagnostics would be performed on the wreck, and both the investigators wanted to be present, not just hear about the findings in one of the meetings on the itinerary.

Both Deni and Sheed were tired and irritable. Neither had had much sleep. Deni had none and Sheed tossed and turned. The tension was palpable. Lisa had been put into a terrible position between her partner and his girlfriend, after having been barged in upon and seen wearing nothing but an angry scowl.

Neither had said a word on the way to Lansing, and neither spoke when Sheed climbed behind the wheel of the electric vehicle. Deni let her drive. They took a few wrong turns before arriving at the hangar that housed the plane that had until very recently been at the bottom of the Atlantic.

Building 80 was yet another massive structure on the Lansing property.

After plugging the electric vehicle into the charging station, the two of them entered the building, having to scan their visitor passes to gain access.

Hardhats and reflective vests were donned, as per the mandate to be in the building. Deni wondered if the Lansing hardhats were like bowling shoes. Someone just sprayed whatever had come off of the head of the previous wearer, making it ready to put onto the next head. His head.

Then he tried not to think about it.

"Hey you can't bring that in here," one of the security guards at the entrance to 80 said. He was pointing at Deni's chest.

"What, this T-shirt?" Deni looked at his chest which had the logo for the band Days of Fire, and graphics for the song *Airplane*.

"The gun. You too," he said pointing to Lisa. He exited his glass booth and stood in front of Deni. "I need to confiscate those."

"I'd like to see you try," Deni said.

The guard reached for his chest, but didn't make it. Deni had taken the taser from the guard's waistband and zapped him with it, sending him backward and smashing into the glass wall of his security booth.

In the center of the hangar was the L530. Or what was left of it. The plane looked like an enormous puzzle that was in the process of being put back together. Most of the plane was pieced back together, but the parts that were missing or damaged beyond being able to be reassembled were many. Some of the outer skin covering the fuselage was missing, exposing the mangled skeletal structure beneath. Deni didn't know what to expect, but what stood in the center of the hangar was not it.

Around the outside of the wreck, was a full compliment of portable scaffolding and heavy equipment. Electric T-matic forklifts by Toyota. Flatbed trailers made by Great Dane were fitted with train wheels and placed on a set of rails that ran various courses around the interior of Building 80. The beds were empty at the moment; four inch wide canary yellow J.J. Keller winch straps, with a three-pound iron flat hook buckle, awaited cargo to secure and move elsewhere. Wires and computer equipment were daisy-chained to a glassed-in diagnostic lab a hundred yards away.

The scene was as if the gigantic machine was on life support instead of being in a morgue to determine cause of death.

Art Connor had arrived ahead of them, the assistant that had been with him twenty-minutes prior at the gate, was absent. He approached as Deni and Sheed made way toward the wrecked plane.

"Are you ready for the walk-through?" Short and to-the-point. Very unlike Monday. Something was quite obviously different today.

"Been ready since yesterday," Deni offered.

"Fine. We'll give you a walk-through, then we will go into the conference room here for a quick briefing, where we'll go over what you missed in the morning IRT meeting. Then the initial diagnostic run. By our mid-day meeting, we might have some initial data to review," he said before turning away from them to climb the stairs on the scaffolding.

The investigators followed but gave their escort an expanded lead.

"So we should probably talk about the elephant in the room," Deni said.

"The plane is the elephant in the room. I'd rather just forget about it," Sheed said.

118

"Still pissed?"

"I'm not pissed, Deni. It's just awkward."

"You want to see me naked? Will that put it to bed?"

"Ugh. No. That's not what's awkward. You saw me naked. Whatever. I'm over it."

"For what it's worth, you look good. I mean, you're in wicked good shape."

"Stop. Idiot. Just ..... Stop. Putting me in the middle of your domestic dispute. That was awkward. That's the elephant in the room. Don't do that again, okay? I don't put you in the middle of me and Reg," she said.

"You talk about what's goin' on with you and Reg all the time."

"Vent. I vent. I don't ask you to persuade her to do something, or not to do something, on my behalf. I feel like I've gotten to know her a little bit. We're friends."

"And I'm not?"

"My friend? Yes. My boss and business partner also. My friend, absolutely. But it's complicated. Just don't put me between my two friends anymore. Got it?"

They had reached the third tier, the third story if you will, on the scaffolding outside the deceased plane and were about to start up the next set of stairs.

"I don't get why she wanted to come in the first place. I seriously don't know why she'd want to stay after the warning note. Ani is much more cautious than that. Fought me for fuckin' hours to stay and I can't figure why. You?"

"You're putting me in the middle again."

"Jesus, She. I'm just askin' your opinion."

"Off the record?"

"Sure."

"This was never about a vacation. She worries about you. About you getting hurt or worse. She wanted to be here to protect you."

"Ridiculous. How the hell is she gonna protect me?"

"She probably can't. But at least she isn't going to be fifteen hundred miles away if something does happen."

"Did she say that?"

"Deni?"

"I'm doing it again?"

"Yes. And we're here."

They'd reached the forward exterior door to the plane, just behind the cockpit. Looking down the exterior of the 530, it didn't look like it had been under water. A crash, to be sure, but not at the bottom of the Atlantic. The plane was damaged beyond salvage, to be sure. But just as surely, it had been cleaned.

The interior was the same as the exterior.

Not a trace of seaweed. No barnacles or coral or any of the things that might be expected. This was not something pulled out of the water on a Jacque Cousteau special on the Discovery Channel, though that is almost exactly what it was. The smell was the only indicator. Whatever cleaner they'd used, it didn't mask the lingering smell of stale beach. And vomit. And bowel odor mixed with cleaning solution.

The aircraft smelled like a college bar restroom. Times ten. Someone had made an effort to make it smell better, but every horrible thing that happened was still an aromatic assault.

"Wow. Who cleaned all this up?"

"We did," Art said. "People wonder why we haven't publicized the findings from an investigation eight months after the crash? Or why we haven't begun to comprehensively investigate the wreck? They think we're trying to hide something. What they don't realize is that it takes time. We had side-scan sonars on remote vehicles scanning the ocean. Ten commercial fishing trawlers. Collection submersibles borrowed from the Department of Defense. Millions of dollars in equipment and experts in oceanic recovery. Then we transported the recovered pieces back here, piece by piece, and a team was assigned to reassemble it. We had another team collaborate with a specialized forensic team to clean it without destroying any evidence that might lead us to a conclusion about causation. It all takes time, that's a fact. A great deal of money, effort, and time. Remember Malaysia Airlines flight 370 in 2014? That Boeing 777 still hasn't been fully recovered, and may never be.

I think we've been rather expedient despite what our naysayers think."

"I just asked you who cleaned it," Deni said with a shrug. "I didn't say anything about time or money or effort."

"Well, I just wanted you to know. I wanted you both to know."

"Great. We're all committed. Can we get on with it?"

"We'll start in the cockpit and move our way toward the tail," Art said.

The cockpit was a mangled mess. Arms and braces were used to keep instrumentation and components in place. Bolts and rivets didn't match up. Metal was twisted. Plastic was cracked and/ or shattered. And yet other pieces were just missing. Wires were zip-tied together and ran from the cockpit, out of the plane, and to the lab where data would be received and interpreted.

"Does any of this stuff still work?"

"No. Most of it, anyway. But what does work we hope will give us readings and data that can be extrapolated to give us enough to piece together a finding. Also, we can study how each item is damaged to determine at what angle the plane hit the water, which gives us more information to indicate how the 530 was configured before the water landing. It's a very complicated puzzle," Connor explained.

"Water landing? That's a bit misleading," Lisa said.

The VP ignored the comment and moved into the front galley.

Deni noticed a large, white phone just outside the cockpit in the flight attendant work area.

"The phone. Did any of the stewardesses make a phone call? If i'm on my way to the ground, I'm probably gonna try and reach out."

"That goes to the cockpit only," Art said. "And they're called 'Flight Attendants' now."

"Whatevah. Why not just open the door?"

"Just 'open the door'? Maybe you've heard of nine-eleven? You can't just open the door from the galley. If there is a situation, hostage or plane malfunction or what have you, the phone is used." Art pointed to the lights above the cockpit door. "The green and red lights indicate the need to either get on the phone, commence emergency protocols, and whatever else the carrier—in this case Preferred—trains their staff to do in those types of unusual situations."

"So they must have used it."

"They did, in fact. The CVR will give us that conversation, among others." Art didn't know if the two investigators remembered what the acronym meant, so he clarified. Cockpit Voice Recorder."

"Have you heard it?" Lisa asked before Deni could ask the same question.

"You'll hear it. Everything will be made available to you. But first we need to finish the walk-through."

"Doesn't really answer the question, does it Arty? Why don't you ever answer our questions?"

Again the VP ignored the jab, progressing aft in the aircraft while pointing to the seating closest to the forward galley.

"There is no such thing as First-Class seating at Preferred. They're philosophy is that every passenger is treated with the same level of luxury. If you want to delve more into that, you'll have to speak with one of our CAS reps ....."

Sheed mouthed the name 'Macy Dunn' to Deni while Art was continuing to speak. The women they'd met at lunch the previous day was the Vice President of Commercial Aviation Services.

"..... In any event, these seats were the first passengers to make contact when the plane made contact with the ocean during the water landing."

"Stop calling it a damned 'water landing'. Everyone died. That qualifies as a crash in my book. Look around you."

Overhead compartments were twisted and mangled, again being held up with reconstructive bracing to hold them in place. Doors were missing. Hard plastic was shattered. Seats were torn, missing a seat-back or arm. Virtually all of the bottoms of the seats were still in place, which Deni found odd.

"All these seats are still in place, Arty. I thought they were used as flotation devices in the event—"

"—PA uses the vests. The seats are secured to the seats and the seats to the aircraft. That's why they're still in place. Some carriers want impact-release.   Some want removable cushions. Some don't. PA doesn't. If they did come loose, they would float, that's a fact. But they're not designed to and they didn't."

Lisa scratched her head.   "Then why weren't more of the passengers found? If they were buckled to the seats, and the seats didn't leave the plane ....."

"With the rate of impact, the seat belts tore them in half."

The gravity of the situation weighed on both Deni and Lisa. Two hundred people were inside this mangled contraption when it hit the surface of the Atlantic, never to be heard from again. Their last moments alive were spent screaming toward their demise. Dreams of seeing sunny-fucking-Florida were traded for prayers of getting out of the predicament alive.   Those prayers went unanswered, many without a proper burial or final goodbyes to those that survived them.

Deni opened one of the few closed overhead bins.   It was empty.

"It's a mess in here, Arty, but where are all the carry-ons and shit?"

"What was salvaged was put into a secure storage facility here at Lansing."

"But not all of these overhead doors are damaged to the point where they don't shut. Not all of the luggage came fallin' out."

"Not all, no. But most. We catalogued the items that we found against the manifest. We then had a forensic team discern what was where and when. Then we tagged them in that seat order when we put them in storage," Art explained.

"We're probably gonna wanna go through all that. And what else have you messed with?"

"Excuse me?"

Lisa intervened. "I think what my partner is trying to say is that we don't exactly have a pristine scene. Good investigative work depends largely upon an untainted scene of the crime."

"Accident. Not crime," Art said.

"Semantics. What we are trying to figure out, what we are asking you, is how much of this aircraft has been edited for viewing?"

"Miss Sheed, I resent the fact that you think that Lansing has some hidden agenda. That we brought you here only to pull some sort of con. We had to clean the plane in order to put it back together so we could begin our investigation. Our legal team insisted that there be signed affidavits by the forensic cleaners. The company that we hired specializes in this sort of thing, and executed their duties with the highest level of integrity. The seaweed is gone, but the mechanical evidence is intact. We are an open book, as I've said to you repeatedly over the past two days."

"And that's a fact," Deni mumbled to himself before saying to Art Connor, "Then let's have a listen to that CVR thing."

Tuesday
11:15 A.M. October 6, 2015

INSIDE THE DIAGNOSTIC LAB A HUNDRED OR SO YARDS away from the crashed L530 it overlooked within Building 80, Art Connor and two technicians sat at a small conference table with the two Boston investigators. In the center of the table was what looked like a hazard-orange, glow-in-the-dark, oversized inhaler for asthma and COPD sufferers. This device was not to administer aerosol Pirbuterol to a giant, however. It was the CVR. The Cockpit Voice Recorder. The device that recorded the final words of Captain Tim Raymond, First Officer Matthew Portman, and the ambient noises inside the cockpit from a third microphone.

The recording would likely rehash what Deni and Sheed had listened to inside the Boston conference room on Boylston Street, called the fishbowl, at Taylor, Higgs & Pratt. They would again hear what was transmitted between Air Traffic Control and 4273. This device, however, promised to provide more insight as to what was happening inside the cockpit. The third microphone, the cockpit mic, picked up voices that were not sent to ATC and would hopefully provide a behind-the-scenes understanding of the two men at the controls and what was happening to the aircraft.

The contraption in the center of the table had wires from it leading to a large set of computers and LED monitors.

"What's that thing?" Deni asked.

"The CVR. It's what you asked to hear. The Cockpit Voice —"

"—I know what CVR stands for. I thought it was the black box."

Everyone in the room who worked for Lansing chuckled, failing in hiding it. Art replied through the laugh.

"There isn't just one black box, remember. Didn't I explain that to you?"

"Yeah, ya did. But this thing isn't even black. Why do they call them black boxes, if they ain't black?"

"It's difficult to find 'black' boxes from a crash site. This is one out of fourteen."

"Have you listened to it?" Lisa asked.

"Many times. As have our techs," Art said referring to the others in the room. One of them took the floor without introducing herself; but at the angle that her badge was turned, Deni could see her first name was Erin.

"We continue to filter and listen to it, specifically the third microphone. Three mics go into this thing and record simultaneously. One for the Captain, one for the First Officer, and one records the cockpit. Any sound inside the cockpit—or loud enough to be heard in it—is recorded real time. We can isolate them, or play them together. We are going to do four run-throughs for you. All together, then one for each mic. The third mic, ambient cockpit, is the biggest puzzle. What they said is what they said, but aircraft noises can be heard on the third mic. Only we haven't been able to figure them out yet. We got the thing down to milliseconds …… It's still a ….. Well, you'll see."

"Are we ready?" Art asked. The two detectives nodded. "Good." He gave the unspoken gesture to move forward.

Another technician tapped a few keys on the computer terminal. He explained that what they would hear was the cockpit version of what they had already heard, with the exception of the NTSBO to the flight crew and other cockpit conversations. The tech explained that at the first indication that something was severely wrong with the plane, and that it was going to be a difficult time to recover, a Nature - Time - Signal for evac - Brace - Other system was enacted.

Art elaborated that the phone and lights outside the cockpit he'd explained earlier when they were doing their nose/cockpit walk-through was used for the NTSBO. The first voices they would hear would be Portman's and a flight attendant, Alice.

As sounds filled the conference room, sound waves moved along a graph on the computer LED screens.

"NiTSBO protocols, Alice." The voice was calm.

"How the hell can he be so calm," Lisa asked. The recording was then paused.

"Pilots are cocky," Art said. "They never give up and even if they have to glide the thing into a landing, that's what they'll do. Did you listen to the recording of the Chesley Sullenberger ditch?"

The name didn't register with either investigator.

"The US Airways Hudson River crash?"

Both nodded. Flight 1549 was in the news virtually all of 2009. The captain of the flight was considered a hero.

"That was an Airbus A320 by the way. And you never hear him say the word 'crash' — because pilots never think 'crash'. It's just a complicated situation that they are trained and prepared for, and that's a fact."

"But they must know. They must know deep-down that if they can't control the plane, it's going to crash," Lisa said.

"They don't give up because they can't give up."

Sheed nodded, mollified if not satisfied with the explanation.

Deni was getting tired of Art Connor defensively pointing out each time a commercial plane crash was referred to, that it wasn't a Lansing jet involved. They were talking about THIS plane, from THIS company, THIS time.

The recording started again from where it had left off, Portman's voice speaking to the flight attendant, Alice. Deni and Sheed stared into the CVR in the center of the table, intently listening.

"The aircraft is—"

"No, it's not turbulence."

"I understand. Is she conscious?"

"How many?"

"We have fifteen minutes to land. Next signal will be five minutes to jumpseat, then the signal evac procedures, then for brace. You know what to do. Just watch the lights. Stay calm and ready the cabin, but only if you can without injuring yourself."

The phone could be heard going back on the receiver, followed immediately by Portman again.

"CHS Approach, this is Preferred Air 4-2-7-3. We have an emergency."

There was a pause while ATC responded. A faint sound could be heard, just as when he was speaking with Alice, but the controller's words could not be made out.

"Request priority clearance for emergency landing in Charleston, if we can get there."

Another pause as the ATC asked the nature of the emergency.

"Wing and fuse damage. Passenger emergency. Trying to recover. When we do, we'll need fifty ambulances on the ground, maybe more."

"Affirmative. At least. I say again, we encountered severe wing and fuselage damage. Power plant is failing. We have severe injuries to passengers and crew."

"Roger, Approach. We need everyone you can get."

"Negative. This is first officer Matthew Portman."

"Negative."

"Affirmative, Approach. Passengers and flight crew are unconscious and possibly dead, but I cannot give you a number."

"Matt. We're losing the deck. Lost power. "

"Get it back, Tim."

"Not going to make CHS. Flash the crew for five to jumpseat and convey."

Another brief pause, presumably while the First Officer multi-tasked his three-way communications. To his Captain, to the ATC at Charleston, and nonverbally with the cabin lights to Alice and what was left of the crew.

"Losing the flight deck. Repeat, losing the deck. FDAU tracking multiple failures. We've just lost pressure and need an immediate place to land. We need an immediate place to land. Repeat. Need an immediate place to land."

"Not going to make CHS. We're looking at a water landing."

"Airspeed over 400 knots. Altitude dropping fast. Rate of Descent 8000 plus feet per minute. Angle at 60. Configuration is dirty."

Static filled the room for a few minutes which seemed like hours.

Finally a loud, deafening static filled the room for one-half of one-second, then nothing.

The tech turned away from his elaborate computer set up to address the room.

"That was all three together. Now we can listen to each individually. First I'll play Captain Tim Raymond's."

"Not for nothin', but what's the point?" Deni asked. "We heard what they said. Like you pointed out, 'they said what they said'. I don't wanna speak for She, but I'd like to hear the third one. The ambient one. Without all the talking."

"You're still going to hear the talking. Even with the two other mics off, you'll hear Tim and Matthew speaking. However, you'll hear the other noises with more volume. I can only isolate them out so much. I can speed it up or slow it down, but you'll still hear them. I can even hone in on the ATC and Flight Attendant if you'd like."

"Maybe Alice. The guy in Charleston isn't gonna tell us shit about what was goin' on inside that plane."

"I'm with Deni," Sheed said.

"You got it." The tech turned around again, made a few keystrokes and the third mic from the CVR played for the room.

"NiTSBO protocols, Alice."

"Wait. Can you go back some? That can't be all this thing has," Deni said as he pointed at the orange nebulizer-looking thing. "What happened before that?"

"It's business as usual except for the 'thud' sound. We've been analyzing that sound for weeks and it has to be the—"

"—Don't worry about that sound, Deni," Art interrupted his subordinate.

"'Don't worry about it'? What kinda bullsh's that? Somethin' happened before all the stuff we just heard, and you say not to worry about it? The 'thud' was the thing that went wrong, right?"

130

"Not necessarily."

Deni looked at the tech. It was an unmistakeable look that inspired fight or flight response.

"'It has to be the what?"

The male tech sitting at the computer terminal looked at the VP, who shot him a look of his own.

Deni snapped his fingers, regaining his attention. "What's the hardest you ever been hit?"

"Excuse me?"

"Simple question.   What's the hardest you ever been hit, guy?"

The tech looked petrified.

Deni moved closer.

The tech winced and blurted out, "It has to be the slats."

He'd obviously weighed the two punishments. An immediate and severe beating outweighed employer disciplinary action down the line exponentially.

"It's the sound of the slats being deployed. Numbers don't lie. Mathematical probability is ….. That's the sound."

"Play it."

"Deni," Art said. "Before you go off on tangent—"

"—Shut up, Arty. You! Play it."

The tech did as instructed, but made a statement of mitigation before doing so. "I was told to leave that part out. Even if the slats extended at cruise, auto would take over and problem solved. I was just doing what I was told by my superiors."

"Tell it to someone who gives a shit. Play it."

Rumble.

Thud.

Clacking.

"Oh shit," Tim Raymond said.

"Auto will correct."

Loud buzzing.

"Nope. Keeps cutting out, Matt. I'm taking over."

Rumble.

Thud.

More buzzing. Several different sounds, indicating different warnings, even to the untrained ear.

"Porpoising. She's not responding. We've got to land it."

A triple ding.

"That's the flight line, Matt. Check the cabin and give NiTSBO instructions."

"Copy."

"NiTSBO protocols, Alice."

"The aircraft is—"

"No, it's not turbulence."

"I understand. Is she conscious?"

"How many?"

"We have fifteen minutes to land. Next signal will be five minutes to jumpseat, then the Signal evac procedures, then one for brace. You know what to do. Just watch the lights. Stay calm and ready the cabin, but only if you can without injuring yourself. Everything is going to be fine."

The phone could be heard going back on the receiver, just as before. Deni motioned to the tech to turn it off.

"It seems to me the 'thud' was the thing. Slats. What's the mystery? Why are you tryin' to cover it up?"

"We're not trying to cover anything up, Deni. Slats don't cause this kind of damage. Ask anybody who knows anything about avionics."

Sheed interrupted. "What's porpoising?"

"It's sudden and violent pitch oscillations," Art said. He held out his hand and made it wave up and down like a dolphin

132

swimming on the surface of the water. "Planes don't really do that at thirty-one thousand feet."

"Or they crash," Deni added.

"No. The pilot lands the aircraft if that's what needs to happen."

"Which you just heard him say needed to happen."

"Correct."

"But it didn't land."

"No, obviously not. Which is why I'm adamant that something else caused the accident. You heard him say 'he lost power' did you not? Slats have nothing to do with power. That's powerplant."

"Uh huh," Deni mumbled. "Likely story."

"I can prove it to you in the simulator if you'd like."

"Why didn't you show us that in the simulator the first time?" Sheed asked.

"Because we would be steering you toward a non-issue. Why even posit the notion of slats for you to run with? The IRT is looking at powerplant."

"Nobody has said, 'powerplant' to either of us. Have they She?"

Lisa shook her head in the negative.

"I believe we told you during our first meeting in Boston. And you would have heard it again today, except you did miss the morning IRT briefing," Art said. "That's a fact."

"Tell ya what, Arty," Deni said as he rose from the table toward the VP. "Let's not pick and choose what information you think we need or don't need. Got it?" Deni opened his jacket, exposing the handle of his pistol.

Art stood up and backed away, visibly concerned for his safety. He was not the only person in the room who shared the concern, yet nobody came to his aid.

"Yes. Yes. Absolutely. Got it."

Tuesday
1:15 P.M. October 6, 2015

THE FOOD TRUCK OUTSIDE BUILDING 80 WAS A POPULAR spot to get lunch. Deni and Lisa shelled out six bucks a piece, with a scan of their ID badges, and each received more food than they could consume, without the need for cash or a debit card. The sandwiches were enormous, the fries that accompanied them were meals in themselves.

Neither wanted to try the executive cafeteria food again, plus they wanted to eat outside. It was a gorgeous day, maybe even a little too hot. This was not Boston in October weather. While they were enjoying seventy-eight degree sunshine, Boston was cold and probably raining.

While waiting in line to order and subsequently to have their orders prepared, they talked about the investigation thus far while trying to disallow another's ability to eavesdrop. They were not the only people at Lansing that wanted to enjoy the food truck and the sun, and so they spoke slightly above a whisper or away from other's whenever possible.

"I told you this case was bullsh, She. These fuckers built a piece of shit plane and they don't want to pay up. They're making us accomplices."

"I don't like being lied to any more than you do. But how can we be sure that this 'porpoising' is what caused forty-two seventy-three? This place has thousands of employees, how many do you think would or could actually keep that kind of secret?"

"It was probably a chain reaction or somethin'. The slats made the thing bob up and down at a couple hundred miles an hour and the pilots couldn't control it down. Or that failure caused others. Point bein' that Lansing has a big problem on their hands, and they want us to help them cover it up."

"Did you not hear me? Thousands of people can't keep a secret, Deni. How many murders have you investigated, cop or otherwise, where one conspirator killed the other because they were a loose end? Any more than one person with the same secret is a recipe for getting caught. Lansing employs what, ten thousand? I'm not sure we have all the facts, because they sure seem confident that they know what they're talking about."

"Then why the cover-up? Why mislead us?"

"Good question. Maybe it's like he said. They thought we'd jump to conclusions, because we kind of are."

"Maybe we can jump ship. I wonder how much the lawyer for the victims would give us for this kinda information. We could help them in their investigation," Deni said.

Sheed pulled out her notepad. "Trey Keating. Victim's Comp litigator's name is Trey Keating. But I know you're kidding, we signed the non-disclosures."

"I'm only half-kiddin'."

They heard the name their food order was under bellowed out from the food truck.

"Reid!"

Deni thought it would be funny to use the name of the Lansing CEO rather than either of theirs. It was also a precaution. There'd already been an attempt to poison him, at least in his mind. Nobody would poison their Chief Executive Officer.

Once they had their food, they looked for an empty picnic table from the six that were located nearby.

They spotted her at nearly the same second she spotted them.

Macy Dunn.

She waved them over to her table.

"I wonder if she's following you. You've got quite the admirer," Deni teased.

"Good grief. Well, we can't *not* go over."

They approached the table for six. Macy was eating alone.

"Sittin' with all your friends, Mace?'

"Deni, don't be rude," Lisa said as she took a seat.

Macy thought it was funny.

"It's a delicate balance, to be sure. I'm not supposed to fraternize with subordinates, but I don't want to spend my lunches with my piers either. Not that they really want me to join them anyway. Real boys club, if you catch my drift."

"You're not 'one of the boys'?"

Lisa kicked Deni under the table.

"Ow! Just kiddin' Mace."

"I know you are. Anyway, you two are the hottest ticket in town. Everybody is running their tongues about you."

"All of it good I'm sure," Deni said before taking a bite from his giant sloppy joe sandwich. He was famished.

"Then you'd be surprised. Just be careful," Macy said.

Deni nodded in the affirmative before wiping his mouth. He used another napkin to cover his chest, hiding the graphic on his T-shirt.

Macy noticed it before he covered it up.

"I see you have a knack for antagonizing people, Deni. I wouldn't do that. Just a fair warning that Lansing is a company that pays well and provides for a great many families in Joplin. Nobody pays as well as Lansing. Not in Joplin anyway. You might want to remember that before you take a stick to the hornet's nest."

"It's a gift," he said with a shrug.

"Just don't say I didn't warn you," Macy said before turning to Lisa. "So how is your day going, honey?"

"It's been interesting. We just heard the CVR from 4273. We heard the slats."

Deni gave his partner a betrayed look, as though she had just divulged a secret. Macy was not somebody that he trusted, though in truth he didn't entirely trust anybody. Actually, he trusted only two. Ani and Lisa. And she just disappointed.

"I see. So you think it was the slats?"

Deni interjected. "Two and two is four, Mace. That rumble sound, then the thud, then a big pop. They lost air pressure and fifteen minutes or so later 4273 was at the bottom of the Atlantic. Gee, I wonder what it was?"

"Sarcasm aside, that's not my area. If you want to know something about Preferred? I'm your gal. If you want to talk parts and maintenance programs, I can help. But if you want me to tell you what caused that particular 530 to crash, I'm afraid you've picked the wrong horse to ride, because I can't help you."

"You wouldn't help them cover this up, would you?"

"Deni, I don't know that that is a fair question to ask her," Lisa said.

"Fair or not, I'll answer. Lansing has given me a lifestyle that I enjoy. I've been here in boon years and bad. Do I have a loyalty to the company? I sure do. Would I help cover up our responsibility, if we have any, to the deaths of two hundred people? Not on your life. I'm a Christian and not only do I have to look myself in the mirror every morning and sleep at night, but someday I'm gonna have to meet my maker. I don't know how I'd look Him in the eye when that day comes with two hundred souls dragging me down."

"So what about Preferred? They tell us that they're squeaky-clean," Lisa said. "But they've told us a lot that has not been exactly true so far."

"By 'they' you mean 'the boys club'?"

"Reid ..... Art ..... "

"Don't forget Timothy Vahn, the finance guy," Macy added.

"Right. We met him in Boston," Lisa said.

"Like I said, they're trying to protect Lansing. Reid Lansing especially. This is his family's legacy we're talking about here. They mean well, believe me. But they're old school. If you ain't wit'em, you're again'em. They don't trust you yet. They may never trust you. But that lack of trust is trickling down through the entire company. Like I said, be careful."

"I heard you, Mace. But you didn't answer the question. Preferred?"

"Oh. Right. Well, it was my team that got them off the ground, no pun intended. It's tough in this day and age to start an airline from scratch. It's easier to buy and merge, like so many are doing. You have to have a niche. Like we did with Emirates. Showers and bars on every flight. With Preferred, they want to provide first-class accommodations for a below-market ticket cost. They've been successful at it, despite the challenges."

"Go on," Deni said, not letting her take a bite of her lunch.

"Well, it's very difficult to compete with a seventy-nine dollar one-way flight like what Southwest offers when you're shelling out money for expansion airports and providing the extras on each flight. Southwest, for example, goes to airport destinations with less expensive airport fees. Those are usually the hidden fees that get tallied up at the end when you're booking your flight. That increases the consumer price of a plane ticket, which forces them to keep shopping and possibly go to another airline. These travel websites and applications make the market very competitive."

"That's business," Deni said.

"But is it *fair* business?"

"I don't follow."

"Neither do I," Sheed said with a mouthful of sandwich.

"I don't want to get sued for slander, but say an airline company—hypothetically like an Eastern or something—is really just a stock scam?"

"Still lost," Deni said.

"They buy some old planes that shoulda been put out to pasture. Then they subcontract out their maintenance so they limit their liability when something goes wrong, and sooner or later it will. You offer cheap fares and use the cash to buy new routes. More airports. It looks great on paper because fares are up, revenue is up, and day-traders can't wait to buy up your stock. Earnings skyrocket and everybody is happy until the accident. By that time they've folded or been merged into another airline, or sometimes they just DBA under a new name."

"Is that what Preferred is doing?"

"No. But that's how some companies compete with sub-hundred dollar fares," Macy said.

"So how *do* they do it? How *do* they make money for expansion and still give a glass of champagne and movie with every ticket?" Lisa asked.

"Volume. By purchasing our jets, they can fit the most passengers on one widebody than any other plane manufactured. Period. It's when those planes aren't full, that's when things get touchy. And like any company, when their planes aren't full, they find ways to cut back. But philosophically, Preferred has not, nor will they ever, cut a cost that affects a passenger. Not in their perception. Maybe that champagne is André instead of Korbel, but you still get champagne. And if you can tell the difference between the two, then you're probably on an airline that has a first-class."

"But would they make cuts in equipment and safety?"

"Highly doubtful. Also we check on them. We send out maintenance suggestions and follow up. If they don't comply, we don't give them any more of our planes and we alert the FAA. There are some things that you just can't compromise on, no matter what the business philosophy."

Deni looked at Sheed. They were both thinking the same thing. And they both knew who had to be the one to ask Macy.

"Would you look into them for us? Please?" Lisa gave a prize-winning smile.

"Quite frankly, we have. Their records are spot-on. But for you? I'll give it another look. A little deeper, if you catch my drift. Give me your number so I can let you know if I come up with anything."

Lisa wrote down her cell number on one of the paper napkins on the picnic table.

Macy gave Lisa a wink as she picked up what was left of her lunch and stood from the table.

"Before you go, Mace, is there a contact over at Preferred? I'd like to look at the pilots, uh—"

Lisa filled in the space.

"—Tim Raymond and Matthew Portman."

"Sure. Stephanie Clark over at PA," Macy said. "I'll text you her number and let her know to expect your call."

After Macy was gone, Sheed turned to her partner.

"You realize after this is all over, I have to change my number. Reg will have my head."

Deni laughed.

"I won't tell if you don't."

"They know about the slats, Reid. They heard it," Art said into his cell phone.

"I thought we agreed that they wouldn't hear that part of the CVR? What the hell are you doing, Arty?"

Connor ground his teeth upon hearing his loathed nickname.

"I'm not doing this. They're doing it, that's a fact."

"It's only the second day they've been here," Reid said from the back of his chauffeured car. Only he wasn't 'here', he was on his way to a Lansing board meeting at the Four Season Hotel in St. Louis. He flew in to give a sort of state-of-the-union to delegates from his other plants, as well as invited guests. Selected members of the media would be present. Government officials in charge of defense spending. He was then scheduled to turnaround and fly back that evening.

"I'm about to speak in front of a packed conference hall," he continued, "in front of cameras for the world to see, telling them that we are free of this mess. That we are continuing our investigation of this tragedy, but that there is nothing that Lansing did or could have done to prevent this.   That our company is moving forward. Growing. Expanding. That we are and will continue to be the best aerospace company on the planet. And now you're telling me that these two morons from Boston are going to prove me a fucking liar?"

"They're not exactly morons, Reid. In fact, I think that we've completely underestimated them.   The dog and pony show isn't working."

"Make it work."

"I can't exactly lie to them. As it is, they don't trust anything I'm telling them anymore."

"It wasn't the slats, Arty. Planes don't crash into the Atlantic fucking ocean because of a slats deploy at cruise. It makes for a bumpy ride, but the thing will land."

"That's what I told them."

"And?"

"And we should have just let them come to a determination on their own with our team. Trying to spin their investigation was a mistake. Now there is nothing I can say that they'll believe."

"Find a way."

"He pulled a goddamned gun on me, Reid."

"Are you giving up?"

"No, Sir. I'm just giving you the facts."

"The fact is, Arty, that these two need to have a come-to-Jesus moment. If you can't do that, I'll find someone who can. Am I making myself clear?"

"Yes."

"Are you sure?"

"Yes."

"Then handle it, Arty."

"I—"

Click.

"—will."

Immediately following the call to Reid Lansing, Art's cell vibrated in his hand.

It was the Joe Ware, Chief of Lansing Security.

"Hello Joe."

"Good afternoon, Mister Connor. I was told to give you a call. I've been making calls all morning trying to figure out what we need to do here. I was told to give them a wide berth, but this can't stand."

"What are you talking about, Joe?"

"The Boston investigators."

"What about them?"

"One of them assaulted one of my guys. In Building 80 this morning."

141

"Let me guess, the male. Warren Dennihan."

"Correct.   Used his own stun-gun on him.   My guy says they're armed.   Both of them.   I was going to send a unit to apprehend them, bring in the Joplin PD—"

"—Don't do that, Joe.   Don't do that.   That won't be necessary."

"This can't stand."

"You're right. It can't."

Tuesday
1:45 P.M. October 6, 2015

THE TWO INVESTIGATORS DECIDED TO SKIP THE MID-DAY, post-lunch meeting-slash-briefing that they'd been told was mandatory when they were given the daily itinerary that morning. The investigators missed the morning meeting and were planning to miss another. Though there would likely be hell to pay for the decision, they both agreed that there really wasn't one.

Art Connor, the Vice President of Quality Assurance for Lansing Aerospace Company, had been leading them by the nose because it was obvious that he had an agenda. A not-so-hidden agenda to protect the company that had raised him. He was not to be trusted, as proven by the latest revelation from the CVR. Slats had caused 4273. There was an involuntary slats deployment at cruise speed and altitude that affected pitch, causing the plane to porpoise. Though the company had made claims that porpoising doesn't cause that level of devastation, it seemed clear that it was the inciting event. Art Connor knew the slats deployed and did his best to cover up that fact. Deni and Sheed, therefore, decided to move forward sans tour guide.

Building 20 held the flight simulator for the L530. The simulator would tell them what happened after the slats deployed. The simulator would give them the answers they sought.

Their visitor badges garnered them access to the building, however the simulator was booked solid through the rest of October. The booker, was quite steadfast in blocking a block of time for the people from Boston.

Lisa had no luck in swaying the young, blonde administrator with subtle persuasion.

It was Deni's turn.

143

"What's your name, hun?"

"Rosie. And could you be more condescending?"

"I'm not tryin' to be a prick, I'm tryin' to get an hour on the machine."

"Which you and your colleague have made abundantly clear. As I've said, ad nauseam, the time is booked. My job is the booker, meaning I'm responsible for scheduling the time, thus my title. I wouldn't be very good at my job if it was a free-for-all, would I? Someone has scheduled the time you're looking for. It's wouldn't be fair to bump them."

"An hour. That's all we're askin' for, Rosie."

"An hour that I can't give you. How can I make that more clear? Shall I call security?"

"I don't think that'll do you much good, hun. Who booked the time?"

"I'm not at liberty—"

"—I've got access to the building. I'll wait around and find out, but it will save us both some time and energy if you just tell me who booked the time."

Rosie pulled a strand of blonde hair out of her face, tucked it behind her ear. Her green eyes were looking around the reception area and her desk as her mind was visibly working through the problem before her. The quickest way around is often through.

"QA. Quality Assurance Division," she finally divulged.

"Really? I happen to know the VP of QA."

"So do I. Shall we give him a call?"

"That won't be necessary, Rosie."

She could see that she had him on the ropes. A welcomed turn of events.

"Oh, I don't know. I think we should," she said as she picked up the phone on her desk. When Art picked up on the other end, Rosie put him on speaker.

"Mister Connor? Rosie from Sim. I have both of the Boston Investigators here looking to book an hour. I've informed them that the simulator is booked through the end of the month, and that your division currently has it on the clock."

"Hi Arty," Deni said loud enough to be heard on the other end of the line. Sheed said hello as well.

"I've repeatedly asked you not to call me that—" Art stopped to calm himself. He then cleared his throat. "—You're supposed to be over here for the briefing."

"Where's here?"

"Admin. Building 10. Don't be coy, Deni. You and I both know that you're supposed to be here. The team is waiting, that's a fact."

"I'm not much for meetings, Arty. Never been the 'sit around and talk about what we're gonna do rather than just go do it' type. Anyways, we both know why we're over here. Should I say it out loud in front of Rosie, here, or do you want to free up an hour."

"How many times do I have to tell you that the slats were not the cause of 4273?"

"Free up an hour and prove it."

"You were shown already. Remember?"

"No, Arty. We were shown how quickly the autopilot took over when there was the problem, not what happens when autopilot didn't fix the problem. Put your money where your mouth is."

"I'll be right over," Art said.

"Not necessary. Just free us up the time and the guys who run it."

"Rosie?"

"Yes, Sir?"

"Who is in the Sim right now?"

"Dave, from your division. He's testing the upgrades for the —"

"—Oh yes, of course. Now I remember. How much longer do they have?"

"Another three hours, Sir."

"Let them know they have another two. The investigators can have the last hour. Okay? Everybody happy?"

"Whatever you say, Mister Connor."

"Happy as a clam, Arty. And that's a fact," Deni said with dripping sarcasm.

"Thank you, Art," Lisa said genuinely.

"Rosie?"

"Yes, Mister Connor?"

"Three forty-five to four forty-five. Not a minute earlier, and not a minute more, am I clear?" It didn't take knowing the man to know that he was speaking through clenched teeth.

"Very, Sir."

Art hung up on his end of the line.

"You heard him. Will you be waiting here for the next two hours?"

"No," Deni said.

Rosie looked relieved.

Deni's first thought was to find another conference room at Lansing, in Building 20 or otherwise. There seemed to be a conference room on every floor, in every building on the massive property. Meetings were held to schedule further meetings where they would discuss what happened in the previous meeting and what was to be discussed in the next. In his view, the rooms were built to waste time.

He was a doer. Action-oriented. If something needed to be accomplished, talking and wishing and delegating was not the way to go.

But Lisa reminded him of the fantastic weather Joplin, Missouri enjoyed in October. Sixty-eight degrees was a whole lot warmer than forty-eight, which is actually warm for Boston this time of year.

Deni agreed and they found another picnic table under one of the few trees on the property. No food truck. Nobody else around to overhear their conversation.

Macy had done as she was asked and text Lisa the number for her contact at Preferred Air, Stephanie Clark. Stephanie was yet another VP, a title most likely given as freely at Preferred Air as it was at Lansing.

The call was expected, Stephanie said. She would help them in any way she could, as long as it was off the record. Preferred had been cleared of any wrongdoing, and she was uncertain as to what the investigators thought they would uncover, but she would provide the employment, service and certification records for both of the pilots. It was purely an act of goodwill on her part, and as a favor to her friend Macy Dunn. Preferred had nothing to hide and had been transparent since the tragedy took place.

Stephanie Clark would continue to keep her company in good light—though she wasn't required to—anonymously.   She would email them personally, presently.

Lisa didn't have her laptop with her, and Deni didn't own one. The two drove back to the rental car at the main gate to retrieve the computer. The email with all attached documents were waiting for her when she opened and rebooted the machine.

They found another shady spot to sit with the laptop.

"She's not gonna send you anything, She. A VP isn't gonna throw her company under a bus, anonymous or not. She told you as much on the phone."

"No, of course not. But the records she sent over *are* going to provide me with information that we can use to do some digging. While my new admirer digs into the PA maintenance, I want to dig into the pilots."

She had their service records and psych evals in a binder in the rental car, but was hoping that the contact at PA was going to send her additional information. Or conflicting. Something to hang her hat on.

And Stephanie Clark had done just that.

A few keystrokes and taps with her fingers on the touchpad, Lisa found what she was looking for.

"See?" She turned the laptop toward Deni.

"Social and DOBs."

"Of course she didn't send me their personal information. But she did send me more information than what Lansing put together in the documents they put together for us. Physicals and checkrides every six months have to be recorded for pilots by the carrier as per FAA guidelines, See? Right here," she said, pointing at the screen, "I got them off the FAA website. Gotta love the Freedom of Information Act, huh Deni?"

"Clever."

"All this and brains too," she said as opened her arms.

"I know. I've seen you naked."

"Shut the fuck up, Deni."

"Now what?"

"Now I dig into their personal lives. Finances. Habits. Clubs. With a date-of-birth, social, and full name? I can tell you everything but their blood-type. Wait. A-neg. Nevermind. I can even tell you their blood-type. You should really learn more about computers, Deni. As an investigator they really are invaluable when you want to completely dive into people's shit."

"Thanks for the tip."

Tuesday
3:45 P.M. October 6, 2015

THE TWO HOURS SEEMED TO FLY BY. For Lisa. While she punched keys and clicked the mousepad on her laptop; Deni attempted to check-in with Alex, give her an update, but she didn't answer. He left a generic message to call when she had a minute. A call to Ani produced the same result. When the short calls were completed, he was relegated to watching Lisa as the in-depth information for both of the dead pilots from 4273 was put together.

Timothy Raymond was divorced three years prior, paying alimony and child support semi-regularly. He never changed his life insurance beneficiaries, so the money he was in arrears for with his ex-wife was more than made up for when he plunged into the Atlantic off the coast of South Carolina.

As a pilot for PA, he worked about fourteen days a month and spent his discretionary time and income with a myriad of women and his Harley Davidson *Fat Boy*—which he just had carbon-fibered before the crash, instead of writing a check to his ex.

The biker club he belonged to consisted of two dentists, a day-trader, a male nurse, a retirement account manager, two regular accountants, a stay-at-home dad, and a pilot—him. These milquetoast men were rough-riders in appearance only. Maybe they'd seen one too many episodes of Sons of Anarchy to avoid a mid-life crisis. Whatever the impetus for their alter-egos, this vanilla lot didn't partake in drugs, excessive alcohol, or vigilantism. Timothy Raymond, however, did get the girls.

Matthew Portman was yet more plain-jane than his first officer for flight 4273. He was a family man who refrained from all alcohol. Church on Sunday. Helped his wife run her soft-serve ice cream shoppe during his fifteen or so free days per month. When he wasn't pouring ice cream and applying sprinkles, he was an assistant coach for his kid's soccer and tee-ball teams—which he would then take to his wife's shoppe after a win or loss, pouring ice cream and apply sprinkles for his young team.

Neither man had severe money issues. Neither man had a gambling issue. No problems with medications. No death wish. No desire for martyrdom. No reason to purposely plunge themselves, and two hundred innocents along with them, into the sea, bye and bye.

Before they knew it, it was time for Deni and Sheed to head back over to Building 20. The flight simulator.

Rosie didn't welcome them back, but Deni made sure to say hello on the way by her desk anyway. The sarcasm was not lost on her.

"Hello again, boys. Time to run that slats thing one more time," Deni said as a way of introduction when he and Lisa entered the observation tower.

"Is that what this is about? I'm telling you, slats did not cause that kind of damage," Greene said.

"Then you won't mind proving it, guy. Get the thing up to thirty-one thousand feet."

"Do we have to go through lift off and all that? Or can I just show the part that's going to prove what I'm telling you?"

"What everyone has been tellin' us."

"Then you'd think you'd understand it by now."

"You'd think," Deni said. "But no. Just cut to the chase and run it."

There were no pilots sitting in the simulator. They were dry-running, entering what a pilot would do into the computer from inside the observation tower. Everyone in the room could see what the pilots would see, if any had been present, on the monitors.

The simulation was at cruise, point-eight-four mach, in short-order, skipping takeoff procedures.

The tech inputed an involuntary slats deployment, and just as it had before, autopilot took over almost instantaneously. The maneuver was but a hiccup in the flight.

"See?"

"Do it again," Deni said.

"Really?"

"Yeah. And this time, make it so auto doesn't take over."

"We don't have a pilot in the simulator."

"And? Didn't the plane get to this virtual place in space and time without a pilot?"

"Well ..... Yes. So you want the computer to act as though a pilot has to fly the plane because auto can't re-engage?"

"Yeah. What you said."

"Oh-kaaay.   But you know that the pilots from 4273 were experienced. Experts. Either one of them could have flown the rest of the way to Florida in that type of scenario, let alone guide it down to a safe emergency landing."

"Just do it," Deni said.

"Yes-sir."

More typing.

The simulated plane again maintained flight after a rough patch lasting a sum-total of eight-seconds.

"Satisfied?"

"No."

"Why the hell not?"

Lisa interjected.

"Have any of you heard the CVR recording?"

The room shook their heads. They hadn't.

Lisa pulled out her cell phone. She went to her voice memos and pressed the play button.

Deni was as shocked as the techs in the room. He hadn't known that his partner had recorded the audio from the CVR when it had been played for them.

"Technology is your friend, Deni," Sheed whispered while the room listened.

When it was over, Greene scratched at the thin stubble on his chin.

"Can I plug your phone into the computer? I want to hear it on louder speakers than your phone."

"Sure." Lisa handed him her phone.

He plugged a chord coming from his computer into her iPhone headphone output. He played it again for the room.

When it was over, Greene and Randle had a brief huddle.

"That rumble and then the thud. The slats were not responding. Autopilot or actual pilot, the slats were not responding. Even if he hadn't said, 'porpoising' - I'd know that sound. We teach that sound. But still ..... Porpoising is not enough to crash the plane. It would have been bumpy as hell and would have beaten the crap out everyone in that cabin, but any competent pilot could have guided her down. Severe injuries? Yes. Crash into the ocean? No."

"Put it in your computer," Deni said.

"Whatever you say, but there's more," Randle said.

"Go on," Sheed said.

"That pop. That's engine. And the stall warning. I heard it on ambient. Even if I didn't know that popping sound, I'd be able to pick out that warning buzz. That's powerplant."

"Where have we heard that before?" Deni looked at Lisa, rolling his eyes.

"And you don't build the engines," Lisa said.

"No. In this case PA wanted GE9Xs. A damn good jet engine."

"So Lansing would be off the hook if it was 'powerplant'," Deni said.

The two techs looked at each other and then back at Deni.

"Well ..... Yeah. But that's what we heard."

"Just run it."

"Okay."

Less than a minute later, everyone in the tower was watching video monitors of what would happen if the slats on the wings involuntarily deployed and would not reset, with autopilot or actual pilot. The nose of the aircraft violently pitched further into the atmosphere, then plunge toward earth with the same violence, repeated roughly a half-dozen times.

Then Randle entered more information into the simulator. Engine two stalled. Eventually, the virtual pilot maneuvered through an emergency landing. The plane was battered but in one piece. Virtual passengers were shaken and battered about the cabin. But the aircraft landed approximately fifteen minutes after the simulated sequence began.

Both of the simulator techs simultaneously swiveled in their chairs toward the investigators.

"Like I said. Beat to hell, but landed."

Deni shook his head in confusion. "But what else could it have been? What other problems could have happened after the slats. We *KNOW* that's what happened. In the words of Arty fuckin' Connor, that's a fact. So why didn't they land the damn thing like it just showed?"

"Engine."

"But it still landed," Lisa said.

"It's a commercial aircraft. A million parts. Literally. Anything could go wrong. But we're talking a Lansing 530 here. For all intents and purposes, a brand new one. Even if I concede that there was a slats issue that couldn't be corrected or maneuvered through—which I'm not—something else happened to cause that crash. Powerplant is certainly something we have to factor here. Those sounds are like fingerprints. The pop and then the warning."

"But it still landed," Deni said again for the room.

"Correct. In the sim, a competent pilot would have landed it," Greene said.

Randle had said very little throughout the simulation but now interjected, "We all want to figure out what that is, believe me. We want to clear our name. Our brand is a good one. A great one. Because we build the best airplane. Period."

Deni shook his head.

"That's what everyone keeps saying."

Tuesday
4:45 P.M. October 6, 2015

IT WAS NEARLY THE END OF FIRST SHIFT FOR ALL THE UNION workers at Lansing, and just as nearly the beginning of the second. The assembly line ran in shifts, as did most manufacturers.

Lansing had tried to move to two twelve-hour shifts a few years before—three days on, three off, followed by four days on, four off—but the UAW pitched a fit. The issue nearly caused a shutdown. Job actions occurred left and right. Tooling had mishaps. Workers were getting hurt and comp claims were rising. Callouts. Production slowed to a crawl.

The shift move would have saved Lansing millions between all of the plant locations. One less shift per assembly faction, meant they could eliminate thousands of unnecessary jobs. Those jobs not only come with salaries, but benefits and 401k's as well. A shutdown, however, would be exponentially worse if it went on for long.

Lansing decided to keep the traditional three, eight-hour shifts with available overtime.

The administrators, however, were salaried. They generally worked Monday through Friday, nine-to-five. Longer if necessary. Those who wanted to keep their cushy positions, or even get promoted to one of the scores of VP positions, found it necessary to come in early and stay late.

After the demonstration in Building 20, Deni and Sheed wanted to take another walk through the wreck. They were in a bit of a hurry because they needed to be back in Building 10, Admin, for the final daily briefing at 5 o'clock. Neither of them wanted to attend, but it seemed prudent not to miss three in a row.

The General Electric vehicle brought them over to Building 80 in under five minutes. Any gasoline-powered vehicle could have made the trip in less than half the time, without the need to put the pedal all the way to the floor. The tiny thing may have been eco-friendly, but it was not-so time-friendly.

Had they been making the trip from 20 to 80 fifteen minutes later in the day, the shift exchange would have made the roads and walkways much more congested and taken three-times as long.

Again their scanned badges got them into the door, unescorted. Fortunately they didn't need to be scheduled for a tour. They moved toward the wreck, noticing a crew spread out on the scaffolding, forklifts, and flatbeds. Like the various assembly lines they'd seen the day before, it was impossible to tell exactly how many workers were in the vast area. It was just as probable that a hundred people were scattered about the aircraft as it was ten.

They ran into only one worker on the way up the scaffolding toward the forward door of the plane. He was busily zip-tying wires to the vertical support beams on the scaffolding, likely his last bit of work for the day. It was quitting time. He didn't seem to care who was climbing said metal stairs toward the cockpit.

The strangers were wearing their PPE, hardhats and vests, badges fluttering against them where they were pinned as they walked, so they must belong.

Once up the stairs and inside the plane, they moved right toward the cabin.

The plane was as they'd seen before. Pieced together with support brackets and wires to put things where they would go if bolts and rivets could be aligned. Something was irking Deni about the seats being the only part of the plane that were in the exact same disposition as when the aircraft had originally left the factory. Only a few random seats were missing.

Deni got down on his knees, looking at how the chairs were fastened to the floor of the cabin. The seats weren't designed individually. They weren't like traditional bucket seats like people have in the front of their cars. It was more like the rear seating in a vehicle. Benches. While each of the three seats looked and felt like individual seats, it was really a three-seat bench-like design. Three seat-backs and headrests, three seat cushions on one bench that is lag-bolted and welded to the floor of the cabin.

He further noticed an 'EASC' logo stamped on the steel bracket under the cushions, which read Elan Aircraft Seating

155

Corporation under the logo. There wasn't a hint of rust on the gray structure. The seat cushions, however, did smell like rotten fish.

"Huh."

"What?" Lisa called from further aft in the plane.

"They shoulda made the whole plane outta these seats."

"I don't get it."

"Look underneath. That's not cleaned and put back together. These seats didn't budge."

"Didn't Art say that earlier?"

"Yeah, but whatevah this Elan company makes these things outta, it's wicked strong. I mean, they didn't budge. Look at all the other things in here. Nothin' lines up."

The ones by the emergency doors did. Look. They moved."

"They're probably designed to," he replied. Then he noticed the seat belts. Most, if not all, were fastened. "Poor bastards were sliced in two."

"Can you imagine?"

"Makes sense. Seats are more rugged than people. At a million miles an hour toward stop, the seats don't move but people do. Arty said the seat belts tore the passengers in two. That's one of his 'facts' that I actually believe. You ever have to do patrol when you were a Trooper?"

"Of course. We all did. Sitting on the Mass Pike all day was the bane of my existence."

"How many accidents you deal with?"

"Too many. I see your point. Let's hope they died of heart-attacks first."

Deni didn't respond. He rose to his feet, walked a few more rows toward the back of plane, closer to Sheed, then took a seat to his left at the emergency exit above the wing. He was on the right, or the starboard side of the plane, aisle seat. He looked out at the wing. He looked up and around from the seat. The amount of damage was undeniable. To his right, the shell of the cabin was sliced where the floor meets the outer wall. On the outside, it would be where the wing meets the fuselage.

He moved toward the window seat and looked out the small window. The wing wasn't attached to the fuselage. The wing was ten feet away, hanging in place from the hangar ceiling with thick, black cable. By his feet, light came through the slices from the hangar.

Deni scrunched down to inspect the slices in the fuselage. He could see light coming in, but the holes were not large enough to see anything outside the cabin.

"Cabin lost pressure all right. I can see light," he said loud enough for Lisa to hear but not sure if she did. He then put his hand on the window seat to help him get to his feet when the notion struck him.

"Hey She!"

"Yeah?"

"Whattaya suppose sliced through the cabin like this? Or did it happen after the—"

He trailed off.

"You have me there. I'm surprised that nobody has given us a theory on that. Well, maybe not. They seem to be keeping things pretty close to the vest, huh Deni? Deni? Deni? Deni!"

She raced up the aisle of the aircraft toward him. He was kneeling on the floor in front of the seats.

"What the hell?"

He handed her a purple and bedazzled cell phone case. It was missing many of the faux stones and didn't seem to work.

"What the hell is this?"

"Phone right? I thought you were the techie?"

"But I don't ..... I mean ..... How the ....."

"It was buried in the seat cushion," he said pointing to the middle seat.

"How is that even possible?"

"Your guess is as good as mine, but here it is. Passenger cut the seat and put it in here? The damn sparkle things cut into the seat and stayed there? I felt it when I tried to get up."

"There's no way this thing works. It was at the bottom of the ocean," Sheed said dismissively.

"Probably not, but we gotta check it out."

"This had to have belonged to a girl."

"Or a boy who likes fairy dust and unicorns," Deni said.

A sudden paranoia struck the two of them simultaneously. They looked around the wreck to see if they were being monitored. It didn't appear as though they were.

"We can't let them know we have this," Lisa said. "At least not yet. Not until we know what we have."

"If we have anything. Like you said, it was under water for eight months."

Lisa looked out the aircraft windows as if looking for an exit strategy.

"Let's get out of here. Like, now."

Tuesday
4:58 P.M. October 6, 2015

THE SCAFFOLDING WAS EMPTY AS THEY EXITED THE PLANE and made way toward the ground floor. Nobody could be seen anywhere, even from their high vantage point. The worker was no longer securing wires. Nobody under the wings. Nobody. It was always difficult to determine how many workers were in an area at any given time because of the shear size of the buildings, aircraft and said workers therein.

But now, there really wasn't anyone around. Building 80 seemed to be deserted, save for the two investigators. A pin-drop could be heard.   The echo from their footfalls on the metal scaffolding reverberated throughout the prodigious building as they made way toward concrete.

Deni, who was first in order as they moved down the stairs, turned to Sheed behind him.

"Odd. You get that?"

"I do. Probably nothing, though. Shift change?"

"Maybe. But nobody? I don't like it."

"You normally like the peace and quiet."

"Sssssssshhhhh. Listen."

They were nearing ground-level. Deni stopped in his tracks, forcing Lisa to do the same as she was not able to pass him on the narrow staircase.

Dead air.

No humming tools. No other footsteps.

"Maybe you're just being paranoid. Like someone trying to poison you?"

"I didn't imagine that note and paranoid is the difference between alive and dead, She," He said in a low voice. "Now be quiet and keep your head on a swivel. We need to get outta here, preferably in one piece."

"I'll play along. Follow me," Lisa said. She moved quickly toward the far-away exit, nearly a quarter-mile in front of them; but rather than follow the designated, painted, safety route as per OSHA regulations, she zigged and zagged through the workstations. Deni was right on her heels, keeping up quickly and quietly while keeping his eyes peeled.

Someone else was keeping up with them from an elevated vantage point. Foot-falls on the metal cat-walk several stories above could be heard echoing throughout Building 80. The exact location of the person was anyone's guess. He or she or they could be heard but not seen.

Deni retrieved his .45 caliber from its holster by his ribs, while continually looking around them in every direction for the person or persons following them. He felt hunted and at a loss. This was not a familiar jungle, though a familiar feeling. He'd done this sort of thing before. Many times. In Boston, and more recently in a Costa Rican rainforest. Instead of insects and snakes and spiders, this jungle was made of metal and machinery and tooling.

The exit was still three hundred-plus yards away with plenty of obstacles in the way.

Suddenly, Deni grabbed the back of Sheed's collar and yanked her backward towards him. She stumbled back into him, choking from where her crew-neck dug into her larynx. Before she could form a thought, much less regain her breath to yell at Deni, a large object fell from above and crashed at her feet just in front of her. The sound of the metallic crash was deafening.

It was a large, red, steel toolbox with locking drawers. The frame was now dented and twisted, but none of the drawers or top hatch had opened to spill the contents. The twenty-by-ten-by-twelve inch, fifty pound box—empty weight, without tools inside—would have crushed Lisa after being thrown over the catwalk railing four stories above them. The BAHCO label stared up at them from the concrete floor at their feet where Sheed's corpse would have been.

Deni fired three rounds at the catwalk above them, footfalls echoed throughout the building once the gun blasts stopped.

Whomever was up there, however many, were moving away from them.

"Still think I'm paranoid?"

"Holy shit, Deni. I almost fucking died."

"They're gonna have another chance if we don't get outta here."

Deni pulled Lisa toward a wide walkway and the two ran toward the exit. The walkway was a more circuitous route, but there weren't any catwalks that crossed overhead. He thought it better to have one less direction in which he needed to be wary of objects coming toward them.

They rounded a left corner to find their path was blocked. A flatbed with tooling on it was rolled across the walkway. There was no way through. They had to go around or again traverse through the workstations.

Deni decided to find away around on the main path.

"That's not supposed to be there," Lisa said between large breaths as she ran.

"No shit. We're being corralled."

"By who?"

"I don't know," Deni said to Lisa before he started yelling into the expanse of Building 80 at the top of his lungs. "Chicken-shit bastards won't show yourselves? Why don't you come out and fight fair?"

But nobody did.

Just the same ticking of feet on the metal catwalk far away and above.

The two investigators continued to run, circumnavigating toward the exit.

When they finally reached the exit, it was locked. The emergency bar on the door wouldn't engage. The door was impenetrable.

"We're locked in, She."

"Pick it. I thought you could pick anything."

"Not this."

"Emergency exits aren't supposed to be locked from the outside."

"You should write a strongly worded letter to OSHA if we ever get outta here alive," Deni said.

Voices were heard.

With the size and echoing in the building, it was difficult to calculate how far away they were, but it sounded like they were to their right. And at ground level.

"Now what?"

Instead of an answer, Deni pulled his partner by the wrist toward the voices.

Another hundred yards in a straight path along the perimeter of the building, they ran toward the voices.

A sea of people were walking into the building. The door held open by the crowds of people entering.

"What the fuck is goin' on?" Deni said to the crowd.

"Work. What's up with you?"

"Work. Whattaya mean?"

"Second Shift. Who are you?"

Deni flicked his visitor badge as an answer and pushed Lisa out the door ahead of him. Nobody commented or saw his gun as the two investigators went through and against traffic.

The seventy-eight degree air felt cool and refreshing. They were outside. And with the crowd that was piling into Building 80, they were likely safe. You can't murder two people in front of countless witnesses and expect to get away with it.

Lisa put her hands to her knees as she tried to catch her breath.

Deni, drenched in sweat, began looking for their electric vehicle. After a few seconds of orienting himself, he realized that it was on the other side of the building. His mind raced as he tried to put together the attempt on their lives, how best to get back to their rental car, and ultimately home.

He looked toward his partner, still bent over and gasping for breath.

"I don't care what Arty says, from now on we don't go anywhere alone or without our weapons. That's a fact."

Tuesday
8:30 P.M. October 6, 2015

THE YOUNG WOMAN AT THE DRURY RECEPTION DESK WAS nice enough to let Lisa use her cell phone adapter. The cell phone that Deni found buried in the seat cushion on the 4273 wreck was an older model, didn't currently have a charge, and might not even work after the ordeal it had been through.

It was all he thought about during the evening IRT meeting. It was all that Sheed could think about. And it was all they could do to keep the possession of such a find to themselves.

But they did.

Then immediately raced back to the hotel after the conclusion of the meeting.

The iPhone 4s that had come from the plane needed a wider connector than Lisa's newer phone. Luckily the twenty-something at reception was holding on to her still useful yet outdated technology, as obviously did the deceased owner of the phone from the wreck.

Lisa peeled off the purple and bedazzled phone case that was made by LIFEPROOF, according to the logo inside the case. The iPhone didn't appear to be leaking water or have any corrosion on the connector, which she felt was a good sign.

Nothing happened when she plugged the charger into the phone. It was the same outlet Lisa was using to charge her laptop, so there was juice. Yet the phone didn't make a sound. The screen didn't illuminate. No indication that the device would charge, let alone provide her with any useful information.

She called to Deni, who was in the kitchen area of Lisa's suite.

"Yeah?"

"This might take a while, if it can be salvaged at all."

"Do you want to see if we can get some food someplace? I'm starvin'."

"Takeout?"

"No way. I wanna watch the fuckers make my food."

"It's after eight, I don't know how long restaurants are going to be open."

"Then we find a grocery store."

An hour later, Sheed entered her suite with Deni in tow after having purchased and eaten their soggy pre-made sandwiches from Price Cutter, the local supermarket. They'd stopped at several restaurants that were still open, but none had an open kitchen which was a necessity for Deni.

Lisa's phone vibrated in her pocket. When she saw the screen, telling her who the call was from, she pressed it toward her chest.

"Give me some privacy, Deni."

"Is that Reg?"

"Just go home for a bit. I'll call you back over after the call."

"How do lesbians have phone sex?"

"C'mon. Just go. I want to get this before it goes to voicemail."

Deni used the connecting door for the two suites and was in his own temporary residence in short order.

He poured himself a Collier and McKeel—it wasn't Redbreast nor Irish but it was growing on him—before trying to get in touch with Ani. She didn't answer. He didn't leave a message.

Alex Pratt didn't pick up either. Her lack of response or attention to the phone calls was beginning to piss him off.

The television produced nothing worthwhile to watch after ESPN highlights had been exhausted. HBO was having a *True Detective* marathon, but the show was complete 'bullsh' in Deni's view. The news was fixated on the presidential race even though it was more than a year before anyone would enter a voting booth.

He thought about hitting the gym, but two whiskeys into a bender was not a great time to workout.

Thoughts of Ani and his dog Hobey crept into his mind and would not leave. Had he overreacted by sending them home? It was for Ani's protection. He missed her.

A knock on the connecting door filled the suite. Lisa opened it without invitation.

Deni turned from the couch, seeing his partner in the doorway. She'd been crying.

"You two have a fight?"

"No. You've gotta see this, Deni."

He looked at the clock. 8:30 P.M. He was exhausted from lack of sleep yet he wasn't going to be able to sleep for another drink or two anyway, so he got off the couch.

"What's up?"

"No words. You just have to see it."

"The phone?"

"Yeah. The phone."

Deni began to sober up, placed the remainder of his fourth drink on an end table before leaving his suite for Sheed's.

The iPhone was connected to her laptop on the small dining table. He pulled up a chair next to his partner after she'd taken her seat. She moved the pointer to the play icon on the media player application. The wobbly video began to play.

It was the interior of the plane. Flight 4273. The Lansing 530 that both detectives had been in earlier in the day. It was unmistakeable even if they didn't know where the phone had come from.

A mid-to-late thirties man was speaking to the camera. It panned from the man over to a young girl, couldn't be more than six or seven.

"Who were you listening to?"

"Nick Jonas."

"Who?"

"Never mind."

"Aria, it's not nice to be dismissive like that. I was just trying to take an interest in what you're interested in."

"You're right. Sorry. Nick Jonas is like super-ho—uh—uh—He's a good singer, Dad."

"Jonas? Like the Jonas Brothers?"

"Yeah."

"Aren't they Disney kids?"

"He grew up."

"Don't they all. Zoe. Do you know the States we have left to travel over?"

The dad was pointing at the screen on the back of the seat in front of them.

The young girl they were calling Zoe, the one that was six or seven, looked nervous.

"Don't worry, Zoe. I'll help you," the cameraperson said. The father had called her Aria.

"Well …. I know that one."

"Everyone knows that one, silly. It's shaped like a penis—uh—uh—Everyone can point out Florida."

"Aria Kane. I don't know that I'm comfortable with the fact that *you* know what a penis is shaped like, let alone your younger sister. Hear me?"

"Sorry."

"Don't be sorry, just think before you speak. It's perfectly fine to not say out loud every single thing that you're thinking."

"Got it."

"Are you video taping me?"

"There's no tape, Dad. It's just video."

"Why are you recording me?"

"Because Mom always defends you when we call you a dork. I want to prove to her that we're right."

Christian looked at his youngest daughter. "You agree?"

The younger girl giggled.

"I have to pee!"

"See Dad? I told you she shouldn't have the window. We better get her out before the cart blocks us."

166

The video panned to the beverage cart that was but a few rows ahead of them in the aisle.

"She's small. Small people have small bladders. You're right, hurry up so she can get out please."

The three of them unbuckled and rose from their seats. For the first time the video showed the cameraperson. Young. Maybe eleven or twelve at most, though it was difficult to tell these days. Kids matured faster now than they used to, especially girls.

Suddenly a loud noise could be heard above all other sounds on the video. Within a second, the video began to violently shake. This was not from an unsteady hand holding a camera.

People were being tossed inside the cabin. Overhead bins were emptying out onto the passengers below.

Screams.

"DADDY!"

"It's okay. Everything is—"

Things were happening so fast. People flying. Luggage and carryons thrown about. The beverage cart seemed to explode.

The father was thrown. Then he seemed to be moving back toward them, then it was completely black. It was still recording, but only audio. The visual was completely blacked out.

The father's voice was cut off as the sound of metal being pierced and air pressure drowned him out.

Determining what was happening from that point on would take much more sophisticated audio equipment. Nothing was discernible.

Screams filled the hotel suite from the small laptop speakers.

The video was dark but was still playing. There was nearly fifteen more minutes left on the timer being shown on the media player navigation bar. The sound was now muffled.

"I think this is where the phone went into the seat. Maybe she was sitting on it? This is all you get until the end of the video. These were the last moments of these girls precious lives." Sheed was crying again. Still.

She looked at Deni. His eyes were getting misty.

"Aria Kane. KANE. Did you hear it?"

Sheed nodded in the affirmative.

"Play it again."

"I've seen it three times now, Deni. It doesn't get any easier."

"Play it again."

Deni watched it two more times before instructing Lisa to make a copy. He didn't stick around to ensure that it was done. He couldn't take anymore of it. He went back to his own suite, poured a triple of whiskey over a fresh set of ice cubes and gulped it down.

He thought about how precious life is. He thought about how it could all end in a second as he poured himself another drink. Those poor little girls. Those poor two-hundred other souls on board 4273. He thought about Ani and how much he missed her. He dialed her number. It again went straight to voicemail. The clock read 10:02 P.M. Her phone was probably turned off. She was most likely asleep.

But he couldn't sleep.

Another drink.

Nothing on T.V.

Music. That would settle him.

The Drury provided a clock-radio on the nightstand in his bedroom.

A country station played the Waylan Jennings song *Luckenbach Texas (Back to the Basics of Love)*.

Deni turned the dial until he heard another song.

I Believe in You, by Don Williams played. Another country song on another country music station. He turned the dial again.

This song sounded more like blues than country. He let it play. He'd never heard the song before, but it spoke to him. The male singer's voice had a raspy quality that was intoxicating.

Deni turned up the volume and poured himself another drink as Chris Stapleton sang *Tennessee Whiskey*.

"..... *I used to spend my nights out in a barroom*
Liquor was the only love I've known

168

But you rescued me from reachin' for the bottom
And brought me back from being too far gone

You're as smooth as Tennessee Whiskey
You're as sweet as strawberry wine
You're as warm as a glass of brandy
And honey, I stay stoned on your love all the time ….."

Wednesday
8:00 A.M. October 7, 2015

LISA KNOCKED ON THE CONNECTING DOOR BEFORE entering, as was the new custom, to make sure that Deni was awake and ready to head to Lansing. It was going to be a big day.

For the first time since they'd arrived in Joplin she felt like she had a firm grasp of the investigation. Progress. There was now momentum and that inertia was putting Lansing on the ropes. Investigations were always about momentum. About keeping things moving forward.

Lisa believed that they were close.   That despite protestations to the contrary, Landing Aerospace had made a plane that failed.

The slats had deployed at thirty-one thousand feet.

In the words of Art Connor, it was fact.

That slat deployment caused the plane to porpoise and violently shake the aircraft and the passengers therein, causing severe injuries. Eye witness accounts confirm what they heard on the voice recorder.

Fact.

The pilots couldn't recover the L530 and the severe porpoising then caused another malfunction. The exact malfunction was unknown, but the CVR proved that within a matter of minutes from the initial incident, the pilots were preparing for an emergency landing. Greene and Randle insisted engine failure.

Fact.

While the pilots were trying to negotiate an emergency landing, the cabin lost pressure due to puncturing into the fuselage under the starboard wing. Where that puncturing occurred could be seen inside the wreck inside Building 80.

Fact.

Fifteen minutes after the loss of pressure, flight 4273 crashed into the Atlantic Ocean near the Pelagic Sargassum Habitat.

Fact.

All of these facts are further proven by the video from the phone Deni had literally uncovered inside the aircraft where that puncturing occurred. A video that Lansing didn't yet know existed.

Both Lisa and Deni had gotten the feeling that the VP who was handling them at Lansing was gaming them. The note and possible poison attempt had been concerning enough, possibly an overreaction on Deni's part. But the attempt to kill them the night before at the Lansing plant was quite real and beyond the pale. She'd almost been crushed. Killed.

It was time to fight back and today was going to be a big day.

Deni was ready to go when she entered his suite. He looked like hell, but he was ready. The red from his retro New England Patriots t-shirt brought out the red in his blood-shot eyes.

"Tie one on last night?"

"Nothin' another pot of coffee won't cure."

"You need to stay frosty. Did you forget that we almost died yesterday? This is day two without any sleep."

He opened his navy-blue blazer to show her his .45 caliber pistol, as if that in some way made his point.

"Just don't shoot me with it."

"Then stop naggin' at me."

"Get your ass into the car and I'll stop nagging."

Lisa drove to Lansing that morning. There wasn't a discussion about it, not that there ever was one. Deni always just went to the driver side whether it was his vehicle or not. But not on Wednesday. He went directly to the front, passenger-side door. Sheed didn't argue or miss a beat. She had the brief thought that maybe her partner was still drunk from his bender the night before, but it passed as the engine turned over.

"Should we talk about how we plan to get through today?"

"We jam that video up their asses."

"Not very subtle, Deni."

"Did you put the phone in your room safe?"

171

"Duh. And I went through it after you left last night. Contacts. Photos. I matched it against the passenger manifest. The Kane family, minus one. Sorina Kane. We heard the name correctly."

"Wife and mother of the two girls. She's the one pressin' the lawsuit."

"That would be the one."

"We should bribe Lansing. Tell'em if they don't settle, we'll give the video to her lawyer. Keating."

"Very funny. Seriously though. What are you thinking?"

"I was kinda serious. But I'm thinkin' I need another coffee."

"You really make it hard to like you sometimes," Lisa said as she turned right onto North St. Louis Avenue.

"I've heard that before. If you don't want to go at them both barrels, then play it close. We tell them about last night in Building 80. We'll have them spin their wheels lookin' to see who came within a few feet of having at least one dead body on the Lansing property, added to the two hundred already on their heads. Meanwhile, we keep digging. We don't have the smoking gun yet."

"Sounds like a plan."

The first hurdle of the day was being allowed further onto the property with their firearms. Art Connor was steadfast in his adamance that they wouldn't be allowed onto the property to conduct their investigation, on behalf of their Boston legal counsel, if they insisted on carry concealed weapons.

Both were wearing sport jackets to conceal them, even in the already nearing eighty degree heat. But unlike on Tuesday, Art had noticed them.

He informed them that he had been made aware of the encounter on Tuesday, where Deni had used a taser on a security guard. They'd been carrying guns then, against a Lansing policy in which they were well-aware. He didn't say 'allegedly'. He said it was a fact.

The two investigators oscillated back and forth in telling the story of how an attempt had been made on their lives in Building 80.

For his part, the VP looked concerned. Neither of them believed his worry was the genuine article, but neither called him on it.

It was make or break. They would have their weapons, or they would go home and tell Alexandria Pratt to push a settlement on Lansing's behalf. A settlement that would cost tens of billions of dollars at minimum.

Art took a few steps away to make a phone call, the result of said call was that they could proceed to the morning briefing with their firearms.

Deni and Lisa watched and waited for the decision. Deni reeked of alcohol, the heat was making him sweat, the sweat seemed to consist of pure whiskey. When the decision was made to allow the weapons; Sheed took off her jacket and pullover blouse, donning only the AG, heather grey, float tank top underneath.

And she was still warm.

Deni kept his jacket for a reason he didn't divulge.

The 9:00 A.M. briefing was a waste of time. Tests were still being run. Data from the tests that had been run by the second and third shifts on Tuesday night were still being compiled. Those reports were promised to be ready by the mid-day briefing. It was another meeting to talk about what was to be expected at the following meeting.

After the hour-plus not-so briefing, Art asked the two investigators to stay behind while the IRT members left the conference room. When it was empty save for the three of them, a portly man was escorted into the room.

He was introduced as Bob Flannery, the UAW rep at Lansing for local 1514, and the investigators were made known to Bob.

"He speaks for the workers here. I called him before the briefing to hear your story about the incident last night," Art explained after the introductions.

"It's not a story," Deni said. "It's what happened. My partner was a few feet from being crushed. If that tool box had smashed open, with God only knows what kind of tools inside flyin' around like shrapnel? I could have been dead right next to her."

"It's a hazardous environment," Flannery shrugged. "Accidents happen all the time. As of today we have seven hundred and forty-two days without a reportable accident at this plant. We keep up with all the safety directives and OSHA guidelines but things happen. I'd say you were both pretty lucky."

"Somebody was above us on the catwalk, ass-hat. The box was pushed over," Lisa explained. Her tone was not lost on the room.

"I can't believe that. Why would one of my guys want to hurt you?"

Lisa looked like she was going to choke him. "Are you for-real? Your 'guys'? We're investigating a plane crash which your 'guys' produced, you misogynist. If we find that there was a manufacturing flaw, guys and girls from this facility alone could possibly be out of work. There's your motive in spades."

Flannery dismissed Lisa and spoke to Deni.

"Accidents happen. You can't get your panties in a twist over it."

Deni held Lisa back as she took a large step toward the man she'd just met but hated with all of her being. It was a role reversal that would be clear to them at a later moment.

"Look, guy. If it was an accident, why didn't the prick that dropped it stick around? They hid in the shadows during a shift change and decided to chase us outta the building." Deni opened his sport jacket to reveal his .45 caliber Taurus. "I got a few rounds off, next time I won't miss. The next time they come at us, they're gonna leave here in a box. Clear?"

"There's no need for threats," Art intervened. "I brought Bob in to tell you, on behalf of the union, that there was no intention to cause either of you any harm."

174

"And I'm sayin' there better not be a next time."

"You'd *betta* watch your tone," Flannery mocked.

Deni took a step toward the rep. Art moved between them.

"Truce. Call a truce. Please."

"I don't take shit from anybody," Flannery said. "Especially from a couple of rent-a-cops. I told you it wasn't my guys, because it wasn't my guys. I don't know where you get off making false accusations."

"Is that what you're goin' with? The party line?"

Flannery looked to the Lansing Vice President. "Why are they even here? This entire thing is ridiculous."

"4273 originated in Boston. It was the survivor of a Boston area family that sought out a litigator who then contacted every surviving family member of every passenger on board to bring about this lawsuit. If it goes that far, the trial will take place in Boston. These two investigators work for the best law firm in Boston, the firm that will be influencing how far the case proceeds. They need to be here or we all lose. And Bob, you need to have your constituents be okay with that."

"My guys made a good plane, Art. A great plane. And you know it."

"I do know it. Everyone at Lansing knows it. They're unbiased and just need to do their due diligence to prove it," Art said, pointing at the investigators. "Bob? They need to be allowed to prove it."

The local UAW rep remained reticent for a time. No one spoke.

Finally, he looked at the investigators instead of his shoes.

"Don't fuck this up."

Wednesday
10:30 A.M. October 7, 2015

AFTER THE MEETING-AFTER-THE-MEETING, DENI AND SHEED made way to the remnants of 4273. They wanted a third look at the plane, this time at the exterior. Between Buildings 10 and 80, Sheed's phone let her know that she'd received a new voicemail.

Someone had called while she was inside the Admin Building, which had gone straight to voicemail. The building's jamming circuits had done their job.

The call had come from Macy Dunn.

She wanted to let Lisa know that she was still conducting her investigation into PA, and that she hadn't forgotten about her. Give her a call as soon as she had the chance.

"I'm never going to be able to get rid of this woman."

"What?"

"Nothing."

"Who was that?"

"Nobody, Deni. Just drop it, okay? Let's just go look at the plane."

"Touchy."

"You look like shit, by the way. Are you going to make it through today?"

"Just getting my legs back under me. I thought you were gonna drop Bob."

"I wanted to."

"I know. I woulda let you, but we need to keep the peace."

"Are you sure you're feeling all right? Are you still drunk?"

"I'm fine, She. I'll scrap it out if I gotta, but ten thousand against two is a bit much. I don't got the bullets."

"Fair enough. What do you think we're going to find in there?"

They had just arrived outside of Building 80. The building which held the plane that claimed the lives of nearly two hundred people. The building that nearly claimed their lives the night before.

"Somethin'? Nothin'? I don't know."

"You're a very enlightened individual, Warren Dennihan."

"Let's just hope this Irish luck keeps rollin'."

Inside Building 80, first shift was scattered about the wreckage, continuing with their forensic work in determining the cause of not only the mechanical carnage before them, but the human toll as well.

The usual ritual of swiping their badges and issuance of hardhats and vests occurred before being allowed to pass beyond building security. Once beyond, they could feel the weight of the stares upon them.

Was it that the workers couldn't fathom that the investigators would have the balls to return?

Or was it something else?

Neither Deni nor Sheed could read the minds of those that watched them as they made way toward the broken L530. They only felt the eyes of the unknown number of people who didn't want them there. Eyes that seemed to come from every direction.

When they eventually reached the plane, after cautiously walking toward it from the main entrance, the scaffolding awaited them. This time they chose to go up the starboard side, the right side of the aircraft. The side that had the fuselage damage near the wing.

Near the top of the stairs, which were likened to fire escapes outside of large city apartment buildings, they reached the landing which garnered them access to the wing. There were three workers walking along it, which was not fastened to the fuselage but rather held in place with rods that hung from the ceiling of the hangar. The wing was steady, and did not move as Deni and Sheed ventured out onto it.

"Watch your step. We wouldn't want you to have another accident," one of the workers said. A mid-thirties male with a handlebar mustache.

Deni was about to say something that would have escalated the situation, but Lisa spoke first.

"Thanks for the heads-up. We've looked at the inside a few times. We noticed the puncture holes. Do we know what all that is from?"

"Consistent with engine blade shrapnel. We don't make those, GE does. Why don't you go harass them?"

"We're not here to harass anyone. We just want to know the truth."

"No. You want to hand Lansing out to dry and put us all out of work."

"Couldn't be further from the truth."

"Why don't I believe you?"

Deni stepped in.

"Listen, you made a good plane. I get it. But it did go down. And everyone here keeps sayin' 'it wasn't the slats'. 'It wasn't the slats'. 'It wasn't the slats.' But the porpoising and everything we've seen says that there was a slats problem."

"Slats don't cause a plane to crash. I don't know where you got your degree in avionics, or aerospace engineering, or any other discipline that would qualify you to come to that ridiculous conclusion. But let's just say that the slats did deploy, and the configuration couldn't be corrected, the pilots still would have landed the plane. It would have been a rough ride, to be sure, but they would have landed the plane."

"Okay, guy. Humor me. Say the slats did flip open or whatever. Bumpy ride. What else went wrong. You said the engines did that?" Deni pointed at the punctured skin on the fuselage below the windows.

The worker moved toward them. The name on his badge said Doug Sweeney.

"It's consistent. We don't have enough of the inside starboard engine to verify."

"But maybe?"

"If the engine exploded. I've read about it happening, but it rarely does. Birds sometimes go through them and chews up the blades, but you never really see an engine come unglued to the point where it throws blades."

"Then why would you say it's possible?" Lisa asked.

178

"Because with aircraft, *anything* is possible. It's a machine. Machines fail. But there are so many redundant systems ….. It's the best guess. But it's just a guess."

"So, for the sake of argument, the slats had a problem and then there was a separate problem with the engine." Deni stamped his foot on the wing over where what was left of the engine hung.

"Okay….. But it's not the only one. Redundancy."

"But if it threw blades into the cabin?"

"At thirty-one thousand feet that would be a problem, yes," the worker said. "But these are GEs. They test these things to hell and back. Throw dead chickens through them. Ice. They set detonators on one of the 24 fan blades to see if it throws them. They don't."

"But if it did. Add that to an already tough flight ….."

"If the engine failed, that's not on us. We put whatever engine the airline wants on their plane. PA wants GE, which is damn good engine. Lufthansa and Quantus want Rolls Royce. Some want Pratt and Whitney. If GE did this, go after them. But you'll have a hard time proving it with what's left of the engine. I'll take you down there to look if you'd like."

Once down a flight of stairs and on the under side of the wing, the threesome looked up at what was left of the GE9X which was held where it was supposed to be with a Toyota forklift. Where it was when the plane had originally left the factory.

"So this is the most state-of-the-art commercial engine ever produced," Doug said.

"What's so great about it? How does it work?"

"I can give you general information, but like I said, we don't make them. We just install them."

"We get it," Lisa said.

"So this isn't like a car engine. A combustion engine. This is a turbofan. It turns fuel into thrust. Action and reaction. Newton's third law of motion. No?"

"Refresh my physics," Lisa said.

"I don't even think I took physics," Deni added.

"Oh brother. Okay. So the force, or action, of the exhaust gases pushing backward, produces an equal and opposite force, or reaction, called thrust that propels the aircraft forward. The fan blades in the front sucks in air—some of which is blown into the compressor, some flows around the combustion chamber to cool it —and blows it out the back to give thrust. Good so far?"

Nods.

"All commercial aviation engines have to be made to the standard set by the FAA, or the European consortium for overseas carriers. Anyway, planes fly when it's raining and cold and in a whole variety of situations over the course of the millions of miles of life they will have to endure. Literally. GE puts their engines through rigorous testing like firehoses being shot into the engines while running at full speed. Ice chips and dead birds, like I said. All during the design process before they manufacture them to be put onto a plane. Any plane."

"But like you said. It's a machine. Machines fail."

"True. But the GE9X is a serious technological advancement. Titanium alloy fan blades that each cost as much as a luxury car. There are twenty-four of them in each engine."

"Titanium?" Deni asked, "So it's like a really strong surgical blade?"

"When that thing is spinning at thirty thousand-plus revolutions per minute, it will cut through anything like it was never there, yes. But again, they test for that. It's called a blade-off test."

"Explain," Lisa said.

"The detonator thing. Are you guys listening to me? During testing, they set up a perfectly good engine with a small explosive device at the base of one of the twenty-four fan blades in the front of the engine. The part that sucks in the air to be combusted. They get that sucker up to full speed and set off the charge. The test is to ensure that the housing around the engine contains the blade so it doesn't tear into the plane. If it did, anything in the path of that thrown blade wouldn't stand a chance. Anything."

"Like the fuselage."

"Exactly."

"So a thrown blade could have easily made those cuts we saw up on the fuselage. And could explain why there isn't much left of this engine."

"Yes. Well ..... It's consistent. But it would have gone through the wing first before it got there. And again, there's just not enough here to support that determination with any degree of certainty. Since you're the expert, what do you see?"

"I don't really know what I'd be lookin' for. But you said before—"

"—Consistent. Yes. Look at the buckling here on the outer engine casing, as well as the shearing. Add to that this carbon blasting ..... The engine may have exploded. It very likely exploded. But again, PA pilots could have landed the plane down an engine."

"But it's gotta be gettin' tougher there, kid. Porpoising and down an engine? I mean fuck me."

"Tough, but not impossible. This is all hypothetical. Evidence suggests, maybe. But we need to keep measuring and testing. GE wants a look at their engines as you can imagine and will have the opportunity to do so. In the meantime, we keep running diagnostics and there just aren't any readings. I'm telling you both—and I'll put my hand on a bible if you need me to— nothing is wrong with the planes we produce. Slats didn't cause 4273. A blown engine didn't either."

"Diagnostics?" Lisa asked. "Readings?"

"QAR."

"Let's pretend I don't know what that is," Deni said.

"Quick Access Recorder. You guys don't know anything, do you?"

"This is Missouri. Show me," Deni said.

Sweeney rolled his eyes and walked them under the nose, where the wheel was located. There was an open compartment just behind the nose wheel where chords and connectors were run up into the plane.

"This is called the forward accessory compartment. It's a quick access area for the maintenance crews to download data between flights." He pointed to an electrical rack that he said was next to something called the hydraulic activator buses. "The QAR

181

records five hours of flight data and then records over itself if there are no 'fail' readings. The ground crew plugs in and gets a quick read if something needs to be looked at or replaced."

"It's a black box," Lisa said as she looked up at it. "Only it's hazard orange with a gray strip." It was a small, seven inch square box that plugged into the electrical rack.

"It's the only other one recovered. The CVR and this. There's no other FDR or DFDR," Sweeney said.

Deni shook his head, his neck was getting red. "Why is this the first we're hearing about this?"

"I don't know. Maybe because it's produced literally nothing of value. It's a paperweight so far. Useless. You'd have to ask someone else why you didn't know we have it. I just work here."

Lisa asked, "What would the QAR tell you if it were in perfect shape?"

"All the major stuff. Altitude, airspeed, fuel, controls—meaning your beloved slats or a threatening to stall warning.....It'd be a major help in other words."

"You think you're going to get it to work?"

"We'll keep trying," Sweeney said with a sigh. "But I doubt it."

Deni and Lisa seemed to think about this latest development for a beat. Then Deni went back to the thrown blade angle.

"A blade-off though? You said a loose blade tearing through the fuselage at thirty-one thousand feet would have done it. We heard the CVR. The cabin lost pressure."

"If that's what happened? Yes."

"So what direction would the blade travel if it came loose?"

"Are you kidding? You're asking which direction a spinning fan blade with the power of a runaway locomotive would take, *if* the housing that was designed to contain it failed?"

"Yeah."

"I have no idea. Ask an engineer from GE."

"What's above this on the wing?"

"Leading edge—"

"—Let me guess," Deni said. "Slats."

"I keep saying the same thing. Slats didn't cause this."

"Everybody keeps saying it. But they did deploy during mid-flight. And they shouldn't have. That's a fact," Deni said, giving Lisa a wink.

Doug didn't hide his frustration. "Come with me."

Sweeney lead them back up onto the wing. He knelt down on the forward area of the wing where several slat doors were located. Some slats were in place, some were missing. The slats that were missing exposed the innards of the wing structure.

There was a series of drive tracks exposed inside—little rails, spaced three feet apart—what the slats would slide out on if they were in place—driven by hydraulic pistons. At the forward edge of the rail was a rocker pin, which allowed the slats to tilt downward. At the back of the compartment were the folded pistons that moved the slats along the tracks. On the missing slats, the pistons were merely metal arms poking out of the wing. It looked complicated to the untrained eye.

"This solenoid sends the signal to the inboard and outboard slat drive mechanisms. Here and here."

He pointed at two disks with hinged arms coming off from them.

"This turns and moves these cylinders this way or that way depending on how the pilot—or autopilot—wants the slats to be positioned. Lift or drag. Binary. On or off. Not complicated."

"But they were on when they shoulda been off," Deni said.

"Even if I agree, which I don't, it just makes for a bumpy—"

"—Ride. I know, I know."

Sheed couldn't help but notice that Doug was distracted as he was reaching into the wing.

"What?"

"Nothing."

"Something. I don't know you, but I know when people lose focus and you just did. What's wrong?"

He motioned for both the investigators to join him on their knees, or at least down at his level. Until that moment, they had been standing over him.

When they were both in a position to see to what he was referring to, he pointed to a tiny metal flange at the back of one of the protruding arms.

"I didn't notice that until now," he said. It was a part about the size of the finger he was using to point it out. Very small in comparison to the size of the plane, or the slat that this part purported to be a part of.

"What are we looking at?"

He moved the part back and forth with his hand.

"It's spring loaded, this flange here. That solenoid that I just showed you actuates this. When the slats retract, this spring loaded pin snaps over this to hold it in place."

The two investigators looked lost.

"It's bent. These are made out of a proprietary alloy. Strong as hell. They're not supposed to bend."

"It looks straight to me," Deni said.

"To you, maybe. But anybody that works here could tell you the same thing. And the hinge here. See where it rubbed? Look at these metal shavings. I can't believe I missed this."

"Metal parts that move. Aren't they supposed to rub together? I can barely see what you're talking about," Lisa confessed.

"Yes, but these are designed to stand the test of time."

"So what are you sayin'?" Deni asked.

"There is a couple of millimeters worth of wear here, on a basically brand new plane, on a part that is supposed to be harder than steel. No metal shavings. No bending."

"So this is kind of a big deal?"

The man said nothing. He looked shocked and confused. Deni thought he was being silent to cover up what he already knew. The damn slats that nobody wanted to admit caused the crash, did cause the crash.

"It's the slats. I want you to say it," Deni said louder than he should have. His voice echoed throughout the vast hangar and was garnering attention from the other workers.

"This isn't our part."

"Of course you'd say that."

"No. Really. It was replaced after it left the factory with an inferior part. This is non-PMA. Not legit. Phony."

"C'mon, guy. Just own your shit."

"Slats are low-speed control surfaces. These pins lock the slats in place."

"How many of them are there?"

"Each slat has one," he said.

"What happened to redundancy?"

"If our part was used, you wouldn't need another one. Look." He pointed at the base of the pin. "All parts have a stamp with a logo and part number stamped on them. With the part number, you can trace the thing back to when it was originally manufactured and which plane it went into. Look at these other ones," he said as he moved down the wing and pointed to another slat pin. It had a small *L* logo with number after it. "Now, go back and look at that one." The worn part had a tiny 大號 symbol followed by the same Lansing part number. The difference, once pointed out, was unmistakeable.

"Somebody swapped out the part," Deni said while Lisa took a photo of it with her phone.

"At cruise speed, .80 to .84 mach, the pilots would have no control over the slat. Or any of the other ones if they had this same faulty locking pin. I have to check the rest of the plane."

Deni nodded his head in the affirmative. "Yeah. Check the rest of the plane. I wonder how many other parts are chintzy?"

"Wait," Lisa said. "Porpoising. You said that couldn't crash the plane. Repeatedly. *EVERYONE* here at Lansing has been saying that. You've all been saying that to us over and over again. Was that all bullshit?"

"It's true. If auto continually tried to deploy the slat. Or a bad signal kept deploying, that's one thing. The pilot would be able to keep engaging and land the plane. It would be a helluva bumpy ride, but a landing nevertheless. Having no control over putting the slat back into position because the lock is broken is another thing all together.

Imagine if your car blew a tire at high speed. You could maneuver the car to the side of road. You'd have some control over the vehicle. Now imagine that instead of a blown tire, the lugs come off and the tire suddenly flies off your car at high speed. You have no tire and no control."

"So this phony part is what did it. This phony part is what killed two hundred people. Right?"

"I'm saying that it could be the inciting event. It would have caused the passengers to be tossed around like they were in a snow globe. If they weren't belted in, it would have been bad. And with the blown engine evidence, they could have limped it into an emergency landing. But if starboard engine one did have a blade-off, and the cabin lost pressure? On top of everything else? Those pilots never stood a chance. If that fuse damage is from a thrown blade, it would mean that they had to have worked the piss out of that engine."

"And the phony part is what caused it all," Deni repeated.

"Hypothetically? In this scenario? Yes. I hope we can get the QAR to calibrate to confirm or contradict this hypothesis of yours. But I think that there's little doubt that this counterfeit part started a chain reaction of events that failed this plane. It failed the passengers."

Wednesday
10:30 A.M. October 7, 2015

AS THE TWO BOSTON INVESTIGATORS LEFT THE
conference room in the Admin Building; Art Connor remained after
the morning IRT meeting. He sat heavily in a chair, and punched the
extension on the room's phone keypad. He heard the line ringing
loudly throughout the conference room and was immediately
reminded to turn off the speakerphone. Reid Lansing's voice came
through the receiver speaker against the VP's ear.

"They just met Bob."

"And?"

"And he denied everything, of course. 'Accidents happen'."

"Good. Did they buy it?"

"No. Not even a little bit. Only now they're armed."

"Yes, I know. This is getting out of hand, Arty. Contain it."

"What would you have me do? They don't scare easily and
they clearly don't have a sense of communal well-being.   Ten
thousand people out of work, minimum, didn't exactly flip a switch.
For either of them."

"If I have to handle this myself, then I don't need you do I?"

"I'm trying to take care of it, but I'm running out of options
that would keep you and the company insulated. If either of them
had actually been hurt or killed last night in 80? We would have had
a real mess. That is a bell that you cannot unring, Reid. And that's a
fact."

"So take a different approach."

"I'm all ears. If you have a suggestion, I'm open to hearing
it."

"Did you call Alex Pratt? Have her call off her dogs."

"Is that wise? With what her investigators know, they might
push her toward settling."

"Just lay it out for her. They aren't working out. Call her."

"I have Reid. Since I called you this morning when they came in with guns literally blazing. She's obviously a busy woman. I've left several messages, but she hasn't returned my calls. Maybe we should use our in-house counsel for this thing. A position that I have maintained since this entire fiasco began, if you'll recall."

"Taylor, Higgs & Pratt is our only play in Boston. There are other firms but they're not as well received or connected. At the end of this thing—this investigation if you want to call it that—if Pratt still says she can get us out of this mess unscathed, then I can take that to the bank and save this company."

"And if she can't? Her investigators are on a witch-hunt. We made the best widebody ever produced. We still do. Lansing isn't responsible for 4273."

"You're absolutely right, of course, but you need to make them see things your way. If you can't reason with them ....."

" ..... Or scare them."

"Who said you can't scare them?"

"I did. They haven't been up until now, Reid."

"If you can't get to them directly, deal with them indirectly."

Art sat in the conference room chair in silence, trying to decipher whatever code his CEO was sending him.

"I'm afraid I don't follow."

"What do they care about, Arty? Family? Loved ones? Pets?"

"You're not insinuating—"

"—I'm not insinuating anything. Make them see the light, Arty. Ten thousand people at this facility alone are counting on you. Your own family is counting on you. I'm counting on you."

"I understand, Sir."

"For all of our sake, I hope you do."

Wednesday
1:30 P.M. October 7, 2015

LISA PUT HER OPEN PALM ABOVE HER HEAD TOWARD Deni in an effort to give him a high-five as he hit the push-bar on the exit door of Building 80. He didn't reciprocate.

"C'mon. Up top. We did it. You didn't think we could do it, and I have to admit I had my doubts in the beginning, but we did it."

"What did we do, She?"

"We solved it. We know what happened to Flight 4273. And it only took us three days.   Not bad for two people with no background in aviation or engineering."

Deni stopped walking, turning toward his partner.   They stood on the walkway in front of the building.

"We haven't solved shit. Another piece of the puzzle maybe, but not solved."

"Wow. You just can't take the win can you? What more do you want? We did our job. Counterfeit parts. Just because you're hungover and haven't slept in two days, don't take it out on me."

"Who installed them? Who put the shitty parts in, She? As far as Lansing is concerned, it's a new plane."

"Relatively new, they said. These things have a million-mile shelf-life. So a thousand miles or whatever to them is like new," Lisa said.

"Hours. They measure in hours and cycles," Deni said.

"Wow, you are paying attention."

"Everybody underestimates me. I can be taught."

"Let's not get carried away, Deni."

"Whatevah. So why the replacement parts? That pin is supposed to last a really long time, that guy just said."

"Sweeney."

"Right. Doug Sweeney."

"It's important to keep these names and conversations straight. Alex may want to depose them," Lisa said.

"If she ever returns a fuckin' call."

"I've been emailing her. She's up to speed. Until now. This is big," Lisa said with excitement. She was almost ready to burst.

"So who put in the chintzy part? And how many of 'em? PA? Or did Lansing cut a few corners and put in a bunch of junk parts? We haven't solved a damn thing, She."

Lisa shrugged as she followed her partner, who had restarted his walk toward a food truck to get some lunch.

Deni decided in that short distance that he needed to strategize with Lisa about how to unveil their findings to the IRT. They'd missed the mid-day briefing—not that they'd actually missed much of anything if the morning meeting was the standard—but the final Incident Review Team briefing of the day promised to be a doozy. They would break the news to the team just before they went home for the day. How to ruin their workday and private night was going to need some strategy.

"I admit that there are still a few holes, Deni, but we did our job."

"Not yet. I want to know who killed those people. The decision to put junk parts in that plane is what caused the crash. That was the first decision in a line of events that crashed 4273. I want to know the who and the why."

"As do I. But do you think Lansing did it? Why would they build a 'state-of-the-art' airplane and install aftermarket parts? What did Sweeney call them, non-PMA? Doubtful. So we did our job. We did as Alex asked us. We proved that Lansing is not responsible."

Deni stopped again. "We don't know that, She. We don't know that for sure. And for the record, our job wasn't to prove Lansing's innocence. Our job is to find out what exactly happened. Unbiased, remember? And we haven't done that yet."

"So you're not exonerating Lansing?"

"Not yet."

"So what now? Are you saying you want to investigate Preferred Air? Or are you proposing we take a trip to China or wherever that locking pin came from? My Chinese isn't what it used to be."

"Funny. Laugh a minute. I'd like to know how many junk parts are on that bird. I'd like to figure out how we're going to handle tonight's meeting. I'd like to ..... Hey. Your friend. Macy. We need to talk to her."

"She's not my friend."

"Don't tell her that. She's diggin' into PA for ya, right?"

"Right."

"Forget lunch. Call Macy. Let's go see what she dug up."

Macy Dunn had a full day of meetings scheduled for Wednesday, none of which included the two investigators from Boston. But subsequent to the call from Lisa Sheed, she had her assistant clear that schedule. She'd been hoping that the term "need her" had meant something different, however.

By 2:00 P.M. Macy had dedicated her personal conference room, adjacent to her office, for the story that lovely Lisa would unfold.

Deni let his partner handle the presentation to Macy. There were some points during the storytelling where he wanted to interject, but he didn't. He remained quiet while Lisa described the counterfeit part—presumably from China, though neither of them could read the characters from the language to authenticate that presumption—and how that decision to install aftermarket mechanical parts had devolved into almost two hundred deaths. Lisa was energetic in the telling, her facial expressions and movements were exaggerated.

Macy Dunn, Vice President of the Commercial Aviation Services for Lansing Aerospace, Joplin Division, was mesmerized.

The shoddy part caused the slats to involuntarily deploy, which then made the flight configuration 'dirty' at thirty-one thousand feet in the air. The flow of air above and blow the wing caused the airplane to nose toward the heavens, which the pilots tried to compensate manually when autopilot couldn't correct the problem.

The plane, nor the pilots, could correct the configuration because the locking pin or pins for said slat or slats were faulty, a system which does not have a redundant system. 4273 then began to violently nose toward outer space, then toward the ground with the same force, called porpoising.

The video from the girls iPhone showed at least a half-dozen different violent pitch changes, though Lisa left out the fact that she had the video footage. She skimmed over the topic by saying, "With a half-dozen or more pitch changes …..

The severe porpoising caused significant G-forces, throwing passengers and other contents around the cabin. Those G-forces are what caused the mass-vomiting, a fact already known and reported by the forensic cleaning team when their tests were positive for 'microscopic human bile'.

The G-force climbs heavily taxed the otherwise perfectly crafted jet engines manufactured by General Electric. The starboard engine, like the others, was worked to the point of failure to keep the aircraft in the sky until it could be landed by what, by all accounts suggested, were more than competent pilots. That starboard jet engine exploded, presumably under the strain.

Despite the extensive testing by jet engine manufacturers to ensure that a thrown fan blade would remain inside the jet engine housing, one or more of said fan blades, at more than thirty-thousand revolutions per minute, sliced through the engine housing and sheered through the starboard side wing and fuselage when it exploded. The breach caused more damage to the wing and a loss of air pressure, both of which were too much for the pilots to overcome.

With an uncontrollable pitch situation, the loss of an engine, control of the aircraft, and finally the loss of cabin pressure due to the fan blade, flight 4273 from Boston to Fort Lauderdale was doomed to crash into the Atlantic Ocean."

Lisa's pitch was over.

"I'm not on the IRT, but that sounds plausible. Do you have proof?" Macy was on the edge of her seat.

Lisa showed her the picture of the counterfeit locking pin inside the wing.

"I've got this. And I have the video of the flight."

Macy showed a stunned expression. "You have a what?"

Deni also was unsure about letting that particular cat out of that particular bag.

"I have a video from inside the cabin. Deni sat in the seat on the right side of the plane where the tears in the fuse were. By the wing. The underside of the wing, to me, shows the tears through the carbon fiber, though that's not definitive. So yeah, I'd say that we have enough."

"And you think Lansing is using inferior parts?"

"That part we don't know. They keep saying it's a new plane, it's a cherry plane, it's brand new, over and over again. Why would PA need to replace parts on a new plane? Especially a part that isn't supposed to wear so quickly. Titanium Alloy is it? We saw the metal shavings, even if we couldn't see the bend. Could be that they weren't legit parts from the get-go."

Macy shook her head in the negative.

"I'm not on the floor, but I can assure you that if any of the workers—which are *union* by the way—were installing non-PMA parts as brand new ..... Let's just say that heads would roll. To put it mildly. I highly doubt it."

Lisa shrugged. "Then it's PA."

"That is much more probable."

Deni finally spoke. "You work for Lansing. Lansing is gonna say that anyway. But for the sake of arguement, did you look into them. Preferred?"

"I did. My assistant and I did some digging. Under the radar. As I think I told you, CAS—my division—helps the carriers with customer support. Integrated Service. Flight Service. You name it, we assist the customers with it."

"A few billion in sales has some perks," Deni said.

"Right. Some of the carriers are established and have all of that worked out. They have their own simulators or companies that they use to train and re-cert their pilots. Their own parts suppliers and distributors. We have an entire division dedicated to fabbing and distributing replacement parts, but some carriers don't want to order direct. Some we make, some companies manufacture them for us and put our stamp on them. Some parts we just buy from a supplier. But whether they need help or not, when you spend seventy-plus million per unit, we want to make sure the customer is getting everything they're paying for and more."

"And PA?"

"Was a start-up. We serviced them to the moon and back. Fleet Service. Financial Service. And Material Service."

Deni was on the edge of his seat. Lisa, who'd been pacing back and forth through her presentation, took one.

"Material Service. Like parts?"

"Like parts," Macy said with a smile.

"Please tell me that they're buying parts from China or Taiwan or some shit. Please. Joplin is nice and all but I like Boston. Tell me you know they're buying shit parts so I can go home." He looked at Lisa. "So *WE* can go home."

"What's the hurry to go home?" Macy winked at Lisa, who looked uncomfortable with it.

Neither investigator gave an answer, so Macy continued.

"I had my assistant send me their financials. Since we're working with them meet their need for new planes and still send positive financial results to their stockholders, we have access to them. As a start-up, that is incredibly difficult."

"Yeah, yeah, yeah, Marce. What did you find?"

"Don't get impatient, Deni," Marcy said. "Let's just say that their mission statement of luxury flights for dime budgets is an added hurdle that most start-up airlines can ill-afford. In order to make it work, they have to cut costs in areas that are not seen or felt by the passengers. Make sense?"

"Kinda. You said stuff about scams the last time we talked."

For the first time, Macy looked frustrated.

"If you provide free beverages on every PA flight, you can't use generic brands, especially after you've been serving top quality."

"Yeah you said somethin' about Korbel or somethin'," Deni said.

"No, no. Listen. What does it say to your passengers when you get a free soda, and that soda isn't Coke or Pepsi but a no-name cola? Or instead of a selection of beer, you offer Genny Cream Ale or something and they can take it or leave it? Or provide a free movie and the only choice is *Ernest Goes to Camp* or some nonsense. After they've been getting top quality amenities since the airline's inception? Quite frankly, the passengers would feel the difference. So they negotiate the best pricing for the top-dollar things that matter, and cheapskate the things that don't."

"And what does any of that have to do with—"

"—The price of tea in China?"

Lisa chuckled.

Deni didn't.

"Yeah."

"Preferred Air has an almost microscopic maintenance expense budget, which is to be expected from a start-up that's buying brand new planes. But they're spending a fraction of what other carriers like what Lufthansa and Quantus are spending in maintenance on *their* brand new planes. If they're buying inferior parts, that might explain it.

Also they're enjoying substantial additional revenues that are not from airfares. Since they don't nickel and dime their passengers with added extras, I found that odd. They have the income listed as 'Outsource Income'. What that means is beyond me. It will take some serious bean-counting to tell you what it is without PA knowing. I would have to get Timothy Vahn, Lansing's finance guy, to look into it."

"I don't know.   We've been getting roadblocks in every direction from the big-wigs here. Except you," Deni said. "I'm not too sure he'd help us."

"It would be for me. And if it helps to clear Lansing …. Quite frankly it's not up to you anymore. If your story is to be believed, and I think that it is, we have to protect our company.

Wednesday
5:00 P.M. October 7, 2015

THE FINAL BRIEFING OF THE DAY WAS NOT THE SAME hum-drum meeting to discuss what tests had been run and were inconclusive or what would be discussed at the next meeting as each had been previously. The Wednesday evening meeting for the Incident Review Team was the opposite of anti-climactic.

As the events of PA flight 4273 were unfolding, Deni and Sheed had decided that the kid gloves were going to come off. They would tell the team what they had found. It was not yet clear who had installed the faulty part, or if there were more of them. Was it PA? Or was it Lansing in an effort to make more of a profit? Macy Dunn had suggested that it wasn't Lansing, but of course she would protect her company, wouldn't she?

And the two investigators were sure that the moment they left Macy's office, that she immediately called Art or Reid.   Or both. Even though Lisa had specifically asked her not to.

"Not yet."

They decided to tell the team what they had found. Just the facts. No speculation. Let the chips fall where they may.

And so they did.

First they played the video from the cell phone of Aria Kane.

Lisa gave them a thumb drive that she informed them that they could keep. She had the original under lock and key. No, the video had not been doctored or edited in any way.

Shock and outrage from the existence of such a video, besides having and concealing ownership of such evidence, filled the room. None in the conference room of Building 10 had seen it, and yet they demanded that it be confiscated from the investigators as Lansing property. If it had come from the wreckage, which was in their possession, from a crash that they were investigating. It was potential evidence from a tragedy in which they were charged with

197

determining causation. Other federal agencies including the FAA and NTSB were going to want the video as well.

Rather than argue the issue, which Art Connor ensured was not dead by any stretch of the imagination, Lisa played it for the room. It was first played on one of the IRT member's laptop, then again on the conference room media system which played the rough footage in high fidelity.

At the first viewing, light chuckles came from the IRT. The video depicted a normal family with normal conversation about normal things.

When the oldest of the two young girls, who Lisa advised was Aria Kane, compared the shape of the state of Florida to a penis to her younger sister and was scolded for it, a few members of the team laughed out loud.

By the conclusion of the video, nobody in the conference room who was watching it for the first time had a dry eye. It was tragic. It was real. And somebody really needed to pay for it.

Anybody but Lansing Aerospace that is.

A short recess took place before the second viewing in order for those that needed time to compose themselves, did so.

The second viewing, this time on a large screen and with much louder audio, was for discovering evidence. The novelty and horror on the initial laptop viewing frustrated the brain's ability to compartmentalize. Separate the emotion from fact. Remove the humanity and see the video for what it was intended. To provide real-time information. Data that could be used to confirm or deny what the inconclusive binary computer tests weren't showing.

Upon completion of the second run-through, the majority of the room determined the cause of the crash was engines. Powerplant. It was as if everyone had selective hearing. Nobody paid any attention to the rumble before the plane started to shake.

Deni spoke to the room, pointing out the rumble from the wing.

The room dismissed it. Slats didn't cause 4273 for the millionth time.

It was the engines. GE made an incomparable product, but in this case they had some explaining to do. Lansing was off the hook. Everyone in the room congratulated each other.

Until Lisa dropped the other bomb.
The photo of the defective slat locking pin.

It couldn't be Lansing. It had to be Preferred Air.

Of course it was. Because if Lansing was installing cheaper parts in an effort to make a bigger buck, they would be the ones to do the explaining. It would be Lansing on the hook for nearly two hundred deaths. The faulty pin or pins, caused the slats which caused the engine to malfunction, which led to the thrown blade, which sliced through the cabin like warm butter and sent the plane and all inside it into the Atlantic.

In legal terms, 'If not but for' the locking pin or pins, none of the subsequent events would have occurred.

So the part with the Chinese-looking letters on it had to be someone else's fault. Because if it wasn't, if Lansing was installing them, the aerospace company was out of business.

Wednesday
8:00 P.M. October 7, 2015

THEY DIDN'T STICK AROUND FOR ANY POST-BRIEFING drama, though there was plenty to go around to be sure. Unlike the conclusion of every IRT meeting prior, fingers pointed and voices were raised. Deni and Lisa left for the day, heading back to their hotel tired and famished.

Their work for the day, however, wasn't yet completed.

After some discussion as they waited for their long overdue meal to be prepared, they decided that it was time to make a phone call. Two phone calls, to be exact.

One was the daily call to Alex Pratt. They had made significant progress on the investigation at her behest and they wanted to tell her personally. Deni didn't think she would answer, but Lisa knew otherwise because they had called from her cell. The call was made before they reached the restaurant to order their food.

She congratulated them and told them to keep at it. She wanted to know where the part or parts had come from. Proof not speculation. Fact. She was beginning to sound like Art Connor.

The second phone call was the one that occurred only after much discussion, and without the knowledge of the recipient of the first phone call. They decided to call Sorina Kane.

After they finished eating their food from P.F. Chang's, Lisa punched the numbers into her phone from the contact list from the phone that was found in the wreck and stored in her in-room safe. The name on the contact was *Mom*.

Sheed would be the one doing the talking. Not because it was any sort of woman thing, but because Deni's accent was so thick that he might not be understood. Even those from Boston, outside of Southie moreover, had trouble deciphering what he was saying at times.   And the Kane's were from Marblehead. Marblehead and South Boston might as well be on different planets, though only thirty minutes up the coast.

The female touch was an ancillary benefit.

Lisa left Sorina Kane's picture up on Aria's phone as her phone rang on speaker inside her suite.   It helped to keep the call human.   Lisa wanted to put a face with the voice whom she would be speaking. A woman who had lost her entire family in one day. A loss that was difficult to fathom, let alone have to live with.

And Lisa was about to open the wound.

Deni and Lisa listened as the ringing on the speaker stopped and a female voice echoed in the suite.

"Hello?"

"Hello. Is this Sorina Kane?"

"It is. Who is this?"

"My name is Lisa Sheed.   I'm conducting an investigation into the plane crash which claimed the lives of your husband and two beautiful daughters."

"Do you work for Trey Keating?"

"No. We, I, do not."

"Then I have nothing to say," Sorina said it sounded like she was about to hang up.

"Wait. Please. I have some information for you that you will want to hear.   Some property that belongs to you as well.   Please just give me a moment of your time."

"Is this some sort of scam? Because if it is, I think that you are sick. I have your number, I'll call the police."

"You can do that, Sorina. Can I call you Sorina?"

"I'll let you know after you say whatever it is you have to say."

"Fair enough.   I have your number from the phone of your daughter. Aria."

Silence.

"Do I have your attention?"

Still nothing.

"Okay. You don't have to say anything. Just listen and feel free to ask questions if you have any. This is a difficult phone call for me as well, though I'm not comparing. I can't even imagine."

"No, you can't," Sorina said. A distinct tremble in her voice. "I lost my husband. I loved that man. And my kids. My kids for God sake. On Valentine's day. You should never outlive your kids. It's not meant to be like that. Do you have any children?"

"No. No, I don't. As I said, I can't imagine."

A sniffle before, "Did you say that you have Aria's phone?"

"I did."

"How?"

"We, rather, I," she said as she looked at Deni in the chair across from her, "found it in the plane. Inside the seat cushion. Where she was sitting."

"I don't understand."

"Your daughter had a very good protective case on her iPhone. It made it through a plane crash and survived a few hundred feet below sea level, inside her seat cushion."

"You were in the plane? I'm confused."

"I'm sorry. I should back up. The recovered plane is inside a building, a hangar, at Lansing Aerospace in Joplin, Missouri. I'm here in Joplin. The plane was transported here, bit by bit, as it was found, and reassembled here. It has taken a long time as you can imagine."

"Do you work for Lansing?"

"No. Well, not directly."

"Not directly? Go fuck yourself!"

"Wait, wait, wait. Are you still there? Don't hang up."

"I should have my head examined for talking to you. You should call my lawyer. Trey Keating. And send me back my daughter's phone. You should be ashamed of yourself."

"I'm not the enemy, Sorina."

"Missus Kane."

"I'm not the enemy, Missus Kane."

"So you say."

"I was hired by a Boston law firm to find out what happened. What caused the plane crash with your family in it. If I found that it was negligence on Lansing's part, then I would present that to the law firm that hired us. That was hired by Lansing. And they would be forced to settle with your lawyer out of court."

"So you do work for Lansing."

"I work for the law firm. Period. Our presence in Joplin could save you years in terms of your civil matter. If we find that Lansing was responsible, they'll pay long before a trial would take place. A trial which could be years from now. Think of me as someone who is going to give you closure, sooner rather than years from now.

"I've gained access to Lansing through the firm. That is how I found the phone, and that is how I have the information that I would like to share with you now," Lisa said.

"How do I know that you are being straight with me? How do I know that this isn't some sort of ploy to get me to call off my lawyer?"

"Because I'm not asking you to. If I were in your shoes, which is nearly impossible for me to imagine, I would want the hide of whomever caused the tragedy. Have their head on a spike on the Zakim Bridge. And I would want everyone in the known universe to see it. That may be Lansing Aerospace. But it may not be."

"Then why are you calling?"

"I'm calling to tell you that I believe I know what caused the crash."

There was no reaction.

"Missus Kane?"

"I'm here. I've been waiting to know since it happened and now that you're about to tell me I don't know if I want to know. This is all just so difficult. Is this even real? Are you even reliable?"

"It is very real and you can trust me. Believe me, Lansing would have *my* head on that spike if they knew I was speaking with you. I've signed a confidentiality agreement, specifically stating that I'm not supposed to talk to you or any of the victims. I'm going out on a limb because I feel it's the right thing to do."

"I'm listening."

"Without getting too involved in the engineering and science behind it, which I've had get a quick and dirty education on myself, there was a part inside the wing that failed."

"So it *was* Lansing's fault? They made a death trap!"

"Mmmmm, that's not so clear."

"Of course you'd say that."

"No, no I wouldn't. I've had the same thought for the better part of a week. If you'll let me finish ...... Will you let me finish?"

"Go on."

"The part inside the wing had a foreign manufacturer stamp on it. Not the original one. The original has a big 'L' logo on it. For Lansing obviously. We still have to trace the part, but the parts that are made for and by Lansing have that 'L' logo on them.

"The one that was inside the wing, right next to where your family was seated, didn't. That caused something on the wing called a slat to fail. That made the entire plane shake violently and climb at a severe angle upward, then back downward. That climb and descent happened several times.

"In and of itself, that isn't enough to crash. The pilots can get the plane and the passengers in it on the ground without killing everyone on board. But the stress of the many drastic pitch changes caused the engine, on the same wing that failed, to also fail. It burst actually. The blade from the fan was thrown from the jet engine and cut into both the wing and the cabin. The loss of pressure caused the crash. With all of the events, it was too much for the pilots to overcome."

It was a time before Sorina Kane could speak. Lisa could hear her soft sobs on the other end of the line.

"So it was this part that started it all?"

"Yes. And it may not be the only one. It stands to reason that since there was one bad part, there are probably more."

"Who made it? Who installed it? Why was it in my family's plane?"

"I still don't know. What I've shared with you is all of what I know at this point. It's all of what *anybody* knows. It may have been Lansing in order to decrease the cost of producing the plane. It

204

could have been the carrier to decrease maintenance costs. We're still looking into it, but I'm calling to tell you that I will find out. I promise. For what it's worth, Missus Kane? I will find out."

"Call me Sorina. I'm flying out first thing tomorrow to meet you."

Wednesday
8:00 P.M. October 7, 2015

THE INCIDENT REVIEW TEAM WAS STILL IN THE conference room at Lansing Aerospace while Deni and Lisa were violating their confidentiality agreement.

Art Connor wanted answers, and nobody was going to get any sleep until he received them.

"I want to know everything there is to know about the plane we delivered to PA. And I want it now," He'd said.

He left the room to make a call to Reid Lansing. This was potentially disastrous news. If someone had decided to move toward less expensive and inferior parts, as the Vice President of Quality Assurance, it was his job to know.

But nobody had made that decision.

And nobody on his team had reported a deviation from spec in their audits.

But if the UAW was up to something, if they were conducting a job action, now or when the plane was manufactured, Lansing was responsible.

Reid Lansing sounded like he was in the throws of a massive coronary when he received the call from his VP.

Bob Flannery didn't answer his phone. Which was unusual.

Connor returned to the IRT room within a half-hour. In that time, the team had scrambled to pull up every shred of 'paper' on the 530 that ended up in the Atlantic Ocean. There was no paper, of course. Everything is computerized. Documentation is an outdated word, because there are no documents. Not unless you need to print them.

Up on the curved screen that hung from the ceiling was seemingly a hundred different windows showing QA reports, parts recs, and the like.

Every one of the 2.65 million parts in every Lansing 530 has a record of; when it was manufactured; who manufactured it; shipping and transfer records, who received it in the parts warehouse, how long it was stored, who requisitioned it and for what plane, who installed it, who ran the QA audit, and—finally—the plane number, test flight information and which customer took delivery.

Once the plane is delivered, each and every one of those more than two and a half million parts is on the clock. There is a maintenance schedule as to when those parts should be checked and/or replaced.

On the screen in front of the IRT members, was every piece of information for the one locking pin on the number one starboard slat for the L530 that flew flight number 4273.

"So where are we people?"

Naomi Spelling, one of Art's top people in Quality Assurance took the lead.

"We pulled all the paper for the pin. You can see here that everything was normal. From tooling to installation, it was a legit locking pin."

"So we can prove that 4273 left here a perfectly designed and manufactured 530?"

"That's correct, Sir."

"So what happened to that wing?"

"We pulled up PA's maintenance logs," Naomi continued. She clicked something on her laptop and the 'documents' changed on the conference room screen."

"Slats locking pins are an infrequent change item. Those pins were brand new and wouldn't need changing unless someone had damaged the wing. PA isn't showing any incident."

"But they replaced it anyway? Why? Gimme the AEP," Art said.

The Associated Equipment Package is a maintenance sub-group of related parts. Each of the more than two million parts on the aircraft have a number of other parts which are connected or interact with the part that is damaged or needs to be replaced. In this case, because they were looking at the Slats locking pin, if a maintenance crew noticed it was damaged on an audit—or damaged one themselves—they would then inspect; the slats drive track, the slats lever, actuator, piston, coupling, and the four sensors that send and receive the signals from the solenoid.

The AEP in this case would include all of the parts for not only the number one starboard slat, but each of the others on the starboard wing, and then all of the slats and AEPs for the port-side wing. There is redundancy built into safety and maintenance as well.

Art Connor was asking for any and all documentation about the associated equipment package, because another part in the package may have been damaged or in need of repair, and therefore the pin as well.

"Here it is," Naomi said.

The screen was blank.

"No record of AEP maintenance."

The VP shook his head while pacing around the conference room table.

"That can't be right. You're telling me that PA replaced a slats locking pin that wasn't damaged and didn't need to be replaced? Anyone with eyes could see the bend. The metal wear. Those shavings would have messed with the sensor reading in the cockpit, that's a fact."

Connor continued to pace.

"And why didn't we notice this before? Rank amateurs came in and ran a clinic right before our eyes. How in the hell …..?"

Nobody spoke. Their boss was right. Why fix what isn't broken or in need of preventative maintenance? And how did they miss it?

"Okay. I want every AEP part, from both wings. Take them out and I want them tested. Report to me ASAP. We'll tear apart that entire bird all over again if we have to."

Thursday
7:00 A.M. October 8, 2015

"YOU LOOK A HELL OF A LOT BETTER TODAY THAN you did yesterday morning," Lisa said to Deni as she made the daily entrance into his suite. She still had wet hair which was wetting the shoulders of her sleeveless rayon blouse. It was going to be even hotter in Joplin today than it had been yesterday. It was in terms of weather as well.

It was an hour earlier than the usual meeting time because Lisa had already been called by Sorina Kane. Kane had notified Lisa that she was currently getting on a plane at Logan airport for Joplin.

Deni was wide awake and ready to start his day. The T-shirt du jour was the cover-art for the People in Planes album, *As Far As the Eye Can See.* He'd had three cups of coffee from the room's Keurig and would welcome another.

Lisa told Deni that Sorina had taken the first flight out of Boston Thursday morning. The flight left Logan airport at 5:05 A.M. and would touch down in Joplin at 7:35. Lisa had told her that they would pick her up at Joplin Regional.

Deni'd not slept like a baby Wednesday night, but he hadn't been up all night drinking with absolutely no sleep like he had the previous two either. Deni poured one drink after the phone call to Sorina Kane, but fell asleep long before he finished it.

Deni ignored the comment. Donning his usual attire and firearm now that it was removed from the room safe, he escorted his partner to the rented Ford Fusion and got into the driver seat without discussion. Things were back to some semblance of normal from Sheed's perspective.

"You're obviously feeling a little better," Lisa said as Deni drove out of the Drury parking lot, headed toward the airport and Lansing.

"Everything is relative."

"Another Zen comment from the all-powerful Warren Dennihan," she joked.

"I don't know why you're in such a good mood, She. Today is gonna get ugly."

"Complicated, yes. But ugly? How do you figure?"

"You honestly think you're gonna keep Sorina Kane at arm's length? This thing was bad enough before you got one of the vics to hop on a plane to breath down our necks."

"I didn't invite her, Deni. It's not like she asked. She said she was coming. You agreed that we should call her."

"Call her. Not tell her where we're stayin'. There's gonna be no avoidin' her."

"What did you expect? We just told her that we have a prized possession of her deceased daughter. That we are getting ever closer to figuring out what nobody else has been able to up to this point. Of course she's going to come out here. What would you do?"

"I'm just sayin' she can thank us from afar. That'd be cool with me," Deni said.

"I think your expectations are a little high—HEY! What are you doing?"

Deni swerved the car and took a sharp right turn, stomping on the accelerator. Lisa practically fell into Deni on the driver's side of the Ford.

"Did you know?"

She pushed herself off of Deni. "Jesus Christ. Slow down. Did I know what?"

"I just saw the Rover."

Deni made another right, never letting off the gas. The tires whined as the Fusion barely held onto the road.

"The Land Rover? You think you saw your Rover? News flash, genius. You're not the only person on God's green earth that can afford a Land Rover."

"With Mass plates?"

Deni weaved in and out of traffic as he got closer to the Land Rover. Even from a distance anyone could see that it did have Massachusetts license plates.

There is no mistaking a Massachusetts plate, front and back, with one stuck on the back of a Missouri vehicle. Both are white, however Missouri's fade into a light blue on the bottom portion of the rectangle with navy blue tag numbers. Massachusetts plates have patriot red and blue on a white field.

Not to mention that the number was the same. It was his Land Rover.

Lisa kept quiet while she white-knuckled the pursuit.

"That's what I thought. You and I ain't done with this yet. I'll deal with her, then you."

"Deni, I—"

"—Shut it. You'll have your turn."

Lisa had heard that tone before. She didn't like it then, and she especially didn't like it now because it was directed at her. She was in deep shit and she didn't have the shoes for it.

The Rover came to a stop in an angled parking spot in front of a coffee shop. Deni was within a few seconds behind it, came to a screeching stop behind, blocking both the SUV and traffic, as Ani opened the driver-side door to get out.

The look on her face was almost identical to Lisa's when she saw Deni exit the Fusion.

"What the fuck?" Deni shouted for the world to hear.

"Oh shit."

"You're goddamn right, 'oh shit'. What the fuck are you doin' here?"

"I haven't left yet," Ani said. Hobey was barking inside the Rover, hind quarters wagging rapidly.

"Couldn't find the time?"

"I was worried, Bae."

"Don't fuckin' 'bae' me. I want you outta here. I want you safe. Ten thousand people are paranoid about their jobs, Ani. They ain't gonna just bend over and take it."

"I am safe. You know nothing's going happen. Stop being so melodramatic."

"I don't know that. Lisa was almost killed."

"And you too."

211

"So you been keepin' tabs? If nothin' is gonna happen, then why are you so worried?"

"Deni, I just don't want to be so far away. If something should go wrong ....."

"Somethin' could go wrong in Boston too. You know what you signed up for with me, Ani. Don't get all maternal on me."

"I can't help it."

"You need to go back to Boston. Seriously."

"I will."

"Now, Ani. I got too much to deal with without having to worry about you on top of it."

"I will," she repeated as she pulled him against her, against the SUV.

"I'm serious."

She kissed him.

"You're not getting out of this with sex. I'm mad," Deni said but meant it less with each peck.

"I missed you," Ani whispered.

"It hasn't been that long."

She kissed him again. "It's been too long."

He kissed her back.

"You haven't been taking care of yourself. No sleep. Drinking. More than usual."

"She really has been keepin' you informed," Deni said. He half-tried to pull away from her to give his partner an evil look, but she held him against her.

"It's not her fault, so don't get all YOU on her. I put her in the middle."

"You shouldn't'a done that. She gave me shit for doin' that."

"So take it out on me," she said before a sultry bite on her lip.

He pulled away from Ani, succeeding this time. Deni walked over to the still idling Fusion.

Lisa reluctantly pressed the button to roll down the window.

"Go pick up Sorina Kane at the airport. I'll meet up with ya later."

"Make-up sex?"

212

"Just go. I'll hook up with you later. I won't be long."

Sheed pressed the button to close the passenger window as Deni made her aware that, "We're still gonna talk about this. For someone who doesn't want to get in the middle ....."

But the window was up before he could finish, Lisa climbing into the driver's seat.

Thursday
7:40 A.M. October 8, 2015

THE POLICE OFFICER IN FRONT OF JOPLIN REGIONAL
Airport was loosing his patience. Lisa had double-parked the rented
Ford by the pick-up/drop-off curb in the front of the airport while
waiting for Sorina Kane. Despite the morning delay they'd had by
running into Ani, Lisa still arrived early.

In most cases it's better to be early than late. But not with an
airport pickup. Not unless she wanted to park the car and hoof it
into the airport in search of the widow.

She'd arrived at twenty-eight minutes after, meaning she was
seven minutes early for the touchdown and who knows how early if
Sorina needed to deal with baggage claim.

The cop had wrapped on her driver side window twice
previously and Lisa could see in her rearview mirror that he was
approaching for a third warning. Three strikes and she was out, she
reckoned, meaning that a ticket was forthcoming.

Lisa put the Fusion in drive and was pulling away from the
curb when she spotted her pickup.

Aria Kane's cell phone was littered with photos of friends and
family, making it somewhat easy to spot her mother from afar as she
walked out of the airport. Sorina was quite beautiful in the photos.
Happy.

As Lisa pulled up, it was as though Mrs. Kane had aged a
decade in less than a year. Her emotional pain had taken a physical
toll. Her aura exuded pain and loss.

The car stopped inches from Kane, who didn't hesitate to
open the passenger door and climb in.

"Lisa Sheed?"

"Yes."

Kane climbed in.

"You're not what I expected," Sorina said. "Where is your partner? You mentioned this morning that you had a partner."

Lisa didn't know what to make from the comment and decided to let it go.

"We had a complication this morning. He'll meet us later if you're still up for it."

"I just flew half-way across the country because of you two. I would like to meet him."

"Fair enough. I'll just warn you that he's, hmmm, how would I put this? Not polished. Great heart but rough around the edges."

"I'm not here to make new friends, Lisa—"

"Missus Kane—"

"—Sorina."

"Sorina. I can't imagine how awkward this must be for you."

"Awkward is not how I would put it. My family was taken from me. All at once. The day before Valentine's Day. One day you're making your kids lunches or hearing about what they learned in school. Wondering which boy is going to notice them, or even if they like boys yet, and the next day they're gone. We were supposed to have a nice family vacation in Florida and then I saw the crash on the news. Do you have any idea what it's like to see that? You pray that it's a different plane. That somehow your family missed the flight and are late but safe. Even when you know different."

"I can't imagine," Lisa said as she made the left onto North Main Street. The airport was just behind them, the entrance to Lansing Aerospace was about to come up on the left, Aerospace Avenue.

"You have no idea how hard it is for me to get on a plane now. Every time I do—Are we going to pull in?"

"Excuse me?"

"Aren't we going to Lansing? You just passed it. I want to look these assholes in the eye," Sorina said.

"Uh....No. I thought we would find a spot to talk. The quieter the better."

"I want to go to Lansing."

"I don't think that is in anybody's best interest, for one. And two, I don't think security would let us through the gate. Your attorney is suing them, Sorina. If they actually did install inferior parts in the plane, ten thousand people are going to lose their jobs. Their probably not going to welcome you onto their property with open arms."

"And you work for them."

"As I've told you, we don't work for Lansing. We work for a Boston law firm that is investigating the plane crash."

"Who was hired by Lansing," Sorina said.

"Correct. But if they were responsible for the crash, then the chips will fall where they fall. We're on the side of the angels here."

"Aria and Zoe."

"I'm sorry?"

"Angels. My girls were angels. Aria and Zoe. Just keep those names in mind while you're investigating."

"Believe me, Sorina. I can't get their faces out of my mind. Your husband. Your daughters....."

Lisa pulled the car over by the coffee shop where they'd seen Ani. It was still packed.

"Damn. I was hoping it would have cleared out by now."

"Do you know where the P.F. Chang's is?"

"Yeah. We've been eating there regularly since we got here. It's on the other side of our hotel parking lot. Why? I'm pretty sure it's not open this early."

"I'm a corporate trainer for Chang's. The chef and kitchen crew will be there now. We can get a table to talk."

Lisa nodded in surprise and agreement, continuing on Route 43 toward the Drury and P.F. Chang's.

Inside of fifteen minutes, Lisa and Sorina were sitting in a booth inside the closed-for-business Chinese bistro chain. The opening manager offered them beverages. Lisa had coffee. Sorina sipped a piping hot White Tangerine full-leaf tea.

The hot beverages weren't necessary for keeping them warm. The restaurant's air conditioning hadn't been turned on yet, the heat from the kitchen added to the warm air inside. It would be eighty-five degrees outside in a few hours, nearly eighty at present.

Sheed set the found cell phone from flight 4273 down on the table between them. Aria Kane's phone was back inside the purple bedazzled case.

Sorina saw the case and tears began to fill her eyes.

"Before you take this," Lisa said, "I need to say two things."

Kane nodded and used her beverage napkin to soak up the now overflowing tears.

"First, I downloaded the contents of the phone for evidentiary reasons."

Another nod.

"Second, this conversation never happened. I signed a confidentiality agreement which forbids me to talk about this case with anyone except the firm that hired me and authorized personnel at Lansing. Letter of the law, I'm committing a civil crime. They could sue me for everything I'll ever have for the rest of my life."

"And the spirit of the law?"

"That's the reason I'm talking to you," Lisa said.

"You don't have any kids."

"No I do not. I think I told you that."

"Husband?"

"Spouse."

Sorina again nodded in understanding. "And if you were me? What would you do? I want these bastards to pay."

"If they did it, they will."

"Of course you'd say that. You work for them."

Lisa decided not to fight her anymore about whom she was working for.

"I have a conscience, Sorina. I'm here talking to you, aren't I? We simply don't know if they did anything criminal yet."

"What *DO* you know?"

"You have to remember, it's still early. We're still digging."

"It's been eight months, Lisa."

"But the plane was just recovered from the bottom of the ocean and put back together. They had to clean.....Never mind. The point is that we just started looking into this on Monday."

"And it's Thursday. What do you know? Anything?"

"Off the record?"

"Lisa, you said this entire conversation is off the record."

"I'm just making sure you understand me."

"I do."

"Deni and I found a counterfeit part, like we told you. I told you. A broken counterfeit part."

"Go on," Sorina said.

"So these planes have almost three million parts. No exaggeration. They have to keep records about these things. Maintenance records. Installation records. Every single part on every single plane has a born-on date and an installation date and a maintenance replacement date, if it has been. And all these parts are either fabricated by Lansing or sub-contracted to a company to produce proprietary parts. Even the subbed-out parts have a Lansing stamp on them, because they designed them. They own them. Nobody else can manufacture them. But this part wasn't. I mean it didn't. It was made in China or something."

Sorina was about to take a sip of her tea. She looked at the cup and set it down on the table. Silence filled the dining room save for the occasional clang of a pot in the kitchen.

Lisa continued to fill the void. Irony not lost on her.

"One fake part does not a crash make. These things have redundant parts and systems to make sure that one thing can't bring the entire plane down. So if I was a betting lady, there are more fake parts on that plane than just the one we found."

"So who put in these parts? How did that make the plane crash?"

"That's the million dollar question. We're looking into it for definitive proof," Lisa said," but we think, thanks to your daughter's video, that we know."

"What did that part, the fake one.....What did it do? You said pitch or something over the phone? It was all such a shock that I was only half-listening."

"I understand. It's a slats locking pin. It's complicated. I've been getting a hell of an education, let me tell you."

"Tell me."

"Well, this pin goes inside the wing. There are parts of the wing that move to control air going over and under the wing. Slats are on the leading edge of the wing. When the plane is in flight, the wing has to be smooth, tucked in, not sticking out of it. Certainly not the slat on the front of the wing. This pin broke. It shouldn't break. It's made of titanium so it won't break. This one wasn't made of titanium. This was a cheap knock-off. It bent and was being shaved by other parts that surround it inside the wing. So the slat wasn't locked into place. It held the slat in place for the beginning of the flight, but when they were flying over the coast of South Carolina, it must have given way. At thirty-one thousand feet, this slat was open and created so much drag that it nosed the plane—Do you really want to hear this?"

Sorina was crying again. Rather than answer, she nodded again. The international signal for 'yes, go on'.

"Okay. So, the pilots for PA, Preferred Airlines, were very good. Accomplished by all accounts. They tried to muscle the plane. Control it. Get it to level off, but it kept pitching. Severely. The pilots would angle it down to level it off, but the slat would catch and send the plane up again, violently. They call it porpoising. The G-forces ..... Anyone not buckled inside the cabin..... But even if they were ....."

Lisa had a hard time in the telling. But Sorina wanted her to continue. It was almost sadistic in her mind. Though there was clearly no pleasure in the pain her explanation was causing.

".....Everything I'm telling you can be seen on the video. I'm not sure you'll want to watch it. It's quite disturbing."

"Just go on. Please. I have to know."

"Well, these severe pitch oscillations were working the jet engines very hard. The G-forces they experienced in the climb, and then the descent ..... One of the engines, the one directly below the wing where we found Aria's phone, and corroborated by the flight manifest showing where they were seated, failed. It threw a fan blade. Again, they're designed not to do that, but it did. The fan blade tore through the wing and through the skin of the fuselage. The cabin lost pressure and it was then that there was no recovery."

Another long pause. Lisa had no more to tell. Not that she could think of.

Finally, Sorina broke the silence.

"So this pin. This fake pin. It caused the crash?"

"It was what was called the inciting event. The sounds and the evidence certainly suggests that everything I've told you is what happened. So yes, in legal terms, 'if not but for' the pin, the engine wouldn't have been overworked and fail, which wouldn't have cut through the wing and fuselage, therefore not causing the cabin to lose air pressure, and not killing your family and nearly two hundred others."

Another nod.

"I want to know who installed that part from China," Sorina said.

"We do too."

Thursday
9:00 A.M. October 8, 2015

BOB FLANNERY ANSWERED HIS INSISTENT CELL PHONE. It was Tommy Ginn, one of his main UAW guys.

The United Aerospace Workers are an international group with a constitution and hierarchy. An annual convention is held to, among other items on the agenda, elect officials. A president, three vice presidents, and a treasurer are elected by a board. The board consists of a predetermined number of officers from each region. Within those set regions, there are always power-plays at the local levels to gain prominence and voice for that region. Shady politics and mob-like sub-rackets are rampant to gain money and power. That money and power buys votes and a larger role in the union.

Joplin, Missouri is in Region 5 of the UAW, as are sixteen other states.

Bob Flannery is the UAW as far as local 1514, within Region 5 is concerned.

Tommy Ginn had wet dreams of someday being Bob Flannery.

"What's up Tommy?"

"Did you hear?"

"Probably. About what?"

"The Boston people. They found an imitation pin. From China they say."

"Who's they, Tommy?"

"Everyone. That's the word. They're sayin' that Lansing puts cheap parts in to make more money. It's gonna kill the plant, Bob."

"I just met with them yesterday. Buried the hatchet. You sure they're comin' after our guys?"

"They're gonna bury Lansing. Just heard it this mornin'," Tommy said. "Diner."

"Those two-faced fuckers. I shoulda known. You can't trust anybody from Boston. Slimy micks."

221

"I thought you was Irish."

"Shut the fuck up, Tommy. We gotta fix this. I mean once and for all. You get me?"

"Sure thing, Boss."

"I mean it. The accident didn't even slow'em down."

"It scared 'em. I saw. Me and Nicky was there."

"You raised a pulse, nothin' more."

"They ran like little bitches," Tommy said.

"Well they're still breakin' our balls aren't they? My point is that you're little accident didn't have the desired result. Can we agree on that?" Flannery shook his head in absolute dismay. *Fucking idiot* is what he thought but didn't say.

"The guy's girl is still here. Saw them both outside the diner this mornin'."

"YOU did? With your own eyes? I thought you said she left. After your little note."

"Yeah. I seen 'em myself. He was pissed at her, Bob. Then I thought he was gonna bone her right there in the street."

"Good. That's the play then."

"I followed 'em. Consider it done."

"You do this and you haven't even seen pissed yet. He came at me at the plant. You probably saw him annoyed, this is gonna make him a very pissed-off individual. He's not someone to fuck with. What I mean is, don't make the mistake of underestimating this guy, Tommy."

"We'll be ready."

"Listen to me, Tommy. Hear me. Do NOT underestimate him."

"I got it. We'll be ready."

"Tommy?"

"Yeah. You need to do it yourself. No 'we'. Nobody can know about it. You got me? Rumors fly 'round here. You get someone else and it'll be the top story on the six o'clock. That's no good for Lansing. No good for your union brothers. Certainly ain't gonna be good if it gets back on me."

"Don't worry, Boss. I'm on it."

Thursday
10:15 A.M. October 8, 2015

THE ONLY THING MISSING FROM THE AFTER-SEX GLOW was the cigarette.

Deni laid in the hotel bed, in the room of the Residence Inn, where Ani had been hiding in plain sight. Ani had her head on his smooth, hairless, tattoo-laced chest in her own state of bliss. Her naked body entangled in his.

Nobody spoke.

They enjoyed the moment and each other while Blake Shelton softly sang *My Eyes* with Gwen Sebastian on the clock-radio beside them.

When the song was over and the local station went to commercial, Deni spoke.

"I used to think that I hated country music."

Ani lifted her head off his chest.

"Who are you and what have you done with Deni?"

"I mean, I still don't love it. But it kinda tells some good stories. I don't hate it. I guess that's what I'm sayin'. I'm getting used to it. That's all they play out here."

"Opening yourself up for new things. I'm impressed. Speaking of which, I have something new for you. For us."

"Ssssh. Hold that thought, hun," Deni said. He heard something at or near the hotel room door. Ani hadn't gotten a suite, it was a very small room in fact. The bed was situated so the door couldn't be seen, because it was around the corner and hidden by the bathroom .

Hobey barked.

Deni swung his legs off the bed and moved toward his clothes and gun, which were strewn about the room.

He didn't get there in time.

The spring-loaded door swung into the room, a masked man charged in with a blackjack in hand.

Hobey charged but was hit with the club and sent out of the room into the hallway. The hotel room door closed automatically, keeping the dog away from the fray. He continued to bark and could be heard from inside their room and others.

Ani screamed and covered up her naked body with the bedsheets, pulling herself and the covers with her to the headboard.

Deni didn't have time to cover up.

The intruder swung the blackjack at Deni, who was able to block it and send his right elbow into the face of the enemy.

The masked man was hurt but didn't go down. Nor did he offer Deni enough time get his gun, which was still covered in clothing somewhere in the room. The man came at Deni, again swinging the club.

The attacker again missed. The continued motion was used by Deni to use the weapon against him. By grabbing the wrist of the hand that held the swinging club as it went past, he was able to put enough pressure on the wrist where the blackjack was to be let go or his wrist would be broken, which it was anyway.

As he let go and groaned in pain under the mask, Deni freed the blackjack and struck the assailant in the neck.

The man fell but recovered quickly. He lunged at Deni, attempting to tackle him at his naked waste.

The attempt failed.

He received a left knee to the face for the trouble. The wet mask left blood spatter on Deni's knee.

This time the man didn't get up. He gurgled. Blood poured from his face onto the carpet.

Deni struck the intruder's left knee with the blackjack. An audible crack could be heard above Hobey barking from the hall, followed by a cry of pain.

"Shoulda thought of that before you fucked with me," Deni explained to the writhing masked man.

He put on his jeans before taking the mask off the intruder.

A white guy with a mullet-esque haircut.

Still covering herself, Ani stepped over the intruder to lock herself in the bathroom.

"Call 9-1-1, hun, will-ya?"

"How can you be so calm? He just tried to kill us. Poor Hobey."

Deni went toward the door, opened it, letting Hobey come into the room. The door was let to close itself. He didn't notice the growing number of people that were gathered in the hall.

Hobey growled at the intruder, who tried to inch away from the dog.

"Stay," Deni said to the Boston terrier.

"Tell me who you are and who sent ya or I'll let him eat ya."

Hobey kept growling and barking.

The intruder said nothing.

"Hobey! Quiet! I want to be able to hear what this prick has to say for himself."

The dog was quiet and went to the bathroom door. He smelled the crack beneath it and once satisfied, laid down.

"Now, tell me who you are and who sent ya. You can start talkin' now."

He remained silent.

"Have it your way."

Deni grabbed the man's hair at the neck, gave the damaged knee a tap with his foot and forced the man to roll over. He then put his own knee on the man's spine while pulling his neck toward him with his right hand. The intruder was being forced into a painful yoga bhujangasana, or snake pose.

His wallet was then removed.

"Let's see who you are, fucker."

Deni flipped open the wallet with his left hand, right still on the intruder's throat. With his thumb, he slid his driver's license out of the slot.

"Thomas Ginn. What the fuck did you wanna talk to me about so bad there, Tommy? You've got my undivided attention."

He did nothing but continue to bleed from the face that produced no words.

From a distance, police sirens were heard.

"You don't have much time before they take you away, fuckstick. How much pain I inflict before they get here depends on you. You came in here. With a billy-club you stupid shit. A deadly

225

weapon. I'm within my rights to fuck you up real bad. Maybe even get away with killin' you. For the last time, who sent you?"

Silence.

"Oh-kay. Just remember. You could have avoided this."

Deni took his knee off Tommy's spine and jammed it into his right side. Repeatedly.

Ribs were instantly broken.

As Tommy tried to fight back, Deni moved into a ground side control position. His elbow pushed down on Tommy's neck forcing his bleeding face into the carpet while continuing to send knees into his already injured side, inflicting ever more damage. Internal organs were suffering irreparable devastation.

"Feel like talkin' yet?"

Tommy Ginn said nothing intelligible. He cried and groaned.

Mr. Misunderstood by Eric Church quietly played on the clock-radio which was still on the country channel.

"This is pointless."

Deni got up from the floor, picking up Tommy's wallet at the same time.

A debit card and two credit cards were flung before coming upon a key piece of identification.

A UAW membership card.

The police were coming down the hall outside the hotel room. Deni heard them just before the knock came on the door.

Time was up, but it didn't matter. Deni had acquired the information he sought.

He looked down at Tommy Ginn.

"I'll let Bob know you said hi, ya cock-sucka."

Thursday
10:30 A.M. October 8, 2015

LISA ENTERED MACY DUNN'S OFFICE WITHOUT AN appointment. Again.

She was let in, and all meetings and calls would have to be cancelled or postponed. Again.

It had been a terrible morning for Sheed until then. First the Deni and Ani thing.

She'd been caught in the middle, asked by Ani to keep her presence in Joplin quiet and to keep her informed about the investigation. It took some convincing. She was loyal to Deni and felt it was a betrayal. But Ani was a friend. A new friend, yet a connection that was as if they had been lifelong chums. In her heart of hearts, she knew Ani wouldn't get away with the deception. And Lisa was going to have to deal with repercussions of her role in it later in the day.

After her speech to Deni about not being put between him and his wife-to-be, she was sure that he was going to have a few choice words for her. The anticipation of that conversation was weighing on her.

Then there was the emotional train-wreck that was Sorina Kane. Not that she could blame her. But not an easy thing nevertheless.

Followed by trying to get rid of her. She wanted to be at Lisa's side for the rest of the investigation. She wanted to be part of the investigation. When she finally realized it was impossible, she insisted on being briefed for any and every new discovery.

Great. More briefings.

Next up, she'd gotten hell for missing the usual morning briefing at Lansing. Art Connor wanted to know where she was and where she'd been. Certainly not on the property. He didn't tell her how he knew that, and of course she couldn't and didn't tell him where she'd been or with whom.

She and Deni had dropped a bomb the previous evening, and Lansing was now at DEFCON 1. Deni and Lisa's presence were required, and yet they picked now to be in dereliction of duty, Connor had said. They needed to protect themselves, now more than ever. More than shit had hit the fan.

The IRT split into two sub-factions earlier that morning. The VP had told Lisa nobody had gone home since the evening briefing on Wednesday.

Lisa found out that each faction was designated a specific set of tasks in order to ascertain the origin and reason for the non-PMA part or parts.

One crew was tasked with searching the rest of the plane for more counterfeit parts. None had been found when bringing the wreck up from the bottom of the Atlantic, nor any at reassembly. But now that they knew that the bunk parts existed and knew what to look for—the microscopic 大號 stamp, which was discovered to be traditional Chinese for the 'L' logo—identifying the imposters would be easier. With size of the aircraft and number of parts, it wouldn't be easy mind you. Just easier.

The second and smaller IRT faction was charged with the engine. The Incident Review Team wanted to know if the GE9X jet engine was defective in any way. If there were any aftermarket parts installed in it. It was plausible that the PA maintenance crews had installed phony parts on the engine as well.

If the pilots could have landed the porpoising plane, it stands to reason that any fault with the engine that threw a fan blade into the wing and fuse would earn the blame for the crash. If PA or GE was to blame, Lansing was not.

Both shifts on both groups reported their findings to the IRT at the morning briefing, where Sheed wasn't present.

Connor informed her that two hundred sixteen parts had the foreign stamp on them. So far. There may be more, but that is where the IRT stood at present. With more than two and a half million parts on a complete L530—some present and some still at the bottom of the ocean in the case of 4273—the current percentage of phony parts was low. Yet each presented a greater possibility of failure, a higher probability of problems in flight.

The group responsible for certifying the GE9X a lemon, came up empty, but they didn't have much to work with. The elevated engine on the forklift was lowered and combed over, what little of it was left to comb. A thrown blade was not supposed to happen, they were designed specifically not to allow a damaged blade outside the engine housing, but it happens. General Electric manufactures the best commercial jet engine and the 9X that blew up had been worked beyond design parameters. To put it in perspective, it was the only damaged engine on the plane. Unfortunately, they would never know if any counterfeit parts were installed in the jet engine.

Art then told her that the QAR data had given them some preliminary data. Snapshots. There were exceedances. The 'black box' had finally delivered some preliminary data overnight which showed climbs of twenty-one degrees. Meaning on the upward climbs because of the faulty slats locking pin, the aircraft would pitch upward at an angle of twenty-one degrees. Nothing on the plane was designed for that kind of G-force. Not the airframe. Not the engines.

A normal takeoff was approximately five degrees, Art explained. Ten degrees would make the passengers notice, probably panic. At twenty-one degrees the passengers would feel like the aircraft was vertical. It wasn't a wonder the engine failed, it was a wonder that all of them didn't.

All during the telling, Lisa could feel Art's anger from the other end of the phone conversation. There was no joy in the new information he was sharing. She was not where she was supposed to be, and she had not supplied a good reason for it.

She drove through the south gate and parked the car. No electric vehicle was waiting for her. It was going to be a long, hot walk over to Building 10, where she would have to meet with Macy Dunn.

And through it all, she'd still not heard from Deni.

"Come on in and have a seat, sweetie. You look like you've had a tough day," Macy said.

"And it's only ten-thirty," Lisa responded. She sat down hard in the offered chair.

"Wanna talk about it?"

"Not really."

"Quite frankly, I'm surprised to see you this early. Pleasantly surprised, but still."

"I was hoping that you had something for me," Lisa said with an exaggerated sigh. "Ive been reaching out to Stephanie Clark from PA. She's not answering her phone or emails.

"I wouldn't expect her to."

"I don't follow."

"I'll get into all that in a minute. Would you like something? Coffee?"

"Macy, do you have something for me or not?"

"Since yesterday? You didn't give me much time."

"I know. I'm kind of taking a shot in the dark."

"You're lucky that I'm well-liked and well-connected 'round here."

Lisa sat upright.

"You do have something, don't you?"

Macy smiled in lieu of a response.

"Please don't leave me hanging, Macy. I've had a real fucked-up day so far, pardon the language."

"Lot's of folks here worked through the night, because of you and your partner. Art Connor's team. Timothy Vahn's team, once I put'em up to it. Five alarm fire and all that. 'The company is depending on you.' Those ego-maniacs eat that stuff up. Anyway, I'll have to rent them a bus and a box for a Rams game as appreciation, if we still have a team. But it will be worth it."

"And?"

"Take it easy, I'll get there. You're sexy when you're eager."

Lisa didn't respond.

Macy sat on her desk in front of Lisa, knees almost touching.

"I also had someone that I know and trust in the QA Department get me all the logs for that plane. Under Art Connor's nose. He passworded everything. Like I said DEFCON 1. If he were to find out, he might have a few words with me."

"And?"

"Patience is a virtue, honey. There is pleasure in anticipation."

Lisa cracked her neck. "I'm really not in the mood for this."

"Preferred Air has been very, very, very bad," Macy blurted. "Thus no calls from Stephanie."

Sheed was ready to explode. She wanted the details and she wanted them immediately.

"Vahn is going to bring what his team found directly to Reid, who will no-doubt have a press-release by mid-day. They may even be meeting as we speak," Macy said as she looked at her oversized, man's watch.

"Add to that the parts logs that Connor's team has been workin' on....."

Lisa could see that the VP in front of her was relishing every moment of the storytelling.

This would be the last time they would meet, most likely. Hopefully, from Lisa's perspective.

But there was still hope from Macy's. Macy was hoping she could spark some sort of interest in the Boston investigator socially. Sexually. Macy was going to milk the time as long as she could.

Sheed read the situation for what it was, and decided to let it play out, though she was reeling inside.

"PA have some clever bean-counters, but not clever enough," Macy finally continued. "They formed a shell company in order to launder money. Remember that odd revenue account I was telling you about yesterday? If you can't make money on passenger sales, you find a new way to bring in money. Sales hide sins. As long as the company is making money, nobody turns over any rocks. The board is happy, the stockholders are happy, and the passengers are happy because they get the world for a shoe-string."

"Macy?"

"Yes, doll?"

"Please?"

"They're selling the genuine parts. Lansing parts."

Lisa's eyes were as big as half-dollars. She knew Macy had said something, but didn't understand what.

"They have a plant in China that reproduces the parts they need at a fraction of the cost because they're junk. All the brand new planes, once PA takes delivery, are stripped of all mandated maintenance parts and their associated equipment packages."

"Stop right there. Explain that."

"Wear and tear parts. We make planes that have a very long shelf-life. Fifty-thousand hours and twenty-thousand cycles. Parts need to be replaced over time. That's inevitable. Service records are kept. You know that, correct?"

"Yes. PA has shown impeccable service records, that was why they were cleared by the FAA and NTSB for the 4273 crash."

"Correct. Only they replaced the mandated parts before they needed to be replaced. They stripped the new planes with parts that were going to need to be replaced over time with their el-cheapo parts, then sold the legit parts taken out of the brand new planes they purchased to other companies that need them. Every part can be traced back to the day it was manufactured. They know that but did it anyway because who would be the wiser? The FAA and NTSB don't have the time to inspect every single plane in the sky. They audit records. If the records, which the carriers and airplane manufacturers house, look legit....."

Lisa's mind was racing.

Macy continued. "Not only did they strip our perfect planes, but they undercut the part sales with the parts they took out. We either manufacture the parts ourselves, or have contracts worth billions of dollars with manufacturers who put our stamp on them. Genuine parts. They're undercutting the parts sales by selling them on the black market. They've made millions."

"I don't get it. Why would they do that?"

"They're business model didn't work. They hung their hat on one assumption that didn't hold. Volume. If you can't make a decent buck on each passenger sale, because you're selling a luxury seat for peanuts, you have to sell that many more seats in order to generate the same income. That's why they bought the L530. More seats. More luxury seating compared to any other widebody. Only the planes weren't full."

"So they decided to make money another way," Lisa said.

"Exactly."

"Why didn't they just sell the cheap China parts? The parts that they're replacing the Lansing parts with."

"Easy question, with a simple answer. Quite frankly, because they can't."

Lisa waited for a more detailed answer to the supposed simple answer.

Macy sensed the need and provided the details.

"We hold the rights to our own parts. You need to replace the specific parts that are mandated by us, with our parts. As I said, every part has meticulous records kept on them. If one were to look long and deep enough, you could trace every part on every plane back to the day it was manufactured. Installed. Replaced."

"Of course. That's right. I know this. It's been explained to me about hundred different ways," Lisa said.

"And PA would have been caught, even if there was a large market for el-cheapo parts. So they started a shell company in order to undercut pricing on actual parts that were being stripped to other carriers. These things have to be replaced. The FAA keeps records. We send out replacement mandates. So these carriers that need the genuine parts are trying to save a buck too, and they were getting legit parts.

"So they purchased locking pins and things from this Chinese shell company instead of us or the approved manufacturer —whichever the case may be. But again, they were legitimate parts. If ever investigated, at least they had complied with the parts mandate."

"But why would they risk their own passenger's safety?"

"*That's* a good one. My guess is they didn't think they were risking safety. Parts are parts. Risk versus reward. Even if they had to replace the part—say a slats locking pin like in this case—three times, it was still cheaper than buying the real part once."

"If 4273 hadn't gone down, they would have gotten away with this scam," Lisa said.

"For a time. There would have been another 4273 eventually. Our parts are more expensive because they work. You get what you pay for. When it comes to the people who are sitting in a contraption that flies thirty-one thousand feet in the air, you cannot skimp."

"Scary."

"There is going to be an industry-wide investigation after this. Because of you," Macy said. She left her desk, placed her hands on the arms of Lisa's chair, and kissed her. The kiss was soft yet firm.

Lisa resisted at first, then returned the kiss.

Her hand left the arm of the chair to run her fingers through Lisa's hair.

Hearts pounded and blood pulsed through them as the intensity grew.

Until Lisa remembered Reg. *How could she forget*?

She tensed but Macy didn't withdraw.

When Sheed's phone rang, she pushed Macy off of her and left her chair as if there was an eject button.

It was Deni. Finally.

"Deni. Perfect timing."

"Where are you?"

"Lansing, where else?"

"Get the fuck outta there."

"What are you talking about?"

"I thought I was bein' pretty clear. Leave. Get the fuck outta there."

"What happened?"

"They came at us. In Ani's room. Not even ours. They went after her, She. They knew she was here the whole time. They been scammin' us."

Lisa looked at Macy who went back to sitting on her desk. She was not embarrassed about what had happened. In fact, she was smiling.

"Uh-huh. I understand. So you'll be here in a few minutes?"

"You can't talk? Who's there? Who are you with?'

"Okay then. I'll see you in a little bit," Lisa said.

"You got your Sig? You're armed right?"

"Uh-huh. Yes. Okay then, I'll meet you there."

She hung up.

Think, Lisa. Think.

Macy was still sitting on the desk.

"I'm not going to apologize for that. I'm attracted to you, and I can feel that you're attracted to me," Macy said.

"Okay, whatever. I'm married. You trapped me in the chair. Let's get back to the topic at hand."

Lisa unfastened the strap on her holster, but didn't remove the Sig. Her pistol remained on her waste but ready if needed.

"Are you going to shoot me?"

"How do I know that Lansing isn't putting in the shitty parts? I'm supposed to take you at your word? Can you prove this shell company theory?"

"What's going on, sweetie? Who just called you? We were having a moment. Admit it." Macy stood but didn't walk closer to Lisa.

"Just stay right there. How do I know? How do I know that you're not scamming me?"

"I'm not scamming anybody. And quite frankly, you came to me. Remember? Alone. You finally came to me without your partner. Alone."

"Macy! Focus!"

"I can prove everything I told you, if I need to. But you and I both know that I don't."

"I'm here to try and help you. Help Lansing. And you're coming after us."

"Who's coming after you? The kiss? I didn't give you anything you didn't want," Macy said. "I'm your friend, remember?"

"I just want to know what happened to 4273, friend."

"I just told you. You saw the locking pin for yourself. And there are two hundred more phony parts on the wreck just like it."

"Which Lansing could have installed," Lisa said.

"Go see for yourself. If you're not convinced, if you're not convinced that PA caused this nightmare, then go check out final assembly. Better yet, you check out the planes coming out of the paint shed. Those green tails are ready to deliver once they get the custom paint. Go see for yourself."

"I will."

Thursday
11:45 A.M. October 8, 2015

TOMMY GINN WASN'T ANSWERING HIS CELL PHONE. Bob Flannery had called no less than 10 times and his henchman wasn't picking up or returning the messages. This was concerning to him to say the least.

This Boston investigator, this Dennihan character, was a problem. He'd told Tommy not to underestimate the scrapper, but clearly he had. Something had gone wrong. Tommy never avoided his calls. And yet he was now.

Flannery then started to make some unofficial inquiries.

He called another one of his reports, Nick Rawls.

Nick hadn't heard from Tommy either but would call Bob when and if he heard from him.

Bob's next call was to a Jasper County Deputy Sheriff. The deputy was a mole. A fixer. If one of Bob's UAW constituents got into a bar fight, a DUI, a domestic dispute, or some other legal scrape, Deputy Dave Merrick would fix it.

Joplin has a police department. The Jasper County Jail, however, is where alleged criminals are held until bail or trial. The Sheriff's Department rules the roost over at the JCJ. Joplin PD could arrest whomever and however many they wanted, but the Sheriff's Department would either hold or release them. You can't make the arrest report disappear, but Joplin PD didn't want to spin their wheels either. What is the point of making arrests if the cases never go to the hoop?

So the sheriff's department was kept in the loop on arrests. Deputy Dave Merrick was in the know, and in a position to help. And he was well-paid to help Bob Flannery.

By quarter 'til noon, Bob had the complete run-down on Tommy Ginn. He'd been arrested and was at Mercy Hospital, handcuffed to his hospital bed. Two detectives were waiting outside his room until doctors gave them the go-ahead to interview him.

Merrick couldn't make this one go away. There were too many witnesses. An ambulance. Bob was told to, "....Forget him. Attempted murder tends to have penalties kind of on the stiff side. Tommy's gone."

Fuck.

Flannery called Nick back.

Rawls answered on the first ring.

"He's cuffed and stuffed, Bob."

"Yeah, I just heard."

"Word is he went after the Boston guy."

"I know. I told him to. They're gonna hang Lansing out to dry. You'll all be outta work, Nicky."

"Holy shit. So what do we do?"

"Do it right this time."

"That's a lot of heat, Bob. What if Tommy blabs? They'll come right at us."

"Tommy knows what to do. He'll keep shut or he knows what'll happen."

"Still. One attempt is one thing. When they end up dead it'll come back on us."

"I need to count on you, Nicky. Our brothers need you. Your union brothers. We'll get you the best attorney money can buy."

"Awwwww, man, Bob. What are ya doin' to me?"

"I'm making you a saint. UAW royalty. Save ten thousand jobs. Don't think about it, just do it."

"Fuck-fuck-fuck."

"Nicky?"

Rawls was breathing heavily on the other end of the phone.

"Nicky?"

"Yeah."

"Make it happen."

"Yeah."

Bob disconnected the call at the same moment he was getting another call in.

It was Art Connor. Flannery let it go to voicemail.

Thursday
12:15 P.M. October 8, 2015

DENI RACED TOWARD LANSING AEROSPACE IN HIS Land Rover.

It had been a fucked up day, and if he didn't get to Lisa before the union did, it was going to get a damn-sight worse.

Joplin PD had done their thing with him. The detectives took his and Ani's statements, as well as those from witnesses in the hallway. He then told the responding officers about his partner, Lisa, and the danger she was in.

Apparently they had too much on their plate with the current murder attempt to take on another. Despite Deni's insistence that she was in imminent danger, there was "nothing they could do."

More like willing to do. They had one suspect, one alleged attacker, two alleged victims of said attack. Case closed.

Tommy Ginn was taken by ambulance to the hospital and was considered to be under arrest. If he didn't take a plea, and took the matter to trial, the detectives informed both Deni and Ani that they would eventually need to come back to Joplin to testify.

Since the cops weren't going to take the ongoing threat to his partner seriously, it was up to Deni.

So he packed up his dog and future wife, locked them in his suite back at the Drury in order to keep them safe. "Don't open the door for anyone, including me."

There was no argument. Ani had had enough excitement for one day. For one lifetime.

Sheed wasn't in her suite. Nor was she answering her phone calls. Straight to voicemail.

Deni then called Art Connor. He answered on the second ring.

"Are you behind all of this, Arty?"

"Deni. I was just about to call you. I wanted to thank you for your work. You and your partner. I don't know how you uncovered something that we've been trying to solve for months, but I guess that's why you get the fees that you charge. I had my doubts, I have to admit. I underestimated you both.   And for that I'm embarrassed and sincerely apologize."

"What the fuck are you talkin' about Arty?"

"PA. Preferred Air. Lisa is here. I'm here with Reid Lansing and Timothy Vahn. Media Relations is preparing a press release. Would you like to speak with Reid? I know he'd like to speak with you."

"If you wanna thank me, stop tryin' to kill me," Deni shouted into his cell phone.

"I'm afraid you have me at a loss," Connor admitted.

"The union.   They work at Lansing, you've seen pictures. The fuckin' union."

"I know what the union is, Deni.   UAW.   United Aerospace Workers. What's your point?"

"That's three times they've tried to kill us, that's my point, *Arty*, and *that's* a fact. Did you say Sheed is still there?"

"Uh. Uh, well, yes." Art took his smartphone away from his face, opened an app, and saw that Lisa Sheed was still in Building 10.

"Last I knew she was here in Admin. Building 10. Is she in some kind of danger? I can have security—"

"—It's the union. Every goddamn employee at Lansing is UAW."

"Deni, I think you might be—"

"—I'm on my way."

"Can you explain—" Art was cut off. Deni had hung up on him.

Before leaving his suite, he asked Ani for help. She was good at technology. He was not. He wanted to track Sheed's iPhone. Lansing was a city within a city. Enormous. Finding her would take some time, unless he could narrow the search.

Ani informed him that tracking her phone was easy. There was an app for that. She left out a jab that she would normally have landed about him being an investigator and the fact that he should know how to track someone's phone. This was not the time for their usual ribbing and jokes. Instead, she installed the PREY application onto Deni's iPhone, then typed in Sheed's cell number.

A map came up where a green dot appeared and then disappeared. Cell service at Lansing was jammed inside most of the buildings, especially those with sensitive equipment. But she was there, Building 10. The VP had told him so.

Deni continually called Lisa while driving to the Lansing facility. She didn't answer. It went straight to voicemail every time. Either her cell was off or, more likely, she didn't have a signal. His Land Rover had bluetooth capability, but Deni didn't know how to use it. He drove at lightning speed with one hand on the wheel and one with his cell against his ear, pressing redial every few seconds.

Traffic was heavy but Deni's honking horn either made the cars get out of the way or he drove around them. His foot was on the floor of the SUV as much as possible.

His Rover careened through a left-hand turn onto East 20th Street, barely negotiating the turn without taking out a stopped car at the intersection in front of the Bel-Aire Shopping Center. At one point he was driving through Murphy Boulevard Park because an accident on the boulevard itself was causing congestion.

He stopped for neither pedestrians, nor traffic lights, nor the security gate at Lansing south entrance.

The tires screeched as he stomped on the brake to park his vehicle, flinging open the door and slamming it closed in a fluid motion.

Now he had to find Sheed.

Her phone still wasn't picking up a cell signal. She was last seen in Building 10, if Art was to be believed.

Deni didn't trust anyone, especially Art Connor, but time was of the essence. His new phone application was of no use. The cell signal was jammed.

He had to find her.

Somehow.

Security personnel crowded around him as he hurried away from his haphazard parking job and toward Building 10, the supposed last place she was seen. Two guards wanted Deni to stop moving in order for their questions to be answered, but he didn't stop. The guards insisted. However they weren't armed with anything more than tasers.

Deni had more firepower.

His .45 caliber semi-automatic pistol was at the ready, ten rounds in the magazine, one in the chamber, another clip in his breast pocket if he needed it, as he ran toward the Admin Building.

Art Connor and Reid Lansing were rushing out of the elevator toward Deni in the main lobby as the investigator entered. They'd received a call from security alerting them to a potential active-shooter situation. Another gaggle of security personnel encircled the would-be terrorist at the elevator, but were motioned to stand down by the two Lansing executives, one of which was the CEO.

"Deni. What the hell is going on? You've created a bit of a situation here," Art said.

"Where is She? Lisa. Is she in the building?"

"No. Not as far as I know," Art said. "What's going on? You said something about the union?"

"I don't have time to explain, Arty. I gotta find her."

"We can help, if you'll just tell us what has you riled up. It's the least we can do," Reid Lansing said.

"Talk and walk then." Deni turned around and speed-walked out of the building, deciding which was the next in a virtual city of buildings he would search for Lisa. The two Lansing executives did their best to keep up behind him.

"Do either of you know a Tommy Ginn?"

Neither of them did, shaking their heads in the negative after looking to other for confirmation. Deni was ahead of them and didn't see their motion, but took the silence for what it was. They claimed not to recognize the name.

"He's a card-carryin' member of the local UAW. He works here."

"Deni, every floor in every building in the plant is filled with, as you say, 'ca-hd carryin' U-A-dub memb-ahs'," Art said. "We have ten thousand employees at this facility alone."

"This one tried to kill me and my girl. In a different hotel room than the one I've been at. We were followed, boys."

"Is that a fact?"

"Fuckin'-A-right it's a fact, Arty. Call the police if you don't believe me. I put that prick in the hospital."

Art stopped walking. His CEO stopped with him. Art looked at his phone. "She just scanned into Building 30," he shouted to Deni who was still speed walking.

Once Deni heard Art say, "Building 30," he set out in a full run.

Stunned, Reid looked at his VP. "Call Bob."

"I'm on it."

Deni was already a good distance away. He was nearing Building 30, the final assembly building.

Thursday
12:15 P.M. October 8, 2015

"YOU THERE! CAN YOU STOP WHAT YOU'RE DOING?"

Lisa shouted to one of the workers on the floor in Building 30. Large flatbeds were moving noses, wings, fuselages, and tails into position for final assembly. Each enormous part of the L530 was either strapped down to the flatbeds; rolled on rails into position, or moved on elevated rails into position, where forklifts and elevators would raise or lower them to be fastened to the aircraft.

The worker looked confused but not stunned.

"What's the deal?"

Lisa flicked the Lansing badge clipped to the highlighter yellow safety vest with her thumb and middle finger.

"Art Connor, you know the Quality Assurance guy?"

"Yeah. Course."

"He sent me over here. He wants to make sure that, among others, the slats locking pins are legit. That they're not being swapped out or initially installed with inferior parts. I want to take a look and see the pins. For starters."

"Really? Now?"

"Now. Right now."

"Whatever floats your boat, lady." The man motioned further down the length of the not-quite fully assembled L530. "Down that way. Talk to Chuck. He'll give you a ride up on the wing."

Sheed walked down the port side of the airplane, toward the wing. When she was just aft of the wing, just behind where an engine would be located, she called out to 'Chuck'. He was yet to be seen."

"Yeah?"

A man up on the wing shouted down to her.

"Are you Chuck?"

"Sure am. Who's askin'?"

"Me," Lisa said. "I was told that you would let me have a look at the slat locking pins."

"Sure. But why?"

"Art Connor sent me."

"I'll be right down."

A few minutes later, the man who was on the wing and responded to the name 'Chuck' was on the floor, walking toward Sheed.

"You're that Boston lady, ain'tcha?"

"I am."

"So what's this about locking pins?"

"Like you don't know?"

"You came to me, you want my help or not?"

"This place is a gossip mill. You can't tell me that you haven't heard about the Chinese imposter parts they found in the wrecked plane."

"I did. And you think we're saving a few pennies by installing shit parts here?"

"No. Well, not really. I'm making sure that Lansing isn't. Right now it looks like PA was running a scam. But I wouldn't be doing my job if I didn't have a look for myself."

"Uh, huh," Chuck said as he eyeballed Sheed, trying to determine if she was on the level. He decided to give her the benefit of the doubt.

For now.

"Let's go up," he said.

Sheed smiled, "Let's."

Several minutes later, Lisa was walking behind Chuck out on the port side wing, which was not yet connected to the fuselage. Connectors from the wing, which would later be connected to the aircraft, were currently connected to a computer system elevated at wing level. Chuck typed onto the keypad and seconds later, the leading edge of the wing opened to expose the inner workings.

Chuck left the computer station and motioned for Lisa to join him.

When they arrived at the first slat, he pointed inside the wing. "See for yourself."

She did. The slat locking pin had a tiny 'L' logo on it. As did the drive track, lever, actuator, piston and the rest of the associated equipment package for slat one.

So did the next. And the next.

As did the packages on each of the slats on the starboard side.

Lisa explained that there were two hundred possible counterfeit parts on planes coming out of finished assembly. Two hundred parts that were found on the wreck, which was a conservative number because they didn't—nor would they likely ever —have a complete plane to examine.

Chuck explained that he neither had the time nor the inclination to walk her through two hundred-plus parts on the plane that was undergoing final assembly; even if the investigator had a comprehensive list of those parts, which she didn't, or if the VP was standing right next to her demanding it.

"..... And this isn't where the final step for these birds anyway. They're green tailed. See?"

The 530 had a lime-green finish on it. There wasn't a carrier logo.

"They go to the paint shed next," Chuck continued. "Once they're painted, then they go through test flights, then to the carriers who bought them."

"So you're saying that you would swap them out over there? At the paint shed?"

"No. We don't use junk parts from China. Period. Why would we? Why would we install our parts here, then pay someone to replace all those parts down the line before the carrier takes delivery? It's ridiculous. What I'm saying is that this isn't the final step, and the pins you wanted to see are the real-deal. But if you're still not satisfied, then go over to the paint shed and bother them."

The point was taken, as was the advice.

Thursday
12:45 P.M. October 8, 2015

DENI RAN INTO BUILDING 30, AGAIN NOT STOPPING FOR security or to scan his badge. He didn't stop to put on a hard-hat, safety vest or any other form of PPE either.

He jogged along the path through final assembly toward the first plane on the line.

A man on ground floor with his back to Deni, turned to notice the investigator as he approached.

"Great. Here comes the other one."

"The other one? My partner was here?"

"Down that way. She's up on the wing. Talk to Chuck."

Deni ran down the length of the unfinished plane, leaving the worker behind him without so much as a 'thank you'.

"You're gonna need to put on some gear," the man said to Deni's back.

As he came closer to the wing, Deni shouted to Lisa, calling both her actual and nickname at the top of his lungs. She didn't respond. Instead, a man called down to him from the port side wing.

"Looking for your partner?"

Deni looked up. "Yeah. She up there?"

"No. Left here a little while ago."

"Where is she?"

"I think she's in the next building over. Thirty-five. Paint shed."

Deni ran in the direction that the guy on the wing pointed toward.

Building 35 may have been considered another building, but unlike the other buildings on the Lansing property, it wasn't a separate entity. Buildings 30 and 35 were connected.

As the Lansing 530s were finished in final assembly, they were wheeled over to the paint shed, where they would receive the specific color and graphics ordered by the purchaser. In order to keep dust and other debris from contaminating the prepared outer skin of the completed aircraft, it was necessary to keep the plane in a controlled environment before detailing.

Deni knew he was in Building 35, not only because of the large numbers overhead, but also because he was forced through a clear plastic curtain and all inside were wearing what looked to him like hazmat suits. He, of course, was not.

Again security tried to halt him, and again he blew by them as if they didn't exist. One guard was more brazen than the rest, running to Deni and attempting to physically stop him.

His effort was unsuccessful. The guard hit the factory floor within a second of laying hands on Deni, who turned to see if others would follow their colleague's lead.

None did. If seeing their fallen friend reduced to flailing in pain wasn't enough to drive his point home, Deni's tapping of his forefinger on his pistol grip certainly did.

The encounter was but a ten-second hiccup in entering Building 35.

Now he needed to find Sheed.

A task that now seemed insurmountable because everyone in the paint shed was covered from head to toe as if they were dealing with uranium. Giant masks with breathing apparatuses. Hazard yellow jumpsuits. Plastic booties covering their feet. Gloves ran up the arms to the elbows. Every inch of every person was covered in neon from hardhat to toe.

Every person save for Deni.

"Lisa! Sheed! She!"

His voice echoed throughout the building. Exhaust fans hummed.

There were dozens of unpainted lime-green planes in the vast expanse.

Nobody responded. They either didn't hear him or refused to acknowledge his existence. The hazmat suits went about their business as usual, though what that business was was beyond Deni. For a building called the paint shed, nothing was being nor had been painted.

"She! Goddammit answer me! We gotta get outta here!"

No response.

Deni hurried toward a line of what appeared to be angle-parked, finished yet unpainted L530s.

"She!"

A somewhat nearby worker pointed in a direction toward another row of unpainted planes without saying anything that Deni could hear.

He ran in the direction the worker pointed.

Not that there were many people in the enormous building, but there seemed to be none in the line of aircraft that was pointed out.

"She!"

Again no response.

Deni traversed through the line of planes at ground level, calling for Lisa every few steps.

He was about to give up, head toward another area of the building all together, when he saw a completely covered person on the wing of an unpainted jet.

"She!"

She waived.

"Fuck. Finally!"

He made way toward her and a metal staircase that he hoped she would come down. He waited at the bottom of the stairs for a minute or so before deciding to climb it after her.

When he eventually got to the top of all of the sets of stairs, he could see the tops of the planes and had a high vantage point to the entire building.

Lisa was walking away from him on the same perimeter scaffolding that he was on, not toward him.

"Lisa! *THIS* way."

She waived him toward her from the distance, again not saying anything that he could hear.

"What the fuck? Did you not hear me earlier? On the phone? We gotta get outta Dodge."

She continued to move away from him.

Deni ran after her, along the perimeter of building, on the scaffolding, trying to get near her.

She obviously can't hear me, he thought. *These damn fans.*

As he gained on her, he continually called to her, but she didn't turn toward him or respond.

"She! Cut the shit. We gotta go."

Lisa slowly moved away from him while he ran at full speed toward her.

When he finally was within arm's reach, he grabbed her shoulder and spun her around. With an upward motion, he flipped her hardhat slash mask off.

It wasn't her.

"What the—"

Something struck the back of his head. Hard.

He heard a gun fire.

Dizzy and kneeling on the scaffolding, he spun to see who'd hit him while reflexively reaching for his pistol.

The person who struck him swung a heavy, metal bar as if it were a baseball bat. Deni got off a shot before the bar hit his hand and sent his gun flying off the scaffolding to land somewhere below.

Deni didn't know which hurt more. His now broken hand or the back of his head.

He heard a muffled scream from under the mask of his attacker. Deni focused long enough to see a red hole in the still masked person's shoulder.

The person he'd mistaken for Lisa was now behind him, trying to choke him. Deni kept sending elbows back into the stranger, but they weren't doing anything to loosen the arm around his neck. He couldn't get his chin down under the choking arm to take some of the pressure off his throat. He was going out.

Another gunshot could be heard. Maybe two. This time the sounds were dull. Maybe they were closer?

He continued to try and free himself from the neck hold. Squirming. Elbowing. To no avail.

As he was about to go to sleep, he felt another hard blow to his head.

Everything went black.

And sleep came.

Friday
4:05 A.M. October 9, 2015

THE INTENSIVE CARE UNIT AT MERCY HOSPITAL WAS EMPTY save for Ani and Lisa. Neither had seen Deni since he'd been taken by ambulance from Lansing Aerospace, Building 35.

Ani oscillated between sadness in the purest form, and rage. Hospital visits were becoming all-to common.   Deni had been involved in a recent altercation on a case after being impaneled on a high-profile Boston jury. He simply couldn't let the case go, just let the authorities do what taxpaying dollars pay them to do. He was involved in the case and wanted to see it through. The case ended with him in the hospital. A head injury and two dislocated shoulders.

And so it was with this case.

Ani hadn't seen him at all since he left her in the room at the Drury. She received a call from Lisa at the hotel suite, a call that haunted her dreams every night since she'd met Deni. Only this call was real. And this time, Deni was hurt very badly.

But Lisa had seen him. She'd seen him and wish she'd hadn't. Deni was tough. Larger than life. The man fought MMA fights and lived to tell the tale. He could both give and take a beating.

And to see him with his brains bashed in was not something that she ever expected to see, let alone have the requisite skills to deal with.

Sheed tried to console Ani who was in another crying jag, put her arm around Deni's future wife. Her arm was pushed away.

"Why couldn't you protect him? You're his partner, Lisa. You're supposed to have his back."

"I tried," Lisa said. She was at a loss for anything more.

The fact of the matter is that she *was* there for him. She was the one firing rounds from the wing of an unpainted 530 while Deni was being attacked above her on the nearby scaffolding. Lisa was the one who shot and killed the two assassins. She had no doubt that when they were finished with him, that they would seek her out.

Deni had been making all sorts of noise, calling her name. Nick Rawls and another goon, Terrence Cole, had gone after him. Ambushed him to be precise.

Neither Rawls nor Cole survived their gunshot wounds. They'd shared a ride to the morgue.

Deni was holding on, last she knew, but barely.

A doctor entered the waiting room. Both Ani and Lisa stood, neither woman could read the look on the doctor's face.

"I was informed that you are both here for Warren Dennihan?"

Both responded simultaneously. "Yes."

"Are you both family members?"

"I'm his wife. Well, I'm going—"

"—She's his wife," Lisa interrupted.

"I'm his fr—"

"—Sister. She's his sister," Ani said.

"Which of you is responsible for making decisions on his behalf?"

Ani almost collapsed. Lisa was there for support and guided her back into a chair.

"She is," Lisa said.

The doctor turned to Ani, but made occasional eye contact with Lisa. "My name is Doctor Lorrie Ling. I'm the chief of Neurology. Your husband has suffered about as bad a case of head trauma as one can experience without immediate death. The MRI indicated that this isn't his first brain trauma. He's had other concussions?"

Ani and Lisa both nodded.

"This one was the whopper. Cerebral Edema. Warren is currently in a vegetative state, how persistent—or how long he will be in that state or if he will recover at all—is too soon to tell. We have him on life support and are seeing very little in the way of brain function."

"Oh my God," Ani wailed. Tears fell. She began to shake.

253

Doctor Ling gave Ani a moment, kneeling in front of Ani's chair, then continued.

"There are two things that are worrisome. The first is brain swelling. The fluid in his brain is pushing against his skull and down on the brain stem. The second is bleeding. Because his brain is bleeding, it's causing portions of his brain to shift, which is also putting pressure on the brain stem. As of right now his situation is too diffuse. Meaning I can't operate to alleviate the swelling because too much of his brain is affected."

Ani was stunned and not responding. Catatonic. It was impossible to tell if she'd even comprehended the information that the doctor had given her.

Lisa took over.

"So he's in a coma. And you can't do anything about it?"

"As of this moment, that's correct."

"Can we see him?"

Doctor Ling looked at Ani who was sobbing but still unresponsive.

"I'm not sure that's a good idea."

Lisa took the doctor by the elbow a few steps away from Ani.

"Listen, if this is the last time that she gets to see him alive —"

"—Alive is a relative term. The machines are keeping him alive. There is no life at this point. He's not responding to any stimuli. The next twenty-four hours is crucial. If we can get the swelling and bleeding under control, he may have a chance at some sort of recovery."

"So even if he comes out of this, he's going to be a vegetable?"

"As someone who studies the brain for a living, I'll tell you the more we know, the less we know. We have surprises. X factors that we don't see coming. I would say prepare for the worst, hope for the best. If you believe in one God or another, a prayer might not hurt."

"That's not very reassuring, Doc."

"But that's the best I can give you right now."

254

"We want to see him."

"Like I said—"

"—I wasn't asking," Lisa said.   Her grip on the Doctor's elbow tightened.

After a pause, Doctor Ling said, "Give me an hour or so. Then I'll come get you. One at a time."

Friday
5:15 A.M. October 9, 2015

THE WAIT IN THE ROOM DESIGNED FOR THOSE TO DO just that was excruciating. No words were spoken after Doctor Ling had checked in with them an hour prior. What was there to say that hadn't already been said?

When last Sheed had seen Deni, he was in very bad shape. And the doctor had said that his situation hadn't changed.

The hour went by slower than a day. They both wanted to see him. They both wanted to see him awake. And both held onto the hope that they would.

Deni wasn't like everyone else. He was stubborn. Strong. A bruin in body armor. Whatever diagnosis, no matter how bad, it simply didn't apply. Deni would be okay.

He just had to be.

For the first time, Lisa noticed that the television in the waiting room was on. Had someone just turned it on? Odd that they had been sitting there for hours, since Deni had been admitted, and it had not been noticed. It was turned to CMT, the country music video channel.

The volume was so low it was hardly audible. Maybe that is why Lisa hadn't noticed it. Or maybe it was because her thoughts kept going over the events of the night. The events of the week.

Deni hadn't wanted to come to Joplin.

Deni wanted no part of this case. But he did it. He did it because she'd talked him into it. If he didn't come out of his coma and make a full recovery, she didn't know what she would do. The guilt would consume her.

Lisa glanced back at the television.

At the bottom of the screen, in the corner, it gave the information about the current music video that was on. Keith Urban. *Break On Me*. From the album with the same title.

Lisa listened to the faint lyrics.   Tears poured down her cheeks.

"....There'll be days your heart don't wanna beat
You pray more than you breathe
And you just want to fall to pieces...."

She turned to Ani, who had her head in hands.   Possibly praying. Probably praying. The lyrics resonated with her. This is what she wanted to say to Ani but couldn't.   Instead, she kept listening. And hoping.

"....And you just need a break
Break on me

Shatter like glass
Come apart in my hands
Take as long as it takes, girl
Break on me
Put your head on my chest
Let me help you forget
When your heart needs to break
Just break on me...."

Doctor Ling entered the waiting room and took Ani's arm.
"Are you ready for this? You don't have to go in there."
"I have to see him."
And she did.

The room was dark.   Machines were hooked up to him, crowding around him. Each made a sound, a sound that meant life Ani hoped.
"I can't give you a long time," Ling said.

"I'll take as much time as you'll give me," Ani responded. She took the chair that was set up by Deni's bed. She took his hand. It was cold and lifeless.

Tears continued to fall and Ani sobbed uncontrollably.

"How could you do this to me, Deni? To us?"

She waited for a response like there would be one. When there wasn't she continued.

"I can't do this alone. I don't want to do this alone. This is not the way it's supposed to be. Not part of the plan. You have to wake up, Bae. You have to wake up and be a daddy.

I'm pregnant."

Headlines from the Associated Press newswire, Monday, October 12, 2015:

Lansing Aerospace Soars after 4273 Exoneration

Thorough internal and federal investigations have declared the Lansing 530, the safest passenger plane in the sky.

Preferred Airlines Executives indicted for 4273 Crash

The CEO and eleven other airline execs were arrested today. The publicly held airline was accused of one hundred ninety-seven counts of depraved indifference homicide, falsifying FAA and NTSB documents, conspiracy, racketeering, money laundering, and numerous other lesser charges. Representatives from PA declined comment.

Preferred Airlines Caught in Parts Scandal

The Airline is accused of switching out critical airplane parts with inferior ones to turn a profit. The switch caused one hundred ninety-seven deaths in the infamous 4273 crash last February.

Headline from the Joplin Globe, Wednesday, October 14, 2015:

Former Lansing Aerospace Employee/UAW Member Knifed in Prison

Thomas Ginn, former employee of Lansing Aerospace and vocal figure in the local United Aerospace Workers union, accused of attempted murder and awaiting trial, was stabbed and killed while being held at Jasper County Jail on Tuesday. A spokesperson for the Jasper County Sheriff's Department said, "While we do our best to control weapons and contact between inmates, it is an ongoing concern and something we need to be better at." Representatives from neither Lansing nor the local UAW chapter 1514 were made available for comment.

Headlines from the Associated Press newswire, Wednesday, November 12, 2015:

Preferred Airlines Files Bankruptcy

The Publicly held airline went belly-up after settling with Boston Victim's Compensation attorney, Trey Keating, for $48B for their gross negligence in flight 4273 last February. Families of the nearly two hundred passengers that died in the February crash will likely only get a fraction of the money owed to them from the settlement once the airline is sold off at auction. The most public of the surviving family members, Sorina Kane, has declared that she "will not rest until every executive [of PA] spends the rest of their lives in prison and is personally sued for every penny they've got".

Headline from the Boston Globe, Friday, November 20, 2015:

Boston Investigator Transferred to Mass General Neuro Unit From Joplin, MO

More than a month after a near-fatal head trauma, former State Police detective and current private investigator was determined to be stable enough for transport to a Boston hospital for further long-term care. Warren Dennihan is still listed as being in a 'persistent vegetative state' by Boston Medical staff, after being wounded during the investigation into the infamous Flight 4273 last February, an investigation that he and his partner, Lisa Sheed of Dennihan Investigation Service, of South Boston, are given credit for solving. While being honored as a hero, his wife, Ani Dennihan, is asking for prayers and privacy. His partner, Lisa Sheed declined comment.

AUTHOR'S NOTES AND ACKNOWLEDGEMENTS

The previous work is one of fiction, any resemblance to specific and true incidents is purely coincidental. The names of real places, people, music, etc. are either coincidental or simply to give the story an authentic feel. None of the events that took place in this novel are real to my knowledge.

Lansing Aerospace is a figment of my imagination, though culled from real research from real aerospace giants. I am forever indebted to the people who allowed me access to their world. Aircraft mechanics, engineering, etc. is complicated stuff. I hope that I was able to explain it in a way that made those that spoke to me proud. If there is any misinformation, the fault is mine.

Parts counterfeiting, in this global economy, is real. And it is really a problem. While airlines continue to try and cut costs while gaining more passengers, it is a problem that is not likely to go away anytime soon. Keep your eyes peeled in the news if you think I'm exaggerating. The next rumble while your in the air might be a cheap part that decided to quit.

In order to give the crash itself credibility, I needed to interview real flight crews, real pilots, real ATCs, and go through the volumes of protocols in the unlikely events I described. I take for granted the things that take place in an effort to transport me from point A to B as quickly and conveniently as possible. A task that is often thankless, but has been successful — else I wouldn't be here to tell this tale. For speaking with me and getting me to my destination safely, I am forever thankful.

Finally, I would like to thank the people of Joplin, MO. A kinder, warmer, inviting place you will not find. My stay with you was invaluable to telling this story. I may have embellished some parts, please forgive me if I did you a disservice.

Thanks to you, the reader, for your time. I hope you enjoyed the story. Maybe you'll think about this tale the next time you get on a plane. For better or worse.

-sw-

ABOUT THE AUTHOR

Photo ©2014 WWPGroup, Inc.
www.WWPGroupInc.com

Scott Wellinger is a well-traveled writer and novelist. He has written many novels, articles, scripts, musical lyrics, and essays under pseudo-names. His more popular novels feature, among others, the fictitious private investigations of Warren Dennihan. A native of New England, he was born in Vermont and was educated in Boston, Massachusetts. He holds a Master's Degree in Applied Economics and when he is not traveling, writing, playing music, cooking or painting, he is on a golf course.

For more author information: www.WWPGroupInc.com

wwpgroupinc@mail.com

Also by scott wellinger:

Use It Up (2015)

The Season for Moths (2016)

Other novels in the **Warren Dennihan crime-fiction series:**

CRASH

A Warren Dennihan Novel (first of series)

Venom

A Warren Dennihan Novel (book 2)

Sinn

A Warren Dennihan Prequel (book 3)

Ebb

A Warren Dennihan Prequel (book 4)

Juror

A Warren Dennihan Prequel (book 5)

These novels can be purchased in Ebook and print wherever books are sold.

Thank You for Reading!

If you enjoyed reading this novel, please help others appreciate it as well.

Recommend it.   Please help other readers find it by recommending it to friends, reader groups, discussion boards, or wherever you purchased the book.

Review it.   You can add your thoughts to Amazon, GooglePlay, iBooks, kobo, Barnes & Noble, at the publisher website (WWPGroup.com), reader clubs like goodreads or LibraryThing, etc., etc. If you do write a review, please share it with either my publisher at WWPGroupInc@mail.com or me directly at scottwellinger@gmail.com (or both) so that I can thank you personally.

Follow me on twitter and Instagram for updates and special offers. @wellinger_scott , and @SCOTT_WELLINGER , respectively.

Best Wishes,

~SW~

The following is an unedited sample of CRASH, book one in the Warren Dennihan series. The novel is available in ebook and print wherever books are sold.

Scott Wellinger

CRASH

a Warren Dennihan novel

PROLOGUE

THE NIGHT HAD DRAWN DOWN like a blanket over the small New England town, tucked in the mountains of southern New Hampshire. A cloudless, late summer sky made the bright stars the only form of illumination, which were little more than pinholes of light off in a distant universe. The pine forest that shot up from the fertile ground gave off a rich perfume reminiscent of Christmas, which was less than half a year to come. Above the tree-line, the natural rock formation known as *The Old Man on the Mountain* was a slight, silhouetted backdrop bidding the tourists a final goodnight whilst he slept. The narrow, windy roads meandering through the hills below that watchful cliff north of Boston, Massachusetts, were fortified with guardrails and graveled pulloffs to accommodate the looky-loo tourist vehicles. The fall foliage leaf-peepers were still a month or so away, but the hiking and camping season was still in full swing. The heavy traffic from the visitors trying to get a last trip in before the arrival of colder nights, was nonexistent in the hours after dusk. The hikers, campers, and naturalists had long since ventured home for the night or abandoned their parked vehicles on one of the pulloffs on the side of the road, as they made camp somewhere in the darkened forest.

The *Old Man* was the sentry for several communities below his perch on the White Mountains; the county and township of Wayland, New Hampshire was by far the most affluent. The old and new money was drawn from the financial hub of Boston in the form of large salaries. The town flourished as the commuters preferred to spend their ample earnings in the sanctity and "tax-free" state of New Hampshire over the Metropolis of Boston which fed them to the South. Another form of income for Wayland was the tourism, but the affluent of the community was torn in that

267

while the outsiders boosted the economy, they trampled over their turf. The people of money from Wayland did appreciate the financial relief from tourism, which was their dilemma in refraining from ousting their numerous intruders. The visitors should be felt yet not seen.

The winters were the most difficult seasons for the citizens in avoiding the onslaught of outsiders. The skiers would come from the flatlands to trample the towns and, in their opinion, the face of their great state. Throughout the rest of the year, they spent their time and income away from the flatlanders at the Wayland Country Club. Golf was just one activity taken in there, and in truth many claimed to play more often than they had a tee-time for. The sanctuary was more for camaraderie and companionship than the activities the club promoted. A place for the wealthy to rub elbows with others of their kind in the same area.

This particular night, those with money were keen to show off just how much they had and were willing to part with. The Gala and Charity event that was taking place in the pavilion was under way, all of the who's-who in place and opening wallets for the silent auction, though whom or what charity would be receiving these sums was anybody's guess. While the sprinklers were misting water over the lush back-nine of the manicured golf course, which could be seen out of the large windows, elegant gowns and tuxedos flattered the bodies of the occupants in the club. Live, light jazz music and the mumbled conversations of the local power couples mingling under the giant chandelier could be heard faintly in the distance, while the rest of the community went about their Saturday night. The well-to-do's had their evening festivities, freeing their assistants and staffers to have theirs.

Arelia Diaz had made her plans weeks prior, when she learned that she would have a rare night off. She was a live-in maid for one of the rich and beautiful, though she called herself a caretaker, and was looking forward to blowing off some built-up steam with a night of dancing with her girlfriends. The initial response from her friends at her invitation for a night out on the town was a jealous decline, until they too were informed that they would have the night off. Her friends in the area were also in the employ of other event attendees and would also have the night free from; babysitting, nannying, serving, cleaning, maintaining, cooking, or the myriad other tasks their employers were too important to perform. A night of dinner; gossiping over the comings and goings of their respective power families, and certainly dancing would be just the cure for the tedium that ailed them. Only one friend, Marina could not make it. She was told that she would have to take care of a child, though her employer didn't have any children.

Arelia was a mid-thirties Brazilian woman who had left her own family back in Recife. Other than her gaggle of female friends, she was alone in the United States. She had no spouse or children, which was the mainspring for many nights of tear-soaked cheeks and a saturated pillow. The oldest of four daughters, she saw limited opportunities in her native village and networked into an immigrant sub-community tucked into the American Northeast almost ten years prior. Alone but not alone, she was content in managing a dream household, though it was not her own.

Ms. Diaz did not consider herself to be what the Americans called a *cougar*, she was too young to be considered for the part, but she was going to be on the prowl this night. All women had needs, this was a rare opportunity, and she was going to make the most of it. She painted on a pair of the most expensive jeans she could afford, her ample bosom bursted out of the front of her new, sparkling, black-yet-shear blouse, exposing her black push-up bra, and donned a pair of high heels which lifted her four inches higher than her usual five-foot-three inch frame. With her raven hair done (in what was coincidentally called a Brazilian Blowout), and her makeup accentuating her big, beautiful brown eyes, she would be turning some heads. She still had what it took to bag any man she wanted, despite her lack of practice.

She would not be bringing anyone back to her suite at her employer's palatial home, this was not allowed, nor did she have any intention of staying with an interested gentleman. Her duties would resume bright and early in the morning. Her employers would likely be as moody as usual, as demanding as usual. Maybe they would even be a little hungover, though they would never in a million years admit that to the help. The agenda for the night would be dinner, *Forró* dancing, and a copious amount of flirting. Unfortunately the line would have to be drawn at flirting.

She was given an older, red, Honda *Civic* to use in her daily errands, which she was using while on her way downtown to meet her girlfriends. It was a small yet able car, in spite of the age, much like Arelia believed herself to be. She had plenty of life left, this was just a means to an end. A way to go back to Brazil with enough money saved to provide for a family she would make, and for their family after she was gone.

Diaz was used to the car and all of the idiosyncrasies that came along with it. She loved the limited freedom that the car provided her, but she loved the stereo system the most. In the ten years of being the caretaker, she was never allowed to listen to her music loud enough to be heard by anyone in any part of the house. Nor was she allowed to use headphones as she was always on call. Always. Failure to hear, much less respond to a call from the main house would mean an immediate end to the life she had built here. Relegated to vehicular sonic therapy, she would blast her beats as loud as the car stereo and tiny speakers could muster.

She had the windows down, feeling the night air through her already blown locks of hair. The outside sounds were competing between the crickets, the sounds of the

Country Club in the distance, and Arelia belting out the Portuguese lyrics over the loud music of her favorite band *Falamansa*. She was blissfully unaware that this would be her final concert.

As she rounded a sweeping blind turn on Wayland Country Club Road, the singing and car-dancing was immediately interrupted by the harsh LED, high-beam headlamps glaring into her eyes from seemingly nowhere, yet everywhere. She knew nothing of candlepower light measurements, but the retina-burning headlamps blinding her surely could have illuminated Fenway Park. Diaz could not see anything, much less navigate the rolling left turn. She could not see the lever protruding off of the steering column to flash her own high-beams at the offensive driver coming towards her. Could not see her bearings on the road. She was desperate to see a yellow line. A white one. Anything to pinpoint if she was in a lane. There were no vibrations from the warning grating on the side of the road, because there wasn't any grating on the side of the road. No reflectors, not that she would have been able to see anything being reflected in the already blinding light. She would have welcomed the grazing of a guardrail, just so she could sort out where she was. Everything was happening so fast. Brakes were unused. The stereo remained at full, deafening decibels. There was no time to turn it down. No time to think. No time to sweat. Was there somewhere she could pull off? But that question did not register in the time it took her to sail off the road.

The little-Civic-that-could missed the end of a guardrail, grabbed the bit of gravel just off of the pavement, bulleted her through the small pulloff. The car continued, severing a maple tree that was contemplating the changing of leaf colors soon, continuing on to impact the base of a large rock formation. The car came to an immediate halt from the forty-plus miles per hour it was traveling just seconds prior. The rear of the car was the last to learn of the immediate stop being insisted upon by the fixed and rooted boulder. It had no choice but to follow the rest of the cars' lead and jetted into the air, rear tire spinning as it tried to continue beyond the mess. It failed.

The sound of the dance music halted, replaced by the sound of mangling of metal and the pulverizing of bone. The jagged metal sliced through flesh which added to the cacophony of horrific sounds. The macabre series of sounds lasted but a beat, but the devastation would be permanent.

Nothing would be continuing beyond the crash. Not the maple tree, not poor Arelia Diaz formerly of Recife, Brazil and more recently of Wayland, New Hampshire. Where her body existed in the cab, where she was car-dancing to her favorite band, singing as loud as her beautiful lungs could project, was a sick sculpture of metal, plastic, glass, rubber and human organs. The front of the car no longer existed. It was impossible to discern car from body, where the red paint from the Honda started, through all the blood, and the end of the former occupant. Her lifeless face rested, burning on part of the steaming engine; searing what was left of her beautiful features, her head and neck was now where the backseat should have been.

The offending headlights stared onto the wreckage for a time, determining what was already known. The lights crept slowly toward the destruction, attached to the black vehicle that was camouflaged by the dark of the night. They would abandon the devastation they had caused. The upbeat, accordion-based dance music and singing, followed by the horrifying reverberations of the crash were no more. The sounds were replaced by the ticking of the cooling, destroyed engine; the sizzling of flesh; the acceleration of the fleeing murderous vehicle. And crickets.

1

UGLY. THE IMAGE APPEARING back at him in the makeshift mirror was ugly. No other word could summarize the reflection and the atmosphere surrounding it; his every thought and emotion. The stainless steel metal above the all-in-one, Willoughby sink-toilet reflected pure ugliness. The image itself superimposed upon the backdrop of the institutional beige walls, the florescent lighting, the grey concrete floor.

Jacob Grantes had never been considered a hunk, nor an Adonis, he was not a physical specimen for which to lust. He had never been compared to the likes of George Clooney but he had been somewhat attractive, smart, confident. His six foot one inch frame, his square jaw, his sea-green eyes were some of the features that admirers had named when defending him as 'a catch'. The image that had once stared back at him, however, had disappeared, morphing into the figure that was reflected back at him in the polished steel. He was splashing water on his face, one push button at a time, but no matter how much water he applied, how much he washed, and how much he scrubbed his face, he could not cleanse away the ugliness, inside or out.

Grantes, inmate #437261, had been a guest at the Wayland County House of Corrections for the past six months, having been denied bail. He had not been in trouble with the law prior to the events leading him to this very moment, which made the denial pending trial quite unusual. Jacob was accustomed to living in a large home, family, and the picket fence; which made the current accommodations all the more intolerable. His cell was an eight by twelve foot concrete room with a double bunk, a small desk and a sink-toilet which he had to share with his celly. The space was tight and the nerves were stretched even tighter. Twenty hours per day were spent in this tiny space. Best friends could be put together in such a way and it would not take long to become mortal enemies. To make matters worse, the door to the cells lacked bars, it was a solid door, which allowed little air flow, with a narrow, horizontal slot at waist-high for food trays to be passed through, or to be handcuffed prior to exiting. The small, vertical window was convenient only for the Correctional Officers who had to execute head counts. This solid metal door was manufactured to make the most loud, God-awful clanks and noises when opened and closed. Studies had been done on this; millions spent, to craft an audible assault on inmates in an effort to make them uncomfortable, on edge, and contemplating the actions that had led them to their current place of residence.

The CO had awoken Grantes with a loud, mechanical unlatching, the grinding of metal as his cell door was sliding open at 5:30 AM.

"Grantes. You got 15 minutes to shit, shower 'n shave. Court. You'll get chow on the ride over."

"Yeah," he said between splashes of water on his face.

His grumbled reply indicated his malcontent, as this was to be a real shit day. It was to be a different kind of shit day, but a shit day all the same. All other days had the exact same schedule; filled with misery, meetings with so-called counselors, and a myriad of conversations with fellow inmates all of whom proclaim to be innocent or screwed by their lawyer. This day would be a shit day of a different color but a shade he knew quite well. Jacob Grantes had previously spent most of his adult life immersed in the muck and mire of the legal system, but on the other side of it. As an attorney, he knew exactly what this day would entail.

The splashing of water on his face would make none of it go away.

"Jesus Christ, can you shut the fuck up? What time is it, bro?"

The shout came from a lump in the sheets, covering the body laying on the top bunk in his cell. Grantes's celly had a very low tolerance for anything beyond sleeping away his bid. This is known in prison as a bed-bid, and he is not the only one trying desperately to dream away the time.

"It's early. Sorry. I have court today. But it looks like you'll have the cell to yourself for the day."

"Goody." He said this without removing the covers which made him appear as though he was levitating five feet above a filthy concrete floor.

"You'll be able to shit in peace at least. I wish you'd spent a little time out of the cell so I could crap without an audience."

"You really gonna shower?"

"Yeah, I'm getting my shower bag ready now."

"That means that the door is gonna open and close a couple more times. Why you gonna shower anyways? Gonna be front and center with a jumpsuit and shackles anyway, clean ain't gonna matter."

"They'll let me change into a suit."

"Ha - you're funny. You're an idiot, but you're funny. Where are you gonna get a suit asshole?"

"I came here in a suit. My lawyer will have another one if they won't let me have that one out of property."

"You're gonna be in a holding tank, good luck getting one of the courthouse COs to let you change. Lazy assholes might have to do extra work," he said. "Whats today anyway?"

"February fif—"

"— the case moron. What part of the case is it?"

"Oh. Discovery and motions. It's when — "

" — I know what it is. Fifteen minutes tops bro. They're not lettin' you change into a fuckin' suit. Two bus rides and a day in the tank for fifteen minutes. Have fun."

"Shithouse lawyers."

It amazed him how much legal knowledge inmates had. Especially those with high recidivism. Grantes's cellmate had a very vast and intimate knowledge of the law from a certain prospective. He was, therefore, known throughout the prison as a good shithouse lawyer. His celly was of course aware that Jacob was a real lawyer, which only caused that many more passionate discussions.

"We'll see."

2

JACOB GRANTES AND HIS BEST FRIEND, Ryan Wells, had started a law practice together fifteen years prior. They had, over time, cornered the bustling criminal and legal market of nowhereville. The small southern New Hampshire town of Barstone, in Wayland County, was considered to be the other side of the tracks by the more affluent locals. Those elevated locals being the residents of the affluent town of Wayland, which was literally just across the tracks of the commuter rail into Boston, Massachusetts. The clichéd delineation was real. The constituents of Wayland Township made it quite clear to all of the inhabitants of Barstone, and really anywhere else for that matter but less vocally, that they were not welcome. The elected Sheriff of Wayland County, his office located in the town of Wayland by design, was well aware of what would happen if the petty crimes and riff-raff of Barstone were to bleed into the backyards of the wealthy community. And so the two towns within the same county coexisted; the town with the same name of the county reaped all the rewards, while the slums went about being the outcasts.

The law office of Grantes, Wells & Associates was strategically located in Barstone, on the border of the two towns. They needed the criminal element, and therefore the business from the Barstonians, and they wanted the much more civilized legal filings of Wayland. The two townships utilized the same courthouse as they were in the same county. Life was never boring for the two attorneys. Defending the proprietors of a Meth Lab one day; filing an uncontested, fourth divorce on behalf of the scorned trophy-wife on the next.

The *Associates* in the name of the firm was a mistruth. JG, as he was called, and Ryan were the only partners, the only lawyers, and there were no others seeking partnership. None would be sought out either as they were not seeking any new blood for such an arrangement. The associates consisted of their part-time private investigator, Warren Dennihan; and their full-time secretary in Ryan's wife, Angie. Warren had his own thriving business, with his own partner, and was subcontracted by the law firm whenever a top investigator was needed. He was rarely, if ever, in the office. Angie was in the office every business day, much to Ryan's chagrin, and she had almost no legal knowledge. What she lacked in legal prowess, she made up for in organization and efficiency. She was invaluable and JG had said in the past, in plain language to Ryan, that whatever problem he had with the arrangement, to get over it.

The arrangement had been Ryan's doing in the first place. He had hired Angie Grummond, as was her name at the time, without consulting JG on the spot at the first interview. Rather than ask the prospective employee out on a date upon their first meeting, which was ultimately what Ryan wanted to do, he decided to hire her instead. The would-be sexual harassment suit in waiting didn't last long, as they were officially an item by the time she was finished her training. JG didn't mind as much as he had initially let on, not even annoyed if truth be told. The headache of starting a firm was a larger migraine than that of an office romance. Besides, Ryan had been JG's best friend since law school, almost for as long as he could remember, and he had never seen his friend so happy.

The startup capital for the small firm came from the money bestowed to Jacob via his surrogate family. His in-laws had been more than good to him, they had filled a hole left in him by the passing of his natural parents. His wife, Anna, had come from money and while she had married for love, her parents could think of no reason for them to struggle financially. They had made the idle threats to rescind the money once they learned that Ryan was to be made full partner from the outset, but all concerned knew the threats were empty. Their apprehension came from genuine concern as they saw their son-in-law, Jacob, as the much more talented of the partnership. With Jacob viewed as having a much higher potential than his friend, especially since he had no money invested in the venture, they felt Ryan was there for the ride instead of the build.

Ryan was not a bad lawyer. He was no Shapiro either. He was talented but he was also a free-spirit. Wells would get caught up in the spirit of the law rather than the black letter. He took flyers. Rather than take on more legitimate claims, he often went to the hoop with little on evidence and heavy on the liberal sentiment. He would often take on the lost cause that was rejected by JG; acknowledging that he might win some, but he would lose more. Ryan was an idealist. He was interested in the law for the good it could do. He actually thought the lady with the scales was indeed blind. He still does to this day.

JG had depended on Ryan to bring in fees not necessarily wins. Winning of course would draw the big cases, but with a location in Barstone, New Hampshire, who was he kidding? JG had the wins, Ryan had the passion. But that was all in the past. What JG needed from his friend and partner now was a win. A big win. He needed him to win the case of his life. For Jacob's life.

3

"All RISE. PLEASE COME TO ORDER, court is now in session. The honorable Judge McCaglia presiding." The bailiff shouted with much too much in the way of volume. There were few people in the fourth session of the Wayland County Superior courtroom. It was entirely unnecessary to shout at that level, but Grantes decided that the loud volume coordinated nicely with the loud color of the neon, hazard-orange prison jumpsuit he was wearing.

He had asked the Correctional Officer, politely mind you, if he could change into a suit that his lawyer had brought for him to wear to court. He even bargained to leave on the shackles, but the request didn't warrant any response. He repeated the question in case the officer didn't hear him. The CO had heard the request because he gave the sternest of looks upon hearing it a second time, though he still gave no response. Ryan involved himself when he'd arrived, but the plea to the Deputy Sheriff was in vain. The officer didn't like the hippie lawyer in the linen suit, and never liked any inmate ever. He was appointed to rid the county of these unwanteds, and this nonconformist was working to free them. Chalk one up for the political right, getting one over on the liberal left.

"You may be seated," said the judge. She was the moderately attractive Judge Grace McCaglia. Wearing the usual black robe, matching black hair that may have been colored to do so, and mystic blue eyes that could virtually see through a person. She confidently presided with a no-nonsense efficiency.

In her late forties, she had accomplished more than most attorneys had in the course of their entire career, in a fraction of the time. In the *Live Free or Die* State of New Hampshire; there were rumors of political favoritism, affirmative action, and sleeping her way into a judgeship. Any explanation was more plausible than that she had earned her position. These whispers did not go unnoticed which is why she once prosecuted, and now presided, strictly but fairly. There would not be any second-guessing her rulings. She would not allow anyone to be justified in criticizing her for not being the right person for the bench.

"Where are we in the matter of the State of New Hampshire v Grantes?"

"Where are Anna and Brady is the better question." JG whispered into Ryan's ear as they sat in their seats at the defendant's table. He looked around the room but with few people in it, it was quite clear that his wife and son were not present.

"No idea. Three messages without a response this morning. Maybe they are giving her a hard time about a four year old in the courtroom?"

Ryan finished whispering the response as he stood to address the judge.

"We would like to request a continuance, your honor."

"On what grounds? This has been ongoing for six months, time is ticking here, sir."

"We are still in discovery, judge. Both theirs and ours."

"Theirs? A Grand Jury was convened and subsequent to Rule 8, they found probable cause to sustain an indictment. The 90-day threshold was met. Do you want to weigh in here counselor?"

She swiveled her chair to her right so she could face the prosecuting Assistant District Attorney. 'Weigh in' was a poor choice of words and she immediately realized it.

Pierce La Fontagne was an enormous man. Fat. He was an unhealthy glutton that could blame whatever or whomever he wanted to regarding his obesity, but it was a fact that he tipped the scales at over four hundred-fifty pounds. He was always disheveled and just as disorganized. How he had lasted as an ADA was a mystery, but his nickname was not so mysterious. They called him Jabba, after the enormous creature in *Star Wars*, behind his back. And he knew it. He spoke with as slow a purpose as his metabolism.

"We have. Ah. Given the defense and have enough to provide the state to move. Ah. Forward with the case, Judge. We. Ah. Don't need much, but we do need a little more time." The fat on his neck jiggled when he spoke. He never looked up to face the judge when he spoke to her, as he was still shuffling papers in the disorganized mess he had created at the prosecutor's table. Besides his disorganization, not making eye contact with her infuriated her. She felt it was a sign of disrespect.

"Does that mean you are ready or not? Kind of late in the game aren't we, counselor? You had enough to sustain the charges, do you have what you need to move forward or don't you?"

"Ah. We feel confident that the current evidence will prove our case beyond the threshold of reasonable doubt."

"I can tell." She had to pause to control her anger. She was a professional to her very core. She swiveled back toward the defendant.

"Mr. Wells. Have you received all of this said evidence? If so, then I'm confused. Speedy trial gentlemen. The defendant has the right to one, he is remanded and sitting in prison awaiting the disposition of this trial. So I would think his lawyer would be more adamant about moving this forward. He pleaded not guilty. ADA La Fontagne and the state requires a speedy trial, and frankly I demand it so I don't get backlogged. Six months gentlemen. This has been going long enough, wouldn't you both agree?

We move ahead forthwith." Efficiency experts could learn a thing or two from Judge McCaglia.

"I agree that six months is a long time, your honor. Especially for my client, who was only remanded due to an imminent threat justification, which we will get to in a minute with the other motion you have before you."

Ryan had filed to have the issue of bail revisited. Jabba had used a justification that argued that Jacob Grantes was an immediate danger to society and should be remanded as to allay any danger to the community. She was already disgruntled with the prosecutor, he was hoping to use that to his and therefore his client's advantage.

"But with all due respect, judge, I do not agree with a forthwith ruling," Ryan continued. "In order to provide a proper defense against the charges, I need to ensure that the burden of proof and all pertaining evidence is met and provided to me by the prosecution. The ADA has just told you and I, after some equivocating I might add, that they now have all the evidence they plan to use when and if this goes to trial. I need time to assemble all the counter-evidence supporting our claim against the charges, and thus proving that my client is innocent."

JG nodded his approval. His friend and partner was doing well. Unlike television and movies in Hollywood, the prosecution cannot come out of nowhere in the last minute of the trial with a damning piece of evidence. It was now time for the assistant district attorney to put up or shut up, and Ryan had just spoken legalese saying so.

"OK. So we are moving forward to trial with this, correct gentlemen?"

The two opposing men nodded in agreement instead of stating it aloud for the court stenographer. The judge didn't make them, she continued instead.

"I don't see a green sheet with any deals on the table as of yet. So, Mr. Wells, how long do you need?"

"We request ninety days your honor."

"Three months for discovery and prep for trial? You are joking right? Nice try. ADA La Fontagne, is there anything else you would like to state before I rule on this?"

"Ah. No, your Honor. I would just like to reiterate that — "

"—No need to reiterate anything, I heard you the first time. You've got thirty days." She turned toward the clerk to dictate. "Let's set a date for pretrial and jury selection at or about one month from today."

"Your Honor with that being settled, I would like to revisit the issue of bail. The motion should be before you," Ryan said.

He was hoping that since things had not exactly gone his way thus far, Judge McCaglia would throw him, and more importantly JG, a bone on the motion to revisit the issue of bail.

"That has already been denied. I denied it six months ago. Is there anything new to bring forth where I would reconsider?"

"He is a prominent attorney in the area, Judge. He has a family, is a husband, and father. He is the sole breadwinner. This has created an enormous hardship. His driver's license has been reinstated at this point, but we would surrender it again in lieu of incarceration if the State is still concerned that he is an imminent threat. But if we are now talking another thirty days before a trial is to even begin, I see no reason or threat to continue to remand him. He has been a model inmate, never been in trouble with the law prior to this case, and he has — "

"—Save it Mr. Wells. You have nothing new here. A woman is dead. The allegation is that she is dead because of your client. Drinking and Driving is serious and a blight on our society. When a child is in the car on top of this, allegedly, it is reprehensible. I continue to believe that he may be an imminent threat. The fact that he is a prominent figure in this community; and that he is an attorney; that has been before me and this court in the past; is not a reason for him to benefit. He cannot garner favor from a court that is supposed to judge his alleged crimes. Any defendant before me with these same allegations would get remanded, remain alcohol-free, surrender their license to drive a motor vehicle, and pending the outcome of the trial matriculate a Substance Abuse Program. I'm sorry Mr. Grantes, but you are to stay at the Wayland County House of Corrections pending trial. Stay in the Substance Abuse Program or there will be consequences, sir. As Mr. Wells just stated it's only thirty more days."

She paused only for a moment while she briefly looked over the rest of the documents regarding this case in front of her.

"So unless there are any other motions, we will resume these proceedings in thirty days. No more delays gentlemen, either one of you. Court is adjourned."

The gavel was only tapped onto the sound block but it sounded as though it was slammed through to the other side by a sledgehammer.

4

THE TRUTH WAS that the hardship the Grantes family was facing was not at all financial. It was Jacob who was suffering the most, but they were all unaccustomed to this torment. Not being able to see his wife and four year old child was all but killing him. Brady was not supposed to be without his father. He hadn't been in his life up to that point. Anna had been distant in recent months but they had dealt with serious difficulty in the past. They would get through it. Their college romance had started blissfully and had some serious downs despite their intense love for one another. Their eventual vows to take each other through good times and bad had taken significant meaning.

Norman and Olivia Craig had done whatever they could to encourage the college romance of their only daughter, Anna. Jacob, not Jake or JG as others called him (his natural parents had taken the time and effort to pick a name for him, and it was rude to bastardize that effort they had said repeatedly), was decidedly the perfect match for their Anna. Especially with the boys she had brought home in previous courtships. True, Jacob's family didn't come from wealth, nor had they built any. They had faith that this legacy would change with Jacob. He had work ethic, was smart, and pre-law. Yes, this is what they had in mind for their girl and they would do whatever they could, financially or otherwise, to support Jacob's goals. As long as Anna was included in the equation.

Jacob was always humbly appreciative, respectful in declining the offers of money or the "just because" expensive gifts, but would relent over time. Anna joined in on the pressure to accept these material tokens of affection for they were deemed as simple manifestations of parental approval. She viewed the entire subject as "only money". Of course it was only money to her, she had been privied to these same gestures and more over the course of her entire life. These were just an extension of her expectations from her wealthy parents.

"You should just get used to it, honey. They won't let up. They love you and they just want to show you how much. Besides, you deserve to live a certain lifestyle even if you don't know it yet," she said in one of their more memorable spats on the subject. There had been more discussions regarding this very subject, all of which she won with some version of the same statement.

Jacob's fight for financial independence with her was a broken alliance, however. He would say things like, "I'm used to doing things for myself, babe. It's not that I am unappreciative of it, but there is something honorable in building a life for ourselves, by ourselves. I feel like I am forever indebted to them."

These declarations would fall on deaf ears and would either reluctantly fade or would be the impetus for a battle royale, depending on the value of the gesture and how much Jacob really wanted to press the issue. Eventually Jacob acquiesced, as he did every time. As the relationship developed, the lifestyle became de rigueur. He had lost every battle and the war as well. In truth, he had built up enormous debt and was very thankful for the financial help. Boston University was not cheap, Boston University School of Law even less so. The money, cars, apartments, the ability to go to Law School (only 11% of those applying to BU School of Law get accepted. The competition is stiff, but Mr. Craig was friends with someone on the Board of Trustees, or so he said).

"It's not bribery," Norman Craig had said. "I love Anna," he also said. It was to ensure that they had a strong foundation on which to build their life together.   Of that, Jacob was sure.

Jacob's biological parents loved him with all of their hearts, albeit with fewer trinkets to show for it.   Actually, there weren't any trinkets.   Reginald and Elizabeth Grantes had to work and toil for every nickel of property or possession they owned, and even then the nickels didn't add up to anything of worth.   They doled out hugs and kisses the way Norman Craig doled out money.   Before the Craigs, Jacob had been a wealthy man.   His parents attended or coached every athletic endeavor their only son struggled to perform.   Neither parent had attended college but made it a priority for their son to get the education they did't have.   They would not, could not, contribute financially. But they were motivating and supportive.

Young Grantes left upstate Vermont to attend Boston University and achieve his and his parent's goals for him. His parents remained there, driving south for visits or sending care packages of sweets to their starving student. They were pleased to learn that as of his sophomore year, their son would no longer struggle financially.   The ends would more than meet.   Unfortunately, in the end, they would never meet Anna.

******

It was the start of Jacob's second semester, of his second year at BU that Reggie and Liz would drive down to Boston to visit their son for the last time.   He had been home for Christmas break and every other sentence was, "Anna this" or "Anna that".

288

He had been a social mingler in high school, never the most popular kid but was a welcome addition to any clique. He was better than averagely attractive. He was polite, and was familiar with many a female as well, in large part because of his standing in a plethora of social circles. He had many dates, with a few sporadically retained as official girlfriends over the years. He certainly didn't have any that he had prattled on about for days on end.

His freshman year had been new and exciting, but also the most difficult endeavor he had undertaken in his life up to then. There were precious few stories regarding the fairer sex as he said there was no time. That was only half true. The other half was that going to University was not about settling down but about exploring, both academically and socially. It was novel that this Anna would commandeer so much of a conversation, which made necessary the trip to Boston.

Interstate 89 is a long, windy, treacherous highway running north-south over and around the Green Mountains, crisscrossing Vermont and into New Hampshire. This is one of two major highways in Vermont, and is the quickest way south to Boston, Massachusetts. The two lanes of patchy, frost-heaved road are tricky to negotiate any time of year; soft shoulders, ice, elevation changes, with notorious fog make it more so during bad weather.

January brings major snow storms almost every year, often dropping several feet of snow in a relatively few number of hours. This particular *Noreaster* should have postponed the trek south to Boston, the storm well-tracked and advised in advance. But in the Northeast, weather personnel and meteorologists were wrong as often as correct, though every weather girl, on every channel, was forecasting the same snow advisory. But the days had been requested off, cashing in vacation and/or personal time, so the show must go on. And so on that January afternoon,

Reginald and Elizabeth Grantes of Burlington, Vermont embarked on their journey south.

Jacob found it odd that his parents had not called him once they had arrived in Boston. They had a reservation with a late check-in scheduled at the Buckingham Hotel on Commonwealth Avenue, as was customary when they visited. When he had not heard from them, the thought of the big storm resonated in the back of his mind. He almost immediately disregarded it, however; his father had driven in the snow his entire life, had taught him how to drive in the stuff. He called the prepaid cellphone they used only when traveling, as cell phones were not the rage with the senior Granteses back then. He could not get through. Their voicemail was not set up, of course. It was not until he called the hotel and been informed that they had not checked in that he began to worry. More phone calls to their friends and to their places of work without a definitive answer to their whereabouts led to panic.

By 10:00 A.M. the following morning, panic became horrified shock. The Vermont State Police informed him by telephone that neither had survived a severe car crash. Neither had been alive when authorities had arrived at the scene.

"We hate to inform you over the phone," they said. "How very sorry we are," they also said. "Please come to Montpelier, Vermont to identify your parents."

They had not made it out of their own state. The reports showed that the snowy weather conditions inhibited sight; mixed with the unplowed snow on top of black ice, with an unfamiliar rental vehicle that was not equipped with all-wheel drive, were some of the elements contributing to the disastrous formula. The guard rail was ill-placed, meaning that there wasn't one in place. A guard rail would have at a minimum kept the vehicle on the road. The lack of this safety measure did the opposite and allowed them to leave the road. The rental vehicle launched off the elevated highway into the icy ravine below. The final element in their premature demise.

The aftershock of the catastrophe had left Jacob scarred both emotionally and financially. Anna and her parents were there to reassemble the pieces as best they could. The financial piece was easy. Norman took care of the massive debt in one phone call. Anna was there for the emotional part. This was not as easy. But they dealt with it.

Reginald and Elizabeth Grantes, formerly of Burlington, Vermont, had loved life. They cared not for money but for the happiness it could provide from joyous memories. They loved each other and they loved their son, and in that they were rich. Realistically, they were not. They lived paycheck to paycheck and didn't manage those very well at all. There were always events deemed too important to pass up, spending money earmarked for bills; spending in lieu of life insurance, savings, or a 401k. They were upside down on their mortgage in part because of the market, but primarily because of the repeated refinancing and remortgaging.

Without life insurance, in their terrible financial condition, and most recently with the cost of their final expenses, they had left their only son with an enormous financial burden. He was already in debt because of his educational loans and the catastrophe would make him more so without a house or substantial property to sell. And so at the ages of 58 and 56, Reginald and Liz respectively, had left their son broken and broke. Had it not been for the Craigs, he would have been broke for the rest of his life.

5

JG WAS ANXIOUSLY AWAITING the arrival of his lawyer at the table in one of the courthouse conference rooms. He was immediately escorted there after his brief legal fray in the fourth session upstairs. Ryan had worked it out to conduct a meeting with his client before he was bussed back to prison, should he not make bail; which to his misfortune, is exactly what happened. Ryan seemed to be taking a long time doing whatever he was doing in the eyes of JG; leaving him alone in the dark, windowless conference room with a court officer standing watch in the corner. It was an awkward silence which made Ryan's absence seem even longer. He was not in any hurry to get back to his cell, nor his celly, but he was overwrought with how his case was progressing thus far. Or not progressing, which consumed his thoughts every minute of every day in prison.

The large wooden door opened with a start, ending the tension that had been building in the small room, adding a different sort of unease. Ryan moved quickly to a chair opposite his client, setting his leather briefcase down on the oversized table between them.

"I'd like to be alone with my client please," he said over his left shoulder to the officer.

"Sure thing. I'll be outside the door when you're finished."

Once the babysitter had left, the lawyer-client pretense was abandoned. "Well, that didn't go very well." The hearing had not gone well, they both knew it, and neither one would sugarcoat it to say that it had.

"Ya think?"

"Look pal, we have them on the ropes, right where we want them," Ryan said.

"Rope a dope, huh? Who's the dope? They're kicking our asses, Ry."

"Well, I don't know what I could have done differently in retrospect. Thoughts? I mean what would the Great Jacob Grantes have done?"

JG's elbows were on the table, head in hands. He needed a lifeline. The sarcasm and mucking it up with his friend needed to cease. He was on the verge of breaking down.

"You did what you did, Ry. I mean you did what I would have done. That woman is a ball-buster."

"McCaglia has always been brutal, you knew that going in. You've been in front of her before. Hell, she was as an ADA, she is now that she's on the bench. She has something to prove, always has, and she doesn't cut breaks unless she absolutely has to. And she doesn't have to here. We don't have anything going for us, and Jabba isn't chomping at the bit to cut a deal either."

"Exactly. So what do we have we going for us?"

"I was just speaking with tons-of-fun upstairs after our hearing. That's what took so long. I've got the 'one and only green sheet' right here. This is the only deal he is offering, or is ever going to offer, he says. It's not a good one, I'll warn you."

He reached into his briefcase on the table, removed the green court document that La Fontagne had given Ryan a few moments prior. It was conveniently on top and quickly slid directly in front of his jumpsuit-clad friend. A green sheet is a bargaining document with legalese and three vertical columns in the middle horizontal third. The form is on No Carbon Required (NCR) paper with three sheets; one for the ADA, one for the defense, and one for the judge. The first column is for the prosecutor, which offers a sentencing recommendation if the defense forgoes the expense of a trial. The middle column is the defense counter offer, which typically chips away at what the State wants. The final column on the right, is the deal formed between the two and goes to the judge. He or she reads the statutory minimums to ensure nobody is ponying up the courthouse, then usually rubber-stamps the deal. When all is said and done, all the judge wants is to clear their docket, keep justice moving just like everyone else. This is called a green sheet for the complicated reason in that the color of the document is a light green. Though it must be signed by all parties, it is only legally binding when and if a formal hearing takes place and agreed to on the record.

"He likes where he is," Ryan continued. "As you can see, the offer is Vehicular Manslaughter, OUI 1 with injury, leaving the scene. He drops the child endangerment, and puts a recommend of eight to ten on the VM, concurrent. Loss of licenses, two years after release on the driver's, law for life because we are talking felonies."

"Not much of a deal."

"You would get fifteen years on the VM alone at trial. Add in the OUI-with, leaving the scene, and indifference would get you another ten-plus separately. Then add the child endangerment back into the charges if we go to the hoop, and you would not be able to see your kid without someone watching over your shoulder until he is legally an adult. Eight to ten, to run concurrent means with good time, two years off the minimum. You've been in for six months already, so you would be out in five and half. No child supervision, no probation. It's not good but it's the best we're gonna get I'm afraid."

The driver's license didn't make that much difference to JG. The loss of his ability to practice law could also be dealt with, he had money and he could always find something to occupy his days. Maybe he could teach. The five and a half years away from his family was intolerable. He could not lose his family for any longer than he already had. Supervised visits with Brady was unacceptable also but at least he would be able to see him other than through glass. These thoughts were going through his mind but he wasn't vocal about them, which caused a long pause. He continued to stare at the offer, lost in the ramifications if he agreed to what was written.

"What's going through your mind? Talk to me. There is nothing saying that you can't be behind the scenes at the firm, you just wouldn't be able to take cases when you get out."

"You think that is what's bothering me, Ry? How long have you known me? You really think that is what's hanging me up?"

"No, I don't. I'm just trying to help. But Jabba isn't going to budge. It's this or we go to the hoop. But you have given me nothing to work with on defense. We go to trial? I think unless we come up with something really damned compelling, you're going to go away for a long time."

"Have you been in touch with Anna yet? I'd like to discuss this with her."

"She isn't, nor was she, here today. No answer either. Voicemail is full. I'm really not sure where she is, but I'll keep trying." He pulled out some other documents from the briefcase, spreading out the pile on his side of the table. "What I would like to discuss is all of this circumstantial evidence and see if anything jogs your memory. Anything we can hammer away at. If we weaken anything he has, maybe the deal gets better."

"We've been through this, I don't remember anything about that night. Well, other than Sully's anyway."

"Yeah well, we are going to go through it again. You admitted to quote, 'being hammered' when they picked you up at your house. You were passed out by the way. Again, Brady was upstairs asleep but unsupervised."

"I can't believe I drove in that condition, much less with Brady in the car. Then left him on his own like that in the house. I just can't believe it."

"Thats what they're going with. I have a statement from the bartender, Jenna, that you left Sully's between 8:00 and 8:15 P.M. You also admitted to being at the bar in the back of the cruiser, which means you had to be really banged up. You, of all people, know better than to say anything to the police after you've been arrested. But anyway, you left and picked up Brady at the Destriers at 8:20 P.M; the servant that was watching him told Chamille Destrier that she put him in his carseat in the back of the running car, that you never spoke or left the driver's seat. She said she found it odd behavior, but this is all third hand through Chamille because the servant doesn't speak English, apparently. The police never spoke to her directly to confirm or deny anything. Chamille was at the charity event next to your wife, so we strike the kid being in the car as hearsay. I think that is why the big-boy is dropping child endangerment, the kind soul."

"Yeah, what a sweetheart."

"Right. So you drove away and must have bounced off a tree, veering into the opposite lane where this poor woman happened to be coming right at you. She goes off the road and plays chicken with a big tree and an even bigger rock. She lost and you went home to sleep it off."

"It's not funny, Ry. Please don't make light of the fact that this woman was decapitated by a smoking-hot engine. I feel awful."

"Sorry, just trying to add some levity. Anyway, they have matching paint from the tree, black sapphire pearl, and the scrape on your Volvo has wood and bark all through it. Exact. No real credible argument there, I'm afraid. Furthermore the rubber zig-zagging on Wayland Country Club Road matches the Michelin 235/60R18s on your ride. Cops investigated your tires, they've got you dead to rights there too."

"Match? *Cops* are matching this all up? Can we get experts to refute them? Volvos are a dime a dozen in New England. Hell, I have two of them."

"Lab techs. This isn't *CSI*, they didn't stop everything they were doing and get top experts from all over the country to fly in on the state's dime, no. But you don't have to be an expert to see that all of this doesn't look good. Picking apart their lab technicians with our expensive ones is not going to win over a jury, if that's what you're thinking."

"That is exactly what I am thinking. The techs are overworked, underpaid, they make mistakes — "

"—This is New Hampshire, JG. They are neither overworked, nor are they underpaid. These aren't MIT grads by any stretch, but they don't have a whole lot to investigate, trust me. Just between you and me, I looked at your car, the road, the tree. You killed this poor woman. If you were anybody else — "

"—So what are we doing here then?"

"You're my best friend. I'm trying to mitigate your responsibility here. I'm trying to help. I don't know, find a technicality. What we're doing here is trying to get the best deal we can."

"Great. Just great. You think five and half is the best I can do?"

"We haven't discussed the 911 call yet. Anonymous, but that is how they nailed you. How they knew to go to your house to grab you."

"What is there to discuss? You've already told me to take the deal, right?

Ryan paused. He shuffled the stack of papers containing all the condemning evidence. He really wasn't sure why he was against taking the deal but he was. He knew his friend, knew him better than any other male on the planet, and something was not right. Endangering the life of his only son, the one they had so much trouble conceiving, was not scanning. True, he had been drinking more in the months before the accident, but to get that blackout drunk was not something he would expect from his friend. He was mister safety. People disappointed. But not JG. Not Jacob Grantes. He had never disappointed. Not until now.

"Look, I'm not telling you to take the deal. At least not yet. We finally have all the evidence that fat-body has compiled; so we put Deni on it and see what he comes up with. I mean, the cops didn't pick you up at your house until 9:45 P.M, which gives you a huge window to get shattered in the comfort of your own home. If everything comes back the way it looks here, which admittedly is really fucking bad, then we pick away at the bartender and the illegal lady."

"Please leave the victim alone. Arelia, right? Jenna too."

"Look. Jenna is a sweet girl, we go there and knock a few back and she is always good to us, but she over-served you. She claims not, but obviously she screwed up and is covering her ass. As far as the victim ..... She's dead. Which is unfortunate. But she shouldn't have been in this country to be dead. She was illegal. I feel for her just like you do, but when it comes to my friend or someone who may or may not even pay taxes? I might be a 'hippie' but I look out for my own. We've kinda got a role reversal here, huh? You're usually the cutthroat."

"Prison changes people I guess. Usually for the worse, not more sympathetic. But, it is what it is."

"Maybe. But if shit goes south, all the cards lead to what we have before us, then we go after the ladies. The bartender has some responsibility here, and so does the vic. This *is* New Hampshire. We don't like drunk drivers but we don't like illegal aliens more."

"Not very Politically Correct of us, is it?"

"Unfortunately, like you said, it is what it is. Peace, love, and get a green card."

"Well, lets hope it doesn't come to that. Just get Deni going because we don't have much time."

"I'm on it. I'm not going anywhere. You need anything?"

"Actually, yes."

"Name it."

"Find Anna."

6

RYAN WELLS WAS JG's longest and closest personal friend. They had both grown up poor but not impoverished, had been instilled with a strong work ethic, and were the first in their respective families to go to college. They had met at BU during freshman orientation and were all but inseparable since. Grantes had been a loyal friend in pulling Wells into the fold of the partnership and Ryan had been loyal in many other ways, including during the death of Jacob's parents. They were each the brother that neither had.

The two were so alike in so many ways that they could have been biological brothers. Ryan was good looking, tall and had what was once an athletic build. They would both be forty this year and had previously made plans for both families to go on vacation together to celebrate. Until the incarceration, all had looked forward to the time away. The only major difference between them was professionally. They were both strong advocates, but the hippie would live in the shadow of his more talented, leaning to the right, brother.

As Ryan left the courthouse, he pulled his iPhone out of his long winter overcoat to call Warren Dennihan, the firm investigator.

"Deni, how are you?" He immediately regretted not using his bluetooth ear device to make the call as he juggled his briefcase, the phone, and his car keys to open his parked car.

"Same shit, different pile. What's up?" Warren Dennihan was from *Southie*, or from the district of South

Boston and had the severe accent to prove it. Bad. Or 'wicked bad, guy'. It was almost like he spoke a different language as *'pahk tha cah in hah-vid yahd,'* just doesn't quite describe how broken his English really was. He didn't pronounce *r's*, unless of course they were not in the word like *drawr* instead of draw. It was work to hold a conversation with him unless you were familiar with him or his kind.

"I just finished up with JG's hearing. It didn't go well."

"I figured. I got my partner workin' my other shit, so how much time do I gotta clear up?"

"Ah shit," Ryan said. He had dropped his phone while opening his car to get it started and warmed up. He had to retrieve it out of the snow but fortunately it still worked. With the new synthetic oils and the fact that he drove an Audi A6, he didn't need to get the car warmed up for performance reasons, but he couldn't get the winter-fighter to work on his cold body until the engine was pumping warm air at him.

"You ok?"

"Yeah, Yeah. I'm here. Just dropped something. So everything we talked about? That's what they've got. The whole shah-bang. We've gotta work on it."

"By we, ya mean me."

"It's been a tough morning, are you really gonna give me a hard time right now?"

"Always. Hey listen. I've been callin' WHOC, I know a few guys over there. Not much I can do to look after him in there. Its all political. He's a lawyer, so nobody trusts him, and he can't gang up. At least he knew not to PC, just take a beat'n like a man if thats what they wanna do."

"If it was going to happen, it would have happened by now."

"Not necessarily, but we can hope. How much longer?"

"That depends on you, Deni. Thirty days if this goes to the hoop. Trial will be probably about two weeks or so, after that depends on what we get. I was hoping we could get enough to kill a trial, maybe enough to get a deal. They are offering eight to ten, which means five and half when all is said and done."

"All depends on me? No pressure. Who's breakin' balls now?"

Ryan was still sitting in his car, which was starting to kick out the warm seventy-four degree air that was set on his in-dash computer. He still couldn't drive, however; the car had not yet picked up the signal for the phone and you cannot drive and talk on the phone in New Hampshire unless handsfree. "Hey where are you?"

"Around the corner from you, I'll be there in thirty-secs or less."

"Good. This might be easier face to face. I have a ton of documents you should look at."

"Do you still drive the silver Audi?"

"Yes, of course. I love this — "

" — I'm behind ya."

"Holy crap. That was fast."

Deni parked his blacked-out Escalade and relocated to the passenger seat of Ryan's vehicle. This was the part that took the thirty-seconds.

"Let's see it all," he said without explanation of how or why he was in the immediate area.

"So this is everything." He handed Warren the stack of evidential material from his briefcase, then continued. "I know we discussed it when this thing happened, and since, but something just isn't sitting right about this case. You think I'm nuts though don't you?"

"I don't think you're nuts, per se, but would you really go through all this bullsh for anybody but JG? I agree that somethin' isn't stirrin' the kool-aid, but you and I both know he did it. He was drinkin' like a fish for months before this all happened. I was thinkin' family trouble at the time, but who knows? That kid is his life, so I can't see him throwing that away. But we all fuck up, doesn't have to be on purpose for it to do damage."

"So does that mean that you are on board? I gotta know that you are on this."

"Loyal as lab, huh? Yeah, me too. I'm in, and you know it. I just need somethin' to work with here, guy."

"Look I never ask how you do what you do, because I'm not sure I want to know, but we are going to need all you've got on this. We need to dig into; Jenna, the bartender we know from Sully's Tavern, the Destrier servant or au pair or whatever she is, the 911 call is a bit wonky, and if all else fails — we make the vic the most despicable person who has ever illegally entered the borders of this country," Ryan said before pausing. "I was kind of hoping for a sliding scale on this one. I know you have to clear your calendar and this is going to take some time, but with me taking this case ..... I have all of *his* cases I have to work, and mine ..... And of course he isn't in the office taking cases so the firm is really financially tight right now and — "

" — Hey relax, buddy. I can't dig up what ain't there, but I'm on it. As legit as possible anyway. As for the fee, don't worry about it. I owe tha kid. He's been good to me over the years."

"So what are you thinking?"

"I've got a couple of ideas. Mostly hunches, but I know people."

"I know you know people, that's why you are so good at what you do. Anyone I know?"

"Stop kissin' my ass, Ry. I wanna check out the bar first. Jenna."

"Business or pleasure?"

"Both."

"I've got another project that's just as important."

"I'm listenin'."

"Find Anna and Brady. They didn't show up at court today and she's not answering phones. It's weirding me out, and JG is really freaking out."

"Huh. Lets go over to the house. You drive."

"Right now? Deni, I've got — "

" — You said it's important. Was that fact or bullsh?"

"Fact."

"Then start driving."